"I kin... backed ...

"You what?" Nancy pushed past the teen and his father and down her front steps. Her Durango had been shoved four feet closer to her porch by the hippo-sized Suburban hard up against its rump. Her rear bumper was dented, the right taillight in shards and her right rear tire was flat. "What on earth happened?"

"My son, here, decided to move the Suburban into our driveway."

"Yeah, I guess I hit Reverse," the kid said. "It wasn't my fault."

"It was the fault of a malevolent universe?" his father snapped. "This unfortunate creature is Jason Wainwright, my son."

"Look, you. I need my car right now—I have an emergency. I've got to help save a dog that was mauled by a pit bull." She grabbed Jason by the sleeve. "Come on. You and your daddy are going to drive me to the clinic, wait for me if it takes all night and drive me home, or I swear to God I'll have you locked up for driving without a valid Tennessee driver's license."

"I can't leave my two younger children alone," Wainwright said.

"Can't your wife look after them?"

"I don't have a wife."

Dear Reader,

Since I began writing about Creature Comfort Veterinary Clinic, readers have been asking me to tell Nancy Mayfield's story. Well, here it is.

Nancy was a professional equestrian until a terrible accident put an end to both her career and marriage. Now after years of struggle, she has a job she loves as a veterinary technician, good friends and neighbors, and her own quiet cottage in a tranquil village.

Until Tim Wainwright moves in across the street with his three strange children.

Suddenly she's fighting desperately to avoid getting caught up in the family's problems at the same time she's drawn to Tim. She was an awful stepmother, and never intends to take on that role again.

Meanwhile, Tim is struggling to be a good father at the same time as he's falling in love with a woman who doesn't want any family, and definitely not one as dysfunctional as his.

Can they get together? Read and find out.

Enjoy!

Carolyn McSparren

OVER HIS HEAD
Carolyn McSparren

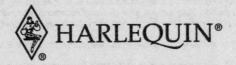

HARLEQUIN®

TORONTO • NEW YORK • LONDON
AMSTERDAM • PARIS • SYDNEY • HAMBURG
STOCKHOLM • ATHENS • TOKYO • MILAN • MADRID
PRAGUE • WARSAW • BUDAPEST • AUCKLAND

ISBN 0-373-71343-6

OVER HIS HEAD

Copyright © 2006 by Carolyn McSparren.

This edition published by arrangement with Harlequin Books S.A.

® and TM are trademarks of the publisher. Trademarks indicated with
® are registered in the United States Patent and Trademark Office, the
Canadian Trade Marks Office and in other countries.

www.eHarlequin.com

Printed in U.S.A.

Books by Carolyn McSparren

HARLEQUIN SUPERROMANCE

CHAPTER ONE

"I LOVED WILLIAMSTON when I was a kid. So will you."

Tim Wainwright turned his Suburban from the highway onto a narrow county road. A small sign said, Williamston, Tennessee, Population 123. He accelerated past it and hoped the kids hadn't noticed that number.

Sometime in the ten years since his grandfather's funeral cortege had wound along this road to the cemetery, the county had paved it. Thank God. After the horrors of the drive from Chicago, even in an air-conditioned Surburban, Tim didn't think he could have faced the last leg of his trip on rutted gravel in a cloud of hot July dust.

His children would mount a full-scale rebellion at the thought of living down a gravel road. He took a deep breath and willed his shoulders to relax. He glanced over at Jason, who stared mulishly out the side window. He'd refused to say a word since they crossed the bridge over the Mississippi River, driving straight through Memphis and out the other side.

Jason's buzz cut would have time to grow so that he wouldn't start school totally bald. He'd fight losing the two earrings in his right ear, but they'd have to go as well. Maybree Academy had a strict dress code. That meant buying him clothes sized for a teenager rather than an African bull elephant.

From what he'd seen of the student body when he came down to interview, Maybree students preferred the preppy look. He prayed Jason would knuckle under to peer pressure and go preppy as well.

He could see Eddy in his rearview mirror, slumped against the armrest, either sleeping or pretending to. As glad as Tim was that Jason had *stopped* complaining, he wished Eddy would say something, *anything* more than to ask for orange juice at breakfast. If only he'd cry. Just once. Stoicism might be okay for Marcus Aurelius, but it was damned unhealthy for a seven-year-old kid.

At least he was no problem to dress. Tim could probably drape a tarpaulin over him without his noticing. He hadn't even played his Game Boy on the drive down. Just sat and stared.

Angie's black hair bounced in and out of his field of vision in the mirror. Usually he forbade headphones. He'd prefer that his children not go deaf before they reached twenty. Today, however, the headphones and portable CD player had been a blessing. She had zoned out on her latest techno-rock band.

"You must admit," Tim said to Jason, the only one who'd be able to hear him, "This is beautiful country. Look at all the trees, the fields, the open space."

"Yeah," Jason said with a wave of his hand. "Look at all the malls, the pizza places, the movie theaters. Yeah, we're gonna love it."

"Look, Jason, I realize this is culture shock, but once you get used to the freedom…"

Tim saw his son actually turn his head to look—no, sneer—at him.

"Freedom. Right. Freedom is not riding to school in the morning with my father, spending all day with him spying on me and riding home with him in the afternoon. Freedom is a new Mustang."

"In your dreams. We'll be lucky if we can afford a thirdhand VW for you. Besides, the legal age for a license is sixteen in Tennessee, not fifteen, and then it's restricted."

"It would be," Jason whispered. "Goddamn prison."

"Watch your language."

"Sure, like you watch yours."

Tim let that pass. There was a certain amount of truth in it.

Since Solange's death he didn't watch his language as much when the kids were around.

This was what *she* had wanted. Maybe not to move to the middle of nowhere in West Tennessee, but to move out of Chicago, find someplace to live with open spaces, a bigger house in a small town. No crime. Kids free to ride their bicycles or skateboards without fear.

Away from Solange's mother.

He hadn't listened. And so she'd died.

Now he was taking control of his family's destiny. Time to haul on the reins and stop the runaway stagecoach before it turned over and killed everybody. He grinned. Even his clichés were turning country. "I've told you how great my summers were down here when I was a kid. You used to think they sounded pretty cool."

"I used to think storks brought babies," Jason said.

"You mean they don't? Okay, I promise you there will be occasional access to malls and movies and maybe even pizza. But you'll have to earn your privileges. Get an after-school job. Earn that VW. Pay for your own gas once you get it. Money's going to be tight. And no more running wild because your grandmother can't keep up with you."

Jason held out his wrists. "Yeah. Freedom, just like you said. Just put the cuffs on now, Mr. Policeman, sir."

"Jason, I'm tired, you're tired, we're all tired. It's hot, we've driven all the way from Chicago, and I've had enough of the sarcasm."

"Shouldn't you call that creative interaction, Mr. Vice Principal, sir?"

"I'm just a lowly English teacher now, Jason." He longed to stop the car, lean across the console separating them and slap the kid silly. He'd always believed in nonviolent alternatives to physical punishment for children and had never raised a hand to his three. He knew their grandmother did from time to time, and he suspected Solange had swatted a behind or two.

Every day Tim worked with abusive parents and abused children. He knew the damage abuse caused both.

Today, however, he was discovering how kids could drive a seemingly rational adult crazy. He took a deep breath. He needed to calm down and chill out before he started yelling. That never did any good and left him feeling guilty afterward.

He took another deep breath, then several more before he said, "Granddad taught me to fish for crappie and catfish in the creek that runs through the farm, and during the summer we took picnics down to the pond and swam. He taught me to paddle a canoe. We can rebuild the dock, buy a new canoe—"

"Skinny-dip with the local milkmaids."

Tim could hear the leer in Jason's voice. Doggedly he kept going. "I had a great bag swing by the pond. You could swing way out over the water and drop. Can't do that in a swimming pool."

"Who'd want to?"

"I have to pee." Angie had taken off the earphones and was leaning against the back of his seat. "Stop at a gas station."

"No gas stations between here and Williamston," Tim said. He didn't remember a gas station within twenty miles of Williamston. Better not tell Angie that. "If you're in real trouble, we'll pull off to the side of the road and you can go behind a tree."

"Eeeew! No way! Gross."

"Then hold on. We're nearly there." He checked her face in the mirror. It was powdered dead-white, made even more dramatic by her hair, dyed so black it looked like a wig. Unfortunately it wasn't. She had bought the dye one afternoon after school, and greeted him looking like an underaged vampire when he got home from school.

"Dad was just telling us about how great it's going to be to swim in some scummy old pond," Jason said. "Water moccasins love little girls. One bite and you swell up and turn green and die."

"Jason!" It was a wail. "Daddy, make him stop. I hate snakes. Are there really snakes?"

Sure there were, but he wasn't about to tell Angie about them right this minute. "Most snakes are harmless. They're more afraid of you than you are of them."

"Want to bet?" Jason breathed.

"Don't think about snakes. Think about how big the house is. After Chicago, it's going to seem like a palace. You'll have a big room all to yourself. And some of the people in the area have horses."

Magic word. Before she had been taken over by the Children of the Night, Angie's one great desire had been for a horse of her own. Not possible in Chicago. Rich people who lived in the suburbs owned horses. Overworked vice principals of inner-city schools did not.

In his new job as an English teacher in a small private school, Tim still wouldn't be able to afford a horse for Angie, but he might be able to give her riding lessons. Maybe he'd offer her a trade. She could have riding lessons if she took off the clown makeup and went back to brown hair.

In any case, the black hair and kohl eyeliner wouldn't be any more acceptable at Maybree than Jason's bald head. He'd have to find out how to remove the dye.

Solange would have known all about that kind of thing. But then if his wife were still alive, Angie probably wouldn't have turned Goth on him.

The only one of his kids who looked halfway normal was Eddy, and he was the most screwed up of the bunch, at least to hear the psychologist tell it.

How could Tim ever teach his children to love Williamston the way he did? He'd regaled them time after time with stories of the wonderful summers he'd spent there. Maybe now that they were here, the stories would take on new meaning for them. They'd never paid much attention before.

The important thing was that he wouldn't be working eighty hours a week as he had in Chicago. He could devote himself to their needs. He'd sacrificed his career, the potential of a princi-palship—all the additional money and prestige—for them. He owed them for the years he'd let Solange raise them practically on her own.

He swung the SUV off the highway and onto a narrow lane lined with big old trees that transformed the road into a sun-dappled tunnel.

He drove past the small rectangular common in the center of the village. The Bermuda grass lawn had turned brown in the heat, and the white fence needed a coat of paint.

The only place to eat in Williamston was a log cabin on the corner of the green. Today a big sign outside read Closed. Tim hoped that meant for dinner and not for good.

One more left, up a hill and past the big moving van. He pulled onto the grass verge at the far side of his grandfather's house and cut the engine.

"Home at last."

"No way," said Jason.

"Way."

"There's supposed to be a town. Where is it?"

"You just drove through it."

"A field and a log cabin?"

"Yuck, some palace," whined Angie, who leaned across Eddy to stare out the window. "No one could possibly expect a human being to live in that—that hovel." She frequently vacillated between teenage colloquial and Victorian supercilious in the same sentence.

Eddy had woken up and was rubbing his eyes.

"Well, Eddy? Care to add your comments?"

Eddy ignored him.

"Gross, gross, gross!" Angie's hands fluttered. "I'll bet you can't even buy a CD for a hundred miles."

"CD, huh! Try a loaf of bread. You said it was a town."

"Williamston *is* a town. Just a very small one. More like a village."

"More like a big fat nothing."

"Looks like an old barn," Jason said as he stared up at the house. "At least I won't have to share a room with Ratso any longer."

"Don't call your brother names," Tim said. Now that he had done this insane thing, had committed his whole family to this change, he was scared to get out of the car. "The house has five bedrooms. One downstairs for me, one for each of you, and one left over for guests."

"For Gran'mere," Eddy whispered from the back seat.

"Yes, Eddy. Your grandmother will come to visit as soon as we get settled."

"No, she won't," Jason said with finality. "Not after we tell her what this place is like." He leered over his shoulder at his brother. "We'll never, ever see her again."

"We will, too!"

"Jason, stop teasing your brother. Eddy, your grandmother will come to visit. She just can't move down here with us. I've explained all that." His voice said he'd explained it until he was blue in the face and wasn't about to try again.

"If she loved us, she'd move."

"Eddy, it's okay, she does love us," Angie said. "Jason, stop being a butthole."

"Angie," her father said, but without much heat. He was too tired of driving and refereeing to be upset by much less than ax murder.

"It's a prison."

"I want to go back to Chicago."

"I'm hungry."

"I want a soda."

"Can't we stay in a motel?"

"I hate this place."

"I have to pee."

He'd decided to feed them a catfish dinner at the Log Cabin. Now he'd have to find someplace else nearby, assuming there was another restaurant this side of Memphis, fifty miles away.

They'd be a captive audience. He'd tell them some more stories of his wonderful summers. Tomorrow maybe they'd all go for a long walk. He really wanted his children to love this place, too.

But he was willing to have them hate it if it kept them safe from crime and gangs and drugs and alcohol and drive-by shootings.

He would even fight his own children to get them to twenty-one sound of mind and body.

CHAPTER TWO

"OH, NUTS. That's all I need," Nancy Mayfield muttered as she turned the corner by the village green into her lane. A huge moving van blocked not only the lane itself, but her driveway. There was no way to reach her garage except by driving across her lawn. Even though the ground was July hard, she preferred not to smash what little grass had survived the drought.

She pulled to a stop a couple of feet from the rear of the van. A large man who seemed to be dripping wet stood on of the tailgate with a psychedelically painted chest of drawers balanced precariously on a dolly.

"Hey, lady, move it!"

She glared at him.

"What're ya, deaf? Back it up. Move it." He waved her back with one hand.

Slowly and carefully she climbed out of her Durango, shut the door softly so as not to wake up Lancelot, snoring softly in the passenger seat, and turned to the man with a sweet smile. "No, you move it, *buddy*. You're blocking my driveway and I would like to park my car."

"Aw, jeez." He yelled toward the house, "Hey, Mac, lady out here wants us to move the van." He laughed. "Lady, ya got to be kiddin'."

"Not at all. Blocking access to a private driveway is a crime in the state of Tennessee. If you remain where you are, I will have a sheriff's deputy here to give you a nice, big citation before you can get that thing down the ramp."

"It's a chest of drawers," said a baritone voice from behind her.

"It looks as if it's been trapped in a riot in a paint store." She tamped down her temper and turned slowly to look at the newcomer. This must be the "Mac" the mover had been calling. No doubt the driver of the van.

This Mac certainly looked as though he could move refrigerators without much effort. He was wearing dirty jeans, equally dirty sneakers and a soggy Chicago Cubs T-shirt that needed a good bleaching. He wasn't quite as tall as Dr. Mac, but he was probably at least six-two.

He might be even brawnier than Dr. Mac. Moving refrigerators no doubt built muscles. His light brown hair was soaked with sweat, and his eyes were concealed behind fancy mirrored sunglasses. Nancy hated not being able to see people's eyes.

He strode up to her as if to make her back down. After everything that had gone wrong today, she was spoiling for a fight. Just let Mr. No-Eyes dare to invade her space and see how far those muscles got him. Heck, she could always sic Lancelot on him.

Behind her she heard the wheels of the dolly begin to roll down the ramp.

"Hey! Heads up! I can't hold her!" shouted the voice behind her.

As she started to turn, the brawny guy with no eyes grabbed Nancy around the waist and swept her to the side. The chest of drawers trundled to a halt on the road where she had been standing seconds before.

The man held her against his chest. She could hear his heart beat. Hers sounded like a trip-hammer. He smelled of male sweat and felt as though he was built of concrete. She struggled out of the circle of his arms.

"You all right?" he asked.

"Fine, thank you." She wriggled her shoulders and realized

the beating of her heart came not so much from the near miss with the furniture, but from the feel of this male body against her. Damn, when a semiliterate roustabout could raise her pulses, she really had been entirely too long without a man. "Now, move your van." She pointed to the gravel driveway across the lane that led up to her small cottage. The heck with *please*. Time to start issuing orders.

"I'm sorry," he said. "I didn't realize that was a driveway."

"Well, it is, and I want access to it."

"Look, miss—um—we're almost finished unloading. If you could see your way clear to park your car where it is for an hour or so, the van will be gone."

Reasonable. Only she didn't feel like being reasonable. She was hot, she was tired, before morning she and Dr. Thorne would probably lose the mastiff they'd operated on this afternoon. She had a blinding headache over her right eye, her neck ached, and she was so sick over losing her dear old neighbors to that nasty man from Chicago that she felt like crying.

On top of all that, she was foster mother to Lancelot for the foreseeable future until the Halliburtons found a place to live that had room for him. And now this truck driver had disturbed her equilibrium in a way she didn't like. It was the final straw.

"Please find the man who hired you," she said as imperiously as she could. Not easy when she had to look up at Mr. No-Eyes.

He smiled. It was a nice smile, no doubt he practiced it frequently on irritated customers. This time it wouldn't work. "I'm afraid I'm the culprit. I'm Tim Wainwright. My family and I are moving in. We're going to be neighbors." He pulled off his leather work glove and offered her his hand.

She felt a wash of heat even greater than the July afternoon. Great. Thank God she hadn't actually called him a semiliterate roustabout. She'd considered it. He'd let her make a fool of herself. Suddenly it didn't matter. Screw the moving van.

Without a word she climbed back into her car, reversed it and drove across her lawn to her driveway and pulled up beyond her dusty azaleas.

She went around to Lancelot's door, grabbed his leash and helped him down. Alarmed by the irrational fear that that Tim person would follow her and try to apologize or explain, she hurried inside the back door.

She unhooked Lancelot's harness, went straight to the refrigerator and poured herself a glass of white Zinfandel. As she raised the glass, her eyes lit on the huge yellow cat who sat on top of the refrigerator. "Sorry we woke you, Otto."

The cat leaped down and padded over to welcome Lancelot. Thank God her cats had known him since he was tiny. She felt fairly certain Lancelot thought he was a cat.

The two old friends trotted after her into her bedroom. A second cat, black and white and even larger, lay curled in the center of her pillow. She kicked off her running shoes and sat on the edge of the bed. The cat on the pillow watched her without moving its head. As she pulled her socks off, he reached out a long arm and swiped at one.

Obligingly she held it out for him. "Okay, Poddy, here you go."

He grabbed the sock, mauled it for a second, then abandoned it and went back to sleep. Yellow Otto crept up on it, pounced and dragged it under the bed. Lancelot tried to follow, but couldn't fit. "You bring that back, Otto," Nancy said without much hope.

She set the glass on the side table and leaned back against her pillows with one arm across her eyes. She heard Lancelot thud onto the rag rug beside her bed. For six whole years this little house had meant peace and comfort, a place of her own, where nobody intruded on her privacy unless and until she wanted them to. The first house she'd ever owned.

The moving van was a symbol—a big monster that got in her way and disturbed her tranquility the way that monster man got in her face with his big sweaty forearms and his ingratiating grin.

And no eyes.

She sat up. His family? He'd said family. How many? Wife, undoubtedly. Children? Aunts, uncles, cousins, grandparents? The house was big enough to hold a small army. Just because the Halliburtons hadn't used the upstairs didn't mean it wasn't there to be used. Williamston was going to be overrun by no-necked monsters, sure as shooting.

"I have enough drama in my life, guys, without coming home to more."

Lancelot looked up at the sound of her voice. Poddy and Otto ignored her.

Then perhaps sensing her mood, Poddy climbed into her lap, walked around in a circle, collapsed and began to knead her thigh. She scratched his ears. "The Calhouns brought their mastiff in with a flipped gut after lunch. If they'd brought him in this morning, we'd have had a better chance to save him. Dr. Mac and I worked on him for two hours, but we had to remove so much necrotic tissue I doubt he'll survive the night."

Otto decided to get in on the act. He hopped up, rolled over beside her and lay on his back like a baby. She scratched his tummy. "Guess who got to tell the Calhouns? Moi, of course. God forbid we let Dr. Mac get near clients he thinks are negligent. If he slugged somebody, he might break his hands, not to mention getting arrested for assault."

She heard Lancelot struggle to his feet. A moment later his nose butted her hand. "No, you cannot get up on the bed," she said. But she scratched him nonetheless. "I only have two hands, guys. I can't pet all three of you at once."

Lancelot's black nose disappeared once more as he sank onto the rug.

"We did do a successful cesarean on an English bulldog," she said. "I got to give some good news. Four healthy pups."

Poddy yawned. He undoubtedly saw no reason to celebrate the advent of more canines into the world.

She lay back on her pillows. Blessed, blessed silence.

The bang of metal crashing against metal brought her bolt upright.

A moment later the doorbell rang.

As she got up to answer it, the telephone beside her bed shrilled.

CHAPTER THREE

"JUST A MINUTE," Nancy shouted at the door as she reached for the telephone. "Mayfield," she answered.

"Nancy," said Mabel, the evening receptionist at Creature Comfort, "we've got an emergency. Mac's on his way. He asked me to call you."

"What kind of emergency?" she stuck her finger in her other ear to block out the impatient ringing of the doorbell. "I just walked in the door." She glanced down at the full glass of wine with longing. No alcohol if she had to go back to surgery. "Is it the mastiff?"

"Worse. The Marshall's Jack Russell. Some idiot let a pit bull out. He got into the Marshall's yard."

"Oh, Lord." The throbbing over Nancy's right eye intensified. "How bad?"

"He's alive, but he's going to need emergency surgery."

"I'll be there in forty minutes unless I run into a Statie with his radar on."

"Drive carefully. I'll get things ready."

"Thanks, Mabel." Nancy hung up and turned to the door. "All right, all right, dammit, I'm coming!" She yanked it open. Mr. No-Eyes stood on the front porch behind a tall, skinny, teenage boy whose head was nearly bald. He looked half sulky, half terrified. "What?" she snapped.

The man thrust the boy forward. "Tell her."

She heard Lancelot behind her, stepped out onto the front porch and slammed the door shut. "Tell me what?"

"I kind of, you know, backed into your car."

"You what?" Nancy pushed past the pair and down her front steps. Her Durango had been shoved four feet closer to her front porch by the hippo-size Suburban hard up against its rump. Over its rump, actually. Nancy ran to her car. Her rear bumper was dented, the right taillight lay in shards, and her right rear tire was flat. "What on earth happened?"

"My son, here, decided to move the Surburban into our driveway." His voice was quiet, but she could almost feel the man's rage.

"Yeah, I guess I hit Reverse," the kid said. "It wasn't my fault."

"It was the fault of a malevolent universe?" his father growled. "Of course it was your fault."

"Look," Nancy said, "I don't give two hoots if it was the fault of a *parallel* universe."

"This unfortunate creature is Jason Wainwright, my son."

"Big whoop," Nancy said. "Look, you. I need my car now, right this minute. I have an emergency. I have to go back to the clinic right now."

"You're a nurse?"

"I'm a veterinary surgical assistant. I've got to get back to help save a dog that just got mauled by a pit bull. And I'm wasting time." She grabbed Jason's sleeve. "Come on. You and your daddy are going to drive me to the clinic, wait for me if it takes all night and drive me home, or I swear to God I'll have you locked up for driving without a valid Tennessee driver's license."

Jason stared at her openmouthed. "Can you do that?"

"If you two don't get your rear ends in gear, you bet I can."

"I can't leave my two younger children on their own," Wainwright said.

"Can't your wife look after them?"

"I don't have a wife."

"Then bring them. Now!" She strode toward the Suburban. "Jason, go get your brother and sister while I move the car."

"Da-a-ad," Jason whined.

"Do it now. Fast." Then he shrugged. "Remember, pizza at a mall."

WHILE JASON ROUNDED up his siblings, Tim carefully backed the Suburban out. It didn't have a scratch. The damage to the Durango's bumper didn't look too bad, but until the light and tire were replaced, and until a mechanic checked the car out thoroughly, she couldn't drive it.

"If it needs bodywork, I could be without a car for a couple of weeks," Nancy said. She stood watching him with her hands on her hips.

He glanced over his shoulder at her. "I'm sure my insurance agent will pay for a rental. I'm truly sorry about this. Jason isn't usually so mutton-headed."

Nancy raised an eyebrow. She suspected she had yet to plumb the depths of Jason's mutton-headedness. "Does he have any sort of driver's license?"

"Illinois Learner's permit. He's fifteen. He's not supposed to drive without an adult."

God help the world's drivers when this kid turned sixteen.

A pubescent vampiress slouched across the road toward them. She was trailed by what looked like a relatively normal small boy. With Nancy's luck, he'd be a kleptomaniac or a Peeping-Tom.

Wainwright started to introduce her to his brood.

"Can we skip all that? Unless you want to be personally responsible for the death of a Jack Russell terrier."

To his credit, Wainwright took her directions down the side roads without question and drove fast and competently. Not fast enough, of course, but then a supersonic jet wouldn't have been fast enough. In the back seat, Jason sulked in a corner, and in front of him in the middle seat, his sister bobbed to the music in her headphones. Wainwright had introduced her as Angie. The blond kid was Eddy. He hadn't said a word.

Nancy pulled the sun visor down to cut out the glare from the westering sun, and caught his image in the visor mirror. He was staring at her.

He doesn't blink. Creepy.

"Down there," she said. "Drive through the wrought-iron gate into the parking lot outside the front doors."

TIM HAD BARELY BROUGHT the truck to a halt when Nancy jumped out, ran up the front stairs and shoved through the glass doors into the lighted reception area. He saw her speak to the woman behind a tall reception desk, then disappear through a side door.

"Can we go find some pizza now?" Angie asked. "I'm starving."

"Stay here." Tim started to climb out of the driver's seat. With a glance at Jason, he reached down and took the keys out of the ignition.

"How do you know I can't hot-wire it?" Jason asked.

"If you can, don't." He took the front stairs of the clinic two at a time.

"May I help you?" asked a motherly woman at the front desk. "We're actually closed now, but if you have an emergency…"

"The woman who just came in is my emergency," Tim said. "We're her new neighbors, and I'm afraid my son put her car out of commission."

The woman's eyes widened, then narrowed. "You're…him?"

"I should have introduced myself." He put out his hand. "I'm Timothy Wainwright." He glanced at the name plate on the desk. "I'm delighted to meet you, Mrs. Uh…"

She touched his hand for an instant. "Huh," she said and turned back to her computer screen.

"Um, I realize hitting Miss Mayfield's car isn't likely to endear me and my family to you, but it was an accident. My son didn't do it on purpose."

The woman didn't look at him. "The way you treated the Halliburtons was on purpose, though."

"I beg your pardon?"

Mabel turned back. "It's your right, of course, but in my opinion it was a wicked thing to do, and I know Nancy agrees with me."

"I'm sorry. I don't know what you're talking about. Who are the Halliburtons?"

At that moment the telephone on the desk rang. Mabel picked it up. "Creature Comfort."

Wainwright hadn't even looked at the name on the front gate of the clinic's parking lot. He was about to go back to his children before they bailed out of the car and fled into the night alone in search of pizza without him when Mabel finished answering a question and hung up. "Um, do you have any idea how long Miss Mayfield is likely to be?"

"Why?"

He gave Mabel his most endearing smile. It nearly always worked on distraught parents. Didn't work on Mabel, however. "I'm her chauffeur until we can get her a rental car."

"No idea. Could be an hour, could be six."

"I'm going to go feed my children some pizza. Where do you recommend?"

Grudgingly she gave him the name and address of a chain pizza place, and directions to get there.

He pulled out a business card. "Here's my card with my cell phone number. When Miss Mayfield needs me to pick her up, just have her call me. I'll be back as quickly as I can."

"Don't bother," Mabel said. "I will personally see that Nancy gets home safely, and I'll pick her up tomorrow morning and take her to a car rental place."

The place was air-conditioned, but the ice in Mabel's voice dropped the temperature another twenty degrees. He nodded. "Thanks, but I'll be back to rent the car for her. My credit card, you know."

"Fine. See that you do."

He started out, then turned back. "Um, could you tell me who the Halliburtons are and what I did to them?"

The woman in front of him actually swelled up. Since she was no lightweight to start with, she looked formidable. "You don't even know the names of your tenants?"

"I'm sorry?"

"They've lived in your house across from Nancy for ten years. They've tried time and time again to buy it from you, and every time you've refused. Then out of the blue, you toss them straight out onto the street like so much trash so you and your family can invade." Her eyes narrowed. "What happened? Chicago get too hot for you?"

Oh, great. He'd only met two people so far and both of them hated him. He'd never even heard the Halliburtons' name. "My agent has handled the property ever since Granddad died." He tried to sound conciliatory and wound up sounding even more arrogant and uncaring. Surely these Halliburtons didn't actually wind up on the street. He'd have to find out somehow. His agent might know. He didn't think this woman was the proper person to ask. "I knew the tenants had tried to buy the house, but it's been in my family for over a hundred years. I'd never sell it."

"You sure as shootin' haven't cared about it for the past ten," Mabel snapped and dismissed him.

He gave up and went back to the car. He hoped his children hadn't ripped up the upholstery while he'd been gone.

Eddy was asleep with his head against the side of the car. Angie was still jouncing to her silent music, but Jason was nowhere to be found. Oh, great. "Where's your brother?" he asked Angie. Twice.

She waved a hand. "He went off that way around the back." She pointed to the edge of the parking lot.

"If you ever expect to eat another pizza, don't move and keep an eye on Eddy." He trotted off around the building.

This clinic stretched a long way back from the modern brick building in front into a large metal building like a warehouse. Lights under the eaves showed him to where more light poured out from open garage doors at the side. He started to call for Jason, then saw him inside the metal building—must be a barn for large animals. He was standing beside some kind of pipe enclosure.

"Jason?"

The boy jumped. "I'm not doing anything," he said sulkily.

Tim walked into the light. In the stall a large gray-and-white sheep stood placidly chomping hay while two—what?—sheeplets? No, kids. Or was that for goats? *Lambs*. He must be losing his mind not to remember. God, he was an English professor—teacher—now. Words were his thing.

He was simply too tired to think straight. The nine-hour drive from Chicago would be enough to exhaust anyone. That same trip with his three children would have exhausted an entire platoon.

"Hey, folks, can I help you?"

Jason started at the voice. A tall young man in hospital greens walked out of the shadows at the far end of the building. Surely he was too young to be a veterinarian.

"Sorry," Tim said. "My son Jason here saw the lights. I came hunting for him. Come on, Jason."

"Dad," Jason said plaintively, "do we have to? I mean, I've never seen a live sheep before."

"Of course you have. At the petting zoo, don't you remember?"

Jason sulked. "It's not the same. And it didn't have babies." He looked up at the young man. "What's wrong with it?"

"Nothing now." The guy grinned at Jason. "Momma had a tough time having those twins. Happens, sometimes. Had to do a cesarean. You know what that is?"

Jason nodded. "Knock her out, then cut across her belly and take the babies out that way. I didn't know you did that with animals."

"We do when we have to."

Tim expected Jason to be grossed out.

"Cool. Is there a bunch of blood?"

"Not much." He turned to Tim. "I'm Kenny Nichols. I work here between semesters."

Tim introduced himself and they shook hands. "You going to vet school?"

"First year. Mississippi State." Kenny smiled proudly.

From somewhere in the shadows a horse nickered. Jason's head went up. "What's that?"

"Sally, a cutting horse. She's recuperating from eye surgery. Want to see?"

"Jason, I thought you were hungry."

He tossed his father a nasty glance and stomped off behind Kenny.

Jason's giant shorts drooped below the waistline of his underwear and almost reached the heavy socks he wore under his high-tops. All that would have to go along with the earrings, Tim thought. Good riddance.

By the time Tim managed to pry his son away from the horse's stall and get him back to the car, Angie was fuming. Eddy was awake, but as usual, he sat without saying a word.

"Jason," Tim said, "tell Eddy and Angie what you saw."

But all Jason's enthusiasm had vanished. He stared out the window.

A lesser man might've lost it by now.

His children certainly thought he'd made a mistake dragging them from Chicago, their friends, their grandmother, their schools, to this backwater.

Tim prayed they were wrong.

MACINTOSH THORN, D. V. M., partner in Creature Comfort Veterinary Clinic, and his surgical assistant, Nancy Mayfield, knew one another so well that they seldom communicated verbally during a procedure. He'd already stitched the Jack Russell's torn throat, now he was working on the gashes along the little dog's side.

"Irrigate, dammit!" he barked. Nancy had already begun to do just that, but she didn't take offense.

"It's a miracle the pit bull didn't snap his spine like a chicken wing," Mac growled.

"Mrs. Marshall told Mabel he managed to squeeze between a packing crate and the garage wall."

"Hell, look at that. Two ribs broken. Got to get the muscle reconnected. Sponge. Sometime this week."

Mac was fast but neat. Nancy slapped instruments into his hand, kept blood and sweat out of his way. Fifty-five minutes later by the big clock on the wall above the oxygen tanks, Mac said, "Gotcha." He looked over at Nancy. "Want to close?"

She shook her head. "I'm so upset I'd probably stitch his ear to his nose."

She saw his eyes widen and his eyebrows rise above the surgical mask.

"No problem."

She always enjoyed watching him stitch. For such a big man, he worked with the delicacy of a silk weaver. After he finished, he touched the small dog's head with his index finger. "You lucky dog, you."

"He'll live?"

"Depends on how tough he is. From what Mrs. Marshall told Mabel before you came, he should make it. Call Big. He'll need intensive care for a couple of days."

Nancy dialed a number on the telephone beside the door while Mac stripped off his surgical gear and tossed it into the bin in the corner of the room. As she was taking off her own greens, the door opened to admit an elephant of a man. He made Mac Thorn look like a child. His white-blond hair was cropped short, and he stared with pale blue eyes at the little dog. Nancy thought he was the gentlest man she'd ever met. He made a tsk sound, scooped the small dog softly into his mammoth arms and shook his head.

"I'll look after him, Dr. Mac," he whispered, as though the dog were not too deeply asleep to hear him. "I flat out hate this. Folks like them ain't got a lick 'a sense, ownin' a pit bull around a baby."

Bigelow Little, man of all work at Creature Comfort, himself owned a pit bull bitch rescued with a number of other wounded animals from a fighting ring. Daisy was the sweetest dog in the world and worshipped Big. Even so, she was never allowed into the area where the sick and wounded small animals were kept. Nancy wondered what Daisy would do if anyone—a total lunatic, it would have to be—tried to harm Big or any of the clinic personnel. She suspected Daisy would go down fighting.

Just as the overmatched little terrier had tried to do.

"What happened to the pit bull?" Nancy asked as she arranged instruments in the autoclave and tidied up the surgical area.

Mac shook his head. "Poor devil. The owners had their vet put him to sleep. Thank God I didn't have to do it."

Thank God indeed. Mac would more likely try to put the owners down. He would certainly feel they deserved it.

"Not his fault, but I can see their point. Mrs. Marshall says they have a two-year-old grandchild."

Nancy shuddered. "The pit bull could just as easily have attacked the child as the terrier." Some two-year-olds could even set off a basset hound.

Nancy followed Mac into the break room. He pulled a couple of diet sodas out of the small refrigerator kept for the staff and handed her one, then sank onto the leather sofa and propped his feet on the scarred coffee table.

"Okay, so how come you're too nervous to stitch up a dog?" he asked. Dr. Mac had a thirteen-year-old stepdaughter, Emma, and his wife, Kit, was heavily pregnant. He was much more aware of other people than he had ever been before he married. Not necessarily more sympathetic—just more aware.

Nancy dropped into one of the chairs at the conference table and took a long pull of her soda. "He's arrived. My new neighbor, the man from Chicago. It's worse than I thought."

Mac raised his eyebrows.

She told him about the afternoon. "So, no car, no privacy, no

Halliburtons any longer and three of the weirdest children I have ever seen in my life."

"Weird how?"

"The one son is almost totally bald, that is, not naturally—and has what looks suspiciously like two holes in his ear where he might have worn studs." She paused to consider that. "And may again. I didn't inquire as to what other portions of his anatomy might be pierced. He also wears shorts that would be too big for Big."

For a moment, Mac looked confused, then he laughed.

"The daughter, Angie, is no creature of light. More like the Angel of Darkness, if you ask me. Black fingernails and dyed black hair and eye makeup she's entirely too young to wear, in my opinion."

"Goth. Okay. You said three children."

"The youngest is a towheaded boy about six or seven who looks perfectly normal, if you consider Damien looked perfectly normal. Mac, he doesn't talk and he doesn't blink. I've been plunged into some kind of Satanic nightmare."

"You're exaggerating. What's the father like?"

She took a deep breath. The father was pheromone central. His ability to arouse her dormant sex drive, however, was not something she could share with Mac. "He's almost as tall as you are, has a nice smile and seems fairly normal except that he's raised a brood of alien monsters and doesn't seem to care." She shook her head. "And he's a professional educator."

Mac finished his soda, crushed the can flat and tossed it into the trash can across the room. "He's a teacher?"

"He is now. Helen Halliburton told me he has a Ph.D. and an Ed.D. from the University of Chicago. He's been some sort of administrator at some school in Chicago, but he's going to be a plain, old English teacher at Maybree Academy starting this fall."

Mac sat up. "Maybree? That's where Emma goes."

"Ah-ha," Nancy said. "Got your attention at last." Mac adored his stepdaughter, who in turn thought he hung not only the moon but the planets. Her biological father, a cop, was never there for her. Mac never missed a school play or a PTA meeting or a teacher's conference unless he was up to his armpits in some dog's stomach. He'd moved Emma from her less-than-adequate public school to Maybree Academy, despite the tuition, which ranked right up there with Harvard.

"How'd she do last year?" Nancy asked.

"Child belongs in Overachievers Anonymous," he said with pride. "Wants to follow in her old man's footsteps. Loves science."

Nancy didn't think he was talking about Emma's biological father.

"Take a warning from someone who grew up with three truly rotten siblings," Nancy said. "Watch out for puberty, drugs and bad company, not necessarily in that order." She put her palms on the table and levered herself upright. One good thing. Her headache was gone. Adrenaline tended to do that.

"So go home to your happy household, and pray that we don't get any more messes tonight." She turned toward the door at the back of the clinic proper that separated the small animal area from the large. "I'll check on the Jack Russell. What's his name?"

Mac snorted. "Miracle."

"If not before, then definitely now."

"I sent the owners home. I'll tell Mabel to call and update them."

The recovery area and ICU were dimly lit. Big had laid the terrier on a thick rubber mattress in the middle of the room, and sat on the floor beside the little dog, stroking its small head and crooning softly.

"He's coming around," Big whispered. "You go on home, Miss Nancy."

She smiled. "Thanks. How's the mastiff?"

Big shrugged his massive shoulders. "He ain't dead. That's something."

She was halfway down the hallway that led to the front reception area when she stopped. "I hope I've *got* a ride home."

CHAPTER FOUR

NANCY TOOK LANCELOT out in her backyard on a leash at about eleven that evening to do his business. He kept pulling her toward her front yard and the lane, grumbling with annoyance. "Lancelot," she commanded. "I know you want to go home, but Helen and Bill don't live across the street any longer. You're staying with me for the foreseeable future."

He peered up at her in the light from her porch as though he didn't believe her for one minute.

"Why do I get the feeling you're smarter than I am?"

Eventually he finished, waddled up her back stairs, waited at the refrigerator until she gave him a bite of cheese—his evening treat was important to him, Helen had said—and settled into his basket. As she climbed into bed, she realized Poddy and Otto weren't waiting for her. She peered around the corner of her bedroom door and saw them curled up against Lancelot's belly. "Deserters," she said, then grabbed her pillow, beat it into submission and propped it under her head.

As tired as she was, she should have slept instantly. No such luck. She felt guilty, as she always did when she was bad-tempered.

Tim Wainwright must think she was the world's biggest bitch. She'd certainly snarled at him like a junkyard dog. She rolled over on her stomach and pulled her pillow over the back of her head. Then she rolled over on her other side. She couldn't get comfortable. Finally she lay on her back, stared up at the ceiling and let herself actually contemplate Tim

Wainwright as a male being, something she'd been consciously avoiding.

She still carried the scent of him in her nostrils. She hadn't been that close to a sweaty male in much too long. Time was when she and Peter used to shower together every night after the horses had been bedded down. She could still remember the feel of his strong hands kneading the kinks out of her shoulders, sliding down her body…

She hit her pillow with a couple of vicious blows. Peter was long gone out of her life. Lord knew how many other women he'd scrubbed since she'd divorced him. She still read about him in the horse magazines as his newly developed riders won trophies and awards.

"I have to thank my trainer, Peter Lombardi, for finding—*insert horse's name*—for me and training us. We owe this win to him." Or variations on that theme. The riders in question were always young, frequently blonde, invariably rich, occasionally talented. She still felt smug that he'd never found another rider who was as talented and fearless as she'd been, who could ride his green horses over fences and make them look like champions. Someone who could ride his crazy jumpers over fences that made the average rider sick with fear.

He'd never married any of the rest of them, either. Well, not so far.

She sat up and leaned against her headboard. She wasn't the least bit sleepy. She crawled out of bed, padded into the kitchen and pulled out the milk jug. Even in summer, a cup of hot chocolate was a guaranteed soporific. After all, she lived in an air-conditioned cottage.

She mixed herself a mug and slid it into the microwave. Two percent milk, nonfat chocolate powder. Unfortunately she'd never discovered a nonfat, nonsugar marshmallow. As she took out her steaming cup, she turned and saw Lancelot's little eyes watching her. "Oh, nuts," she said and poured a little chocolate into a saucer, blew on it, then set it down in front of him. The cats weren't allowed to have chocolate, but they didn't like it anyway, and Lancelot wouldn't be caught dead sharing. He set to with pleasure.

She took the hot chocolate out onto her front porch, sat in one of the old white cane rockers and pulled her feet up under her. The temperature had dropped to a respectable eighty degrees, and there was a fresh breeze blowing through the leaves of the big oak that shaded her roof. She blessed her mother's genes that kept the mosquitoes from biting her.

The house across the street was dark. She wondered where Tim slept. She hoped he didn't wear pajamas. She'd always thought men who slept in both top and bottoms were kind of wimpy and old-fashioned, but then she thought of male teachers as pretty wimpy on the whole. Hers certainly had been. Teaching high school must be a real comedown for somebody like that. She wondered if he was running away from some sort of scandal.

The kind of strong muscles she'd felt when he'd wrapped his arms around her didn't come from sitting behind a desk all day talking about Shakespeare and Tennyson. He must run, swim, lift weights—something to keep in shape. That kind of man probably slept nude.

The rocking chair seemed to have increased its speed. She shuddered and throttled it back. When the vision of an attractive man laying naked in bed brought her nipples to full attention and darned near tossed her out of the rocking chair on her nose, she knew she'd been alone in her own bed far too long.

One of the few good memories from her marriage was sleeping curled against Peter's naked back. Peter only wore pajamas to bed when Poppy, her stepdaughter from hell, or as Nancy called her, "The Worst Seed," stayed over.

Tim Wainwright apparently was raising at least two bad seeds of his own. Maybe three if Eddy was as weird as he seemed.

More reason to avoid the entire family. "If you're lousy at

something," Dr. Mac always said, "quit doing it and take up something you're good at."

She felt incompetent to deal with other people's children, and was absolutely, positively the world's worst stepmother. She hoped she hadn't scarred Poppy for life, although Poppy had inflicted some deep wounds of her own. Nancy swore she'd never give anyone a chance to slice and dice her again, nor did she intend to be responsible for even partially rearing anyone else's kids.

She just had to arm her libido against Tim Wainwright and the heady way his touch had made her feel.

She'd slept alone too long. She'd almost forgotten how it felt to have a man inside her, driving both of them higher until the explosion of pleasure took them over the top.

Hoo, boy. Enough of that.

She sighed and went to open the front door. Before she could get inside, she felt a sharp little foot on her instep.

"No! Lancelot." She shoved him back, slipped in and shut the door. "You're staying here, understand? Helen and Bill will come over to visit, and you'll be going to your new home with them before you realize it." She set her cup down in the sink, picked up his dish and put it to soak, then went and climbed back into bed. This time she absolutely, positively must get some sleep. Tomorrow looked like it was going to be one god-awful day.

SHE WOKE UP AT DAWN as always, even on Saturday. When she started to sit, she realized her neck was giving her fits. She'd been too tense the day before. Now she'd pay for it. She pulled on a sleeveless T-shirt and a pair of threadbare low-rider cutoffs and padded into the kitchen barefoot to take Lancelot out for his morning potty break.

Poddy and Otto slept curled together in the pet bed, but Lancelot wasn't in the kitchen. "Lancelot, if you're in the living room making a mess, I swear I'll barbecue you," she called. The cats each opened one eye, then went back to sleep. She rounded the corner and saw at once that the front door was ajar. She must not have latched it properly when she'd come back in. "Oh, no," she whispered. She grabbed Lancelot's leash and harness and ran out onto the front porch. He was nowhere in sight.

"Damn! I'll bet he's gone back home." She raced down the steps, taking care to slam the door behind her so that Otto and Poddy couldn't wander. The asphalt of the lane already felt hot on the soles of her bare feet, but she ignored it, hopping a couple of times when she stepped on pebbles, as she ran across Tim's lawn to his back door.

She nudged the pet door with her toe. It moved, so he hadn't locked it, although she didn't think the Wainwrights had a pet. She bent down, swung it open and tried to see into the kitchen. Next, she tried the back door. Locked.

Most of the people in Williamston left their doors open when they were home.

She peered through the window in the door, shading her eyes to see into the gloom. No sign of Lancelot. He must be inside somewhere. He'd probably scare those children into catatonia.

She raced around to the front of the house, tiptoed onto the front porch and tried to see into the room the Halliburtons had used for their master bedroom. The curtains were drawn. She could see only a sliver of a foot of the bed.

Okay, Okay, she thought, *what do I do*? Bang on the door, ring the doorbell, wake those city folks up at five on a Saturday morning to tell them they have an intruder? Somehow she didn't think they'd be pleased. Besides, Lancelot was her responsibility, and this was her fault.

Only one thing to do.

She went to the back porch again. "Please, Helen," she prayed. "Please have left the spare key over the door." She stood on tiptoe and felt around. Her index finger touched something metallic.

She dislodged it, saw the key fall, made a grab for it in midair and missed.

It clinked on the porch steps. She dived after it and caught it before it could clink again. Now on her hands and knees bent over the step, she wondered whether she'd actually have the nerve to use it.

She and the Halliburtons had looked after each other's property a million times. They knew where she hid her spare key, and where the spare keys to her storage shed and car were kept in the kitchen. She'd watered Helen's house plants when they were out of town, and taken in their mail and newspapers. Helen and Bill had fed the cats when she was gone.

But this wasn't Helen and Bill. New owners often changed locks. Maybe the key wouldn't even fit.

Tentatively she slid the key into the lock. It went in. She began to twist it slowly. It turned. The lock clicked.

Now what? Barge in, call out, "Yoo-hoo, it's Nancy!" and assume Tim hadn't had time to get a handgun permit yet? Technically she wasn't breaking in, but she was definitely entering.

She took a deep breath, put her hand along the jamb to keep the door from squeaking, opened it and stepped into the kitchen.

The refrigerator door stood ajar. On the floor in front of it was a bottle of Perrier. Intact, thank the Lord. So far as she knew, Lancelot had not yet learned to open screw caps. She put the sparkling water back. The refrigerator was empty except for several more bottles of Perrier and a couple of big bottles of soda—also screw-on tops. Lancelot must have been extremely disappointed. He could open any pop-top can he could reach.

She closed the refrigerator softly and looked around for evidence of destruction.

The kitchen looked clean. Cluttered, of course. At least a dozen cardboard boxes sat on the counters waiting to be unpacked, but Lancelot hadn't been able to reach high enough to pull any of them off in his lifelong quest for treats.

She stood in the archway leading to the living room and listened. For a moment, there was nothing but silence, then she heard a soft snore from across the living room and down the hall. Tim must be sleeping in the Halliburtons' master bedroom. She prayed Lancelot had gone in there and not up the stairs to join one of the children.

Slipping silently across the wood floor, she edged around the boxes and furniture in the living room and started down the hall. The door at the end was open and the snoring was louder now.

Five feet from that door she saw the figure in the bed. Wainwright.

He was not alone.

Beside him, spooned against his belly, head on a pillow, lay Lancelot.

He was the one snoring.

Wainwright lay under a single sheet, his naked shoulders exposed, his arm thrown casually across Lancelot's back. He was breathing evenly.

She got down on her hands and knees and crawled into the room.

"Lancelot," she whispered. "Get down here."

No response. She crawled closer. "Lancelot!" It was hard to whisper with menace, but she tried. "Get down here this instant."

Lancelot raised his head and stared at her unperturbed.

"Now!"

"Wha…?"

She froze. *Please, God, don't let him wake up.*

Tim sighed.

She shut her eyes and began to back out on her hands and knees.

"What the hell!"

He sat straight up in bed. No pajama top. No pajama bottoms, either. Apparently, he saw her on her hands and knees two feet inside his bedroom at the same time he registered that his bed buddy was not the houri he'd no doubt been dreaming about.

He didn't exactly shriek. The sound was too deep and male

for that. He gave a sort of combined gurgle and yelp and lunged sideways off the bed.

His feet hit the floor. He grabbed the sheet and held it waist-high in front of him, but not before she had a glimpse of a well-muscled hairy stomach.

For a moment he simply gaped at her.

"Hi," she said, and wiggled her fingers at him.

Lancelot, thoroughly awake now and aware that he was sleeping with a stranger, squealed, fell onto the floor and tried to wedge himself under the bed. Since the bed was low and modern, he only made it as far as his snout.

"*That* is a pig," Tim said, pointing to the bristly butt sticking up on the far side of the bed. He sounded very, very calm.

"Uh-huh." Nancy sat back on her heels. She held up Lancelot's harness and leash.

"I'm sure there's a simple explanation why he was sharing my bed. Is it a he?"

She nodded. "His name is Lancelot."

"And an equally simple explanation why you're crouching at the foot of my bed at dawn."

She nodded. "I was after Lancelot."

"I see. Apart from the obvious question of how he wound up in my bed, it occurs to me to wonder if you've ever heard the term 'doorbell.'"

Oh, boy. This guy was a good deal more annoying when he was in the right. She pushed herself up to a standing position and took a deep breath. "I didn't want to wake you."

"Isn't that kind of you."

"Well, you're the one who left the pet flap unlocked."

"My mistake. I should have realized I'd wind up in bed with a pig. Sorry."

"Listen, you. It could have been a possum or a raccoon or God forbid a skunk. Not to mention a copperhead or a water moccasin."

"I'm curious. Did you also crawl in the dog door? Frankly you don't look as though you'd fit." He ran his gaze from her head to her toes.

She wished she'd taken the time to put on her sneakers, let alone a bra and underpants. She felt her face flame. She knew damned well her nipples were standing out to here, and her shorts not only bared her navel, but covered precious little below it.

"No, I did *not* crawl in the pet door," she said with hauteur. "I used the spare key over the back door."

"Ah. The spare key over the back door. My, I wish someone had mentioned that to me."

"Here it is," she said and tossed it onto the rumpled bed.

"Thank you."

"Now, if you don't mind, I'll put Lancelot's harness on and take him home."

He waved a hand, nearly dropped the sheet and clutched it in front of him again. At that moment, she realized he was standing in front of a full-length mirror that had been propped against the wall beside the bed. The sheet might be concealing the family jewels, but she was learning a good deal more about Mr. Wainwright's backside than she had thought she ever would. It was an extremely nice backside. Better than nice. Great. She felt her temperature rising just looking at him. If only he knew.

She gulped and grabbed Lancelot. She had to get away from that mirror before he caught her staring and turned around to see what had riveted her. "Lancelot belongs to the Halliburtons, the tenants you *evicted*," she said. "The poor baby's staying with me because they can't have pets in the poky little apartment they're stuck with in Collierville, while they *try* to find a house they can afford closer to Williamston. He just wanted to come home where his people loved him." She hoped she was laying it on thick enough. Although she doubted he'd care.

She clipped the leash to Lancelot's harness, stood and began to haul him toward the bedroom door. "It won't happen again. I apologize for our intrusion."

"No problem."

Now she had to turn her back to him. She knew her shorts weren't much less revealing of *her* backside than what she'd seen in the mirror of his.

"Do you always go barefoot?" he asked.

"In the summer, often. Seldom in January." Better than bare-*assed*, she thought, and despite all her efforts, began to snicker. "Come on, Lancelot, bad pig," she said and pulled on his leash. He squealed and yanked back.

She made it all the way to the back steps before uncontrollable laughter broke the surface. She sank onto the back steps, hugged Lancelot to her and laughed until the tears ran down her cheeks.

At the same moment that Nancy began to laugh, Tim dropped his sheet and turned around. It took him a moment to process what he was seeing in the full-length mirror—and to realize what Nancy Mayfield had been looking at for the past five minutes.

That's when he heard her laughing.

CHAPTER FIVE

NANCY HAD BARELY dragged Lancelot home and fed him and the cats when her doorbell rang. She froze. It had to be Tim Wainwright. No doubt infuriated. No doubt accusing her of burglary, being a Peeping Tom and assault with a deadly pig.

Might as well face him now. After all, he was supposed to drive her to the car rental agency. If he didn't, she was stuck, and she needed to check on the mastiff and the Jack Russell at the clinic. Not to mention the usual Saturday grocery shopping. She opened the door prepared for a frontal assault, no pun intended.

The kid—Eddy, was it?—stood on the doorstep. He stared up at her with those blank, unblinking blue eyes. He was cradling something in his arms.

She caught her breath. All puppies looked pretty much alike at this age except in size, but this one had come from small parents and would probably stay small itself. Possibly some mixed variety that included Jack Russell terrier and dachshund.

Eddy held it out to her. "Please?" he said. His voice sounded rusty from disuse, deep and gravelly for a child his age.

She feared the pup was dead from the way it lay in the child's arms, but when she took it, she felt the flutter of a small heart. And the warmth of blood on her palms. She turned and raced for her kitchen, as she called over her shoulder, "Come in, shut the door behind you tight so the animals don't get out."

She heard the sound of the lock clicking into place and then the patter of bare feet on her floorboards.

She grabbed a dry dish towel off the rack beside the sink and laid the pup on it. Poor little thing, it was too traumatized or too hurt to fight. "Hit by a car, probably," she said as she gently lifted the satiny brown baby hair away from the place she had felt blood.

She gasped. The flesh was raw, the burns so deep she could see blistered muscle tissue. The pup wriggled and mewed more like a small kitten than a dog. Instantly Poddy jumped onto the drain board. "Down, Poddy, go 'way. I'm not hurting it."

She felt rather than saw Eddy beside her. "Please," he whispered again.

"Did you do this?" she asked sharply without taking her eyes off the pup. She ran cold water over a dish towel and, folding it, placed it over the wound, then turned to glare down at him.

He shook his head. Those blue eyes stared into hers, and for the first time she saw expression in him. A single tear ran down his cheek, cutting a swatch through the dirt. "I found him." He reached out and touched the brown pup's little skull tentatively. "Please don't let him die." Without warning, he began to shake his head fiercely and backed away from the sink. "Mustn't die, mustn't die!"

She caught his shoulder. He was thin, but wiry. He was as tense as a crossbow. Probably just as ready to snap. "I won't lie. He's in shock. Otherwise you'd never have been able to carry him. He'd have bitten you."

She turned back to the sink. "Somebody's poured lighter fluid or kerosene on him and lit it, but they did a lousy job. He must have broken loose and put out the fire in the damp grass. He's brown. He wouldn't have been easy to spot in the dark once the fire was out."

"Somebody hurt him? On purpose?"

As she talked, she gently cleaned the debris and grass away, then placed a dry towel over the pup to keep him warm. "It's nasty and deep, but you did the right thing bringing him to me. Let's see what I can do."

Her voice had gentled frightened animals for years. *Let's see if I can gentle this little Eddy beast*, she thought as she went to get the first-aid case she kept at home. She was used to opening the door to neighbors with baby squirrels or birds that had fallen from nests, hurt cats and dogs, momma possums hit by cars with their bellies still full of their young—everything including snakes and cows…even the occasional fawn. So her kit was extensive.

By the time she came back, Poddy was sitting on the counter beside the pup. Wonder of wonders, Eddy was stroking him, not a liberty he allowed many people. Lancelot watched them from his basket. She didn't think Eddy had noticed him yet. "Okay," she said, "let's spray a bit of painkiller over that wound, so we can clean it up and see what we've got." She looked down at Eddy. "Won't your father wonder where you are?"

He shook his head without taking his eyes off the pup or his grubby, small hand off Poddy. "He's asleep."

"I don't think he is." Probably calling the cops. "You sure you want to watch?" she asked. "Then we'll call your father so he won't worry."

"Not watch. Help."

She dealt frequently with people who didn't want to watch or even to help when their animals were in pain, and many parents who felt junior's tender sensibilities couldn't take watching the birth of the kittens or the excision of a sarcoid tumor on a horse's flank. As far as Nancy was concerned, if a child was old enough to ask to watch, he was old enough to know the truth about the event. She didn't particularly enjoy children, considered herself hopeless with them, so she treated them like adults. It was all she knew to do.

"Okay," she said. "Hold his jaws together gently. He's warming up and really starting to hurt. He's small, but he can still bite." The pup had begun to whine and scrabble. She was afraid to give him a shot—any amount of sedative could kill him. She pulled on latex gloves and sprayed the wound with a solution that would deaden the tissue at once.

Eddy stood beside her with his fingers around the pup's jaw. Without asking, he took the pup's four legs in his other hand to keep the pup still, as Nancy clipped what remained of singed fur and trimmed off the seared skin around the deepest part of the burn.

Give the kid credit. He didn't back off from the blood or the stench of burned hair and skin. On closer look, the blisters weren't as deep as she'd thought. The actual muscles hadn't been attacked, nor had any of the major blood vessels. She finished cleaning and treating the pup with antiburn salve, antibiotics and more painkiller, then bound the wound around the pup's belly. "Okay, kid, that's got it for the moment," she said as she peeled off her gloves and tossed them into the wastebasket.

"Will he be all right?"

"No idea, but I think so. He's going to need care. He's probably eating on his own, but his mother may still suckle him as well. Did you find any others like this?"

Eddy shook his head.

Nancy shuddered. Please God let's hope this was the only victim. The mother and other pups might not have been so lucky. "Where'd you find him? And what are you doing up so early anyway?" She slipped her hands under the pup, towel and all. "Go into my bathroom. Linen closet's the little door on the left. Bring me a couple of towels. We'll make him a bed."

Eddy didn't ask questions. He stiffened for a moment when he spotted Lancelot, and edged warily around his bed, but he got the towels. Together they settled the pup on top of a folded blue bath towel, and covered him with another to keep him warm.

"Ever nurse a puppy?"

Eddy shook his head.

"Then it's time you learned." She fetched one of the small nursing bottles and a box of dry puppy milk formula from her case, mixed up the formula with warm water and put the nipple on. She handed the bottle to the child, who immediately hunkered down beside the pup.

"Snuggle him in your lap, towel and all."

Eddy did as he was told, and within seconds the puppy was suckling contentedly.

She was certain Lancelot would intrude the moment he smelled the milk. Amazingly he seemed to understand that this was one time he shouldn't. He didn't take his eyes off Eddy, but he stayed in his bed and confined his comments to the occasional snuffle.

She sat on the floor beside the boy. "Now, where'd you find him? Do you know who did this?"

He shook his head. "I went out in the yard. You fix animals, so I brought him."

He must have been outside while she'd been trying to spring Lancelot from Tim's bed. She wondered how he planned to get back into the house. The back door locked automatically when it was on the latch as she had left it. He probably hadn't thought that far ahead.

The Halliburtons' yard—she had to stop thinking of it as the Halliburtons'—was surrounded by thick woods that went down to the lake. Hers, across the lane, had a ten-acre pasture behind it with an old barn. The rest of the fifty acres she owned was covered in equally dense woods.

The nearest house directly behind Eddy's was probably a couple of miles south of the village on the side road. She'd have to go over to those woods to see if she could find any other wounded animals and the scene of the crime, because it was a crime. She'd call Mike O'Hara, the sheriff, and notify him they had a mutilator in the neighborhood. He could alert the rest of the community.

"Do you know what happened to it?"

Eddy looked up at her. "Why would somebody burn it?"

She had to admit the possibility that he'd done it himself, then become frightened of what he'd done and tried to save the animal.

Nancy didn't think so though. She'd seen kids and adults who mutilated animals for what they considered fun. They felt nothing except annoyance that they'd been caught. Animal cruelty was one of the first symptoms of a psychopathic personality—a Ted Bundy in the making. She couldn't remember the other symptoms—that spelled trouble.

That Wainwright guy ought to know. "Eddy, do you know if either Jason or Angie went out of the house last night?"

His head jerked up. "They like animals."

Smart kid. Knew precisely why she was asking.

"Angie's horse-crazy. Jason even liked the sheep."

Nancy had no idea what sheep, but for the moment, at least, she respected Eddy's take on his siblings.

"He's finished," Eddy said. "See?" He held the empty bottle up.

"Okay, rub his tummy until he piddles and poops." She reached under the sink for a new roll of paper towels, took a couple and handed them to Eddy.

He didn't hesitate. He simply set to work until the pup had evacuated satisfactorily. Nancy took the neatly folded paper towels from him. They'd go outside in the trash.

"Do you have any idea who he belongs to?" she asked. Stupid question. If she didn't recognize the pup or its parents after six years in the neighborhood, he couldn't be expected to know after one night.

Eddy shook his head and laid the sleeping pup and his nest back into the corner.

"That presents a problem. If I take him to the clinic, it costs money, and I suspect he's a stray."

"Can't he stay here? I'll look after him."

She knew absolutely, positively that she shouldn't even consider agreeing. "At his age he needs to be fed every four to six hours, and his bandage changed morning and night. We'll get him onto puppy food soaked in milk, and after he starts getting better he'll need to go outside to the bathroom."

"School doesn't start for a while," Eddy said with what passed for enthusiasm with this child. "I can do it."

"I'm sure your father won't want you spending all your time looking after the pup."

"Sure he will." Then he ducked his head and all enthusiasm vanished. "He said we couldn't have a dog yet. I could keep him here." He stroked the pup's head. "And I can pay you. My Gran'mere will send me some money if I ask her."

When he looked up at her, she wondered how she could ever have thought he was expressionless. Such longing, such sadness, such hope! What had happened to this child to make him close down? She'd have to find out. And if that Wainwright fellow had anything to do with it, she'd see him rot in hell.

As if in answer to her summons, the doorbell rang again. Eddy jumped. "That's my daddy," he whispered.

"Stay here."

"Do we have to tell him?"

"Don't worry, Eddy, I'll handle it."

When she opened her front door, Wainwright stepped in without asking. "Have you seen my son? I can't find him."

"He's here," she said, and turned back to the kitchen.

"Eddy," Tim rushed past her.

Eddy hunched over the puppy's nest.

Tim squatted beside his son. "Eddy, don't you ever do that again, you hear me?" Then he hugged the boy.

If he was an abuser, he was good at concealing it. Nancy saw tears in his eyes.

He held Eddy at arm's length. "Son, you're filthy. And no shoes. Where've you been?"

"I went out. I thought I'd be back before you woke up." Then, as if realizing he'd actually spoken more than a few words at a time, he seemed to shrink into himself. "I'm sorry."

She saw Tim gulp convulsively.

"It's okay, son. It's good that you wanted to go out and explore. Just don't go out alone again without telling me. Even if I'm still in bed, I'll get up and go with you. Maybe we'll all go. We definitely need to explore our land, but this is the country. There's a whole bunch of new stuff you're not used to—snakes and fast trucks and woods and streams. You could have gotten lost." He drew back and glanced over his shoulder. "And what are you doing over here bothering Miss Mayfield?"

No mention of their previous meeting. Thank God he chose to ignore it.

Eddy looked down at the nest. The only visible portion of the pup was an inch of charred brown ear.

"How about I make some coffee," Nancy said. "I've also got OJ and a coffee cake. Sit down and let Eddy tell you about it. He's a real hero."

Eddy gave her a grateful look. She winked at him. Whether Tim Wainwright liked it or not, his son had a dog. If she had anything to say about it, he'd keep it.

CHAPTER SIX

TIM SIPPED HIS COFFEE and watched with wonder as his son wolfed down his third piece of coffee cake. He was on his second glass of orange juice, as well. In the past year, Eddy had grown thinner and thinner. Tim gave him vitamins, made certain his mother-in-law kept the house filled with fruit and lunch meat as well as pastry and tried to believe the doctors who told him his son was perfectly healthy. Physically, maybe he was.

Didn't stop Tim from worrying. On the one hand, he had to watch his mother-in-law to keep her from stuffing Angie, already verging on pudgy, with French pastry. Jason could eat Chicago without gaining an ounce. Every calorie went straight up. Eddy seemed to have lost his sense of self-preservation when he lost his mother.

Now, here he was swigging orange juice and actually kicking the rungs of the kitchen chair like a normal kid. He opened his mouth to admonish his son, then clapped it shut. If it didn't bother her, it shouldn't bother him.

"So you see, he's a hero," Miss Mayfield said.

"I'm going to look after him while Nancy's at work," Eddy said. He met his father's eyes as though daring him to object.

"The lady's name is Miss Mayfield," Tim said automatically.

"Nancy," she said, "I hate being called Miss Mayfield. Makes me feel as old as my grandmother." She smiled at Eddy, who actually smiled back. "Nobody in Williamston stands much on ceremony. We all live too close to one another." He saw her give a convulsive gulp as though she realized what she'd just said. She quickly poured Tim another cup of coffee without being asked and turned her back on the table.

Lancelot had managed to stay on his good behavior until he smelled the coffee cake. He sat at Eddy's feet and gave an occasional soft oink. Tim saw that Eddy was sneaking him bits of coffee cake under the table. He seemed to accept Lancelot as casually as he did the cats.

Lancelot pushed his snout against Tim's leg. One look into those eyes and Tim was forced to give him a bit of coffee cake himself.

So far the only eyes he'd managed to avoid were Nancy's. She seemed to be cooperating by avoiding his as well. Good. Better to forget the entire incident with the pig and the mirror. God that sounded like a fairy tale. Despite his previous resolution to stay aloof, he found himself grinning down at Lancelot.

Besides, he couldn't stay aloof when he was so elated that Eddy had found something worth fighting for.

"Wonderful coffee," he said. "Chicago coffee tends to be dark auburn unless you spend a fortune for it at Starbucks." Actually the coffee could probably strip the bristles off Lancelot's back, but at the moment, that was what he needed. He wasn't used to 5:00 a.m. crises.

"Thanks," she said. "Be back in a minute."

He watched her go into what must be her bedroom. He could see the corner of a high, unmade bed through the doorway.

She still wore her cutoffs and a T-shirt. Even seminaked and embarrassed in his bedroom, Tim had appreciated the sight of his new neighbor as she dragged that blasted pig down his hallway. A man who didn't enjoy looking at her long legs and tight rear end would have to be dead. Tim wasn't quite dead. He was, however, turning into a randy old man. Celibacy tended to do that to the male of the species.

He realized he was getting hard, took an almighty gulp of

coffee, scalded the roof of his mouth and drank half of Eddy's orange juice.

"Hey!" Eddy protested.

Tim laughed. In the past eighteen months Eddy hadn't cared enough about anything to feel proprietary. Even a little thing like begrudging his father a swig of orange juice was a major victory. He put down his son's glass and topped it up from the pitcher on the table. "You realize you've drunk an entire orange grove there, son."

"Oh." Eddy looked away and set his glass down untouched.

Tim wanted to kick himself. "Joke," he said. "Tell you what. We'll bring Miss Mayfield—"

"Nancy," Eddy corrected.

"—Nancy a gallon of OJ from the grocery."

At that moment Nancy came back into the kitchen. She had combed her short, brown hair, but those delectable nipples were still very visible under the thin cotton of her T-shirt.

"I called Mike O'Hara," she said. "He's the sheriff. Lives a couple of miles outside town. He's going to stop by on his way into the office. He wants to talk to you, Eddy, find out exactly where you found your pup."

Eddy's terrified eyes went straight to his father's face. "Do I have to?"

"He's a great guy," Nancy explained. "He's proud of you, too." The look on Eddy's face didn't change. "Say, I thought I heard a whimper. You better go check on your puppy. Why don't you move his bed into my bedroom?"

Eddy slipped off his chair, went over to the corner, scooped up pup and towels, and disappeared through Nancy's bedroom door without a word.

"Of course what was done to the dog is a crime," Tim said. "I should have realized."

"A felony. There may be more hurt dogs out there that weren't so lucky as Eddy's puppy. He needs a name, by the way."

Tim started to say that the dog wasn't actually Eddy's, but stopped. Of course the puppy was Eddy's. It would remain Eddy's even if he had to fight half of Williamston for possession. "Eddy will come up with something."

Nancy took the chair across from Tim. "Okay, what gives with Eddy?"

Tim sat up. "That's hardly your business."

"The minute he dragged that burned puppy into my house, it became my business. At first I thought he must have burned the puppy himself—"

"Eddy loves animals! He'd never—"

"Calm down. I said at first. Nothing like this has happened in Williamston in the six years I've lived here."

Tim felt his temperature rising. "Then the first night we're here, somebody burns a puppy in my yard?"

"You do have two other children."

Tim wanted to snatch Eddy, stalk out and slam the door after him.

"I'm not accusing you," Nancy said.

"The hell you're not."

"You think Mike's not going to ask these questions? You're supposed to be this hotshot educator with degrees up the wazoo. You must know about kids who like to torture animals."

"Not my children." Suddenly he felt his anger evaporate. She was right, although he didn't like to admit it. He walked over and looked into Nancy's bedroom. Eddy slept on the rag rug beside her bed with the puppy's bed in the crook of his arm. Lancelot had moved to snuggle into the crook behind his knees and was fast asleep as well. The two cats, he noted, were curled up together on the foot of the bed where they could oversee everything. Tim closed the door softly and went back to his place at Nancy's table.

"A year ago my wife was killed in a drive-by shooting."

Nancy caught her breath. "Oh, I am so sorry!"

"It's been hard on all of us, but especially Eddy. He was the youngest and the closest to Solange, I think."

"Solange? Is that Angie's real name?"

He nodded. "Her father brought his family to Chicago from St. Nazaire in the fifties. He was a chemical engineer. Solange was born in Chicago."

"Of course I hear about drive-by shootings, but I guess nobody ever thinks it will happen to them."

Tim took a deep breath. "After she was killed, we did grief counseling, went a couple of times to groups for people who've lost loved ones to violence. The kids hated it. You can see how Angie reacted." He laughed ruefully. "The day she dyed her hair jet-black, I thought her grandmother would have a stroke." He glanced at Nancy. "Solange's mother has been babysitter and substitute parent since Solange was killed."

"I'm surprised you didn't bring her down with you."

"She wouldn't have come. She thinks *Chicago* is barbaric. God only knows what she'd make of Williamston." He wondered whether Nancy would notice his tense. He hadn't actually asked Madame to join them. One of his reasons for leaving Chicago was to get away from her.

"Anyway, Jason seemed to be doing okay bar the oversize clothes. Then his grades started falling, I caught him smoking—only tobacco, thank God—and he started hanging around with some local gang wannabes. Then he took up skateboarding. You've already seen the hair and the earring holes. The next step would have been tattoos. He's basically sound, but I was afraid he wouldn't stay sound if I didn't get him away."

"And Eddy?"

"Eddy shut down. He's been a little ghost. Never speaks unless he's spoken to, does what he's told, makes A's in school. A Stepford kid." He ran his hand over his short hair. "Even the psychologists couldn't get through to him. I certainly couldn't." He nodded at her. "But you did."

"Not me." She nodded toward the bedroom door. "What's the fancy academic phrase for therapy dog?"

CHAPTER SEVEN

SHERIFF MIKE O'HARA loved being sheriff nearly as much as he loved his fine herd of Red Brahman cattle. He liked to tell everyone who would listen, he either had to run cows or take bribes to keep his kid in private school. "So far I prefer cows," he'd say. "Nobody's offered me a good enough bribe yet."

He looked like one of the bulls he raised. He was only about five foot ten, but red hair covered his head, arms, knuckles and probably his back. Nancy had never seen his back and didn't want to. He was built like his bulls as well. Big neck, big shoulders, thick chest, which was only beginning its inevitable slide south of his beltline, the thighs of a football lineman and huge feet in highly polished ostrich boots. Since today was Saturday, he wore a tan polo shirt stretched tight across his chest and cowboy cut jeans worn extra long and crumpled over the ankles of his boots.

Nancy caught Tim's dismay when Mike walked into her cottage. The heels of his boots cracked against her hardwood floors. Even though he was shorter than Tim, he looked formidable. Tim was no doubt afraid that the sight of this wide man with a gun on his belt would terrify his fragile son.

"Hey, Dr. Wainwright," Mike said as he extended his hand. "Glad to have you in Williamston."

Nancy grinned at Tim's surprise. Mike O'Hara's voice was a sweet, gentle light baritone that made listening to the choir at the Williamston Baptist Church on Sunday a real pleasure. Still, to be on the safe side, she warned him again about Eddy. She did not, however, mention the death of Tim's wife. That was up to Tim.

Tim started to follow him as he went toward Nancy's bedroom, but Mike shook his head. "Don't worry, Doc. I won't scare him."

They watched him hunker down beside the child, who was already stirring from his nap. When Mike spoke to him, he rubbed his eyes, then sat up quickly the moment he glimpsed the sheriff looming over him. Nancy saw Eddy's startled expression, watched him shrink closer to the bundled puppy, then relax as Mike's voice flowed over him. Mike scratched behind Lancelot's ears as he talked.

Five minutes later, Mike came back with his arm draped across Eddy's shoulders. "Boy here's a real hero, Doc. Got yourself a good young'un. He's gonna show me right where he found the pup."

"I'll come with you, if you don't mind," Tim said. Nancy could tell he didn't give a damn whether Mike minded or not.

"Me, too," she said. "Soon as I get some shoes on. Eddy, how's your pup doing?"

"He was whimpering a little, but I calmed him down." He nodded. "He's breathing real good."

"I'll check on him first," Nancy said. "By the time we're finished he'll probably need another bottle. You game?"

"He's *my* puppy."

Eddy was right. He was breathing well. She sprayed some more pain killer on the gauze that covered his burns, stroked his small, brown velvet head, pulled on a pair of deck shoes and ran across the street to find the men.

Mike was saying, "Probably some teenage idiot and his drunken buddies." He turned to her. "Nancy, looks like the pup may have been tossed out of a car." He shook his head. "Somebody's idea of a Roman candle. Rolling in the grass probably saved his life, and the high grass and those soft baby bones probably kept him from breaking up when he hit."

"You can't find any others?"

Mike shrugged. "Let's hope he's all there were." He glanced at Eddy, then at Nancy and raised an eyebrow. She got the message.

"Eddy, you know where the puppy formula is," Nancy said. "Wash out the bottle really well and rinse it a lot before you mix up the formula. You okay with that?"

"Uh-huh." He started to run across the lane, but his father grabbed him.

"Eddy, this may not be Chicago, but cars do drive this road. You know better. Look both ways and don't run."

"Yes, sir." Eddy looked both ways, then dashed full tilt across the street and into Nancy's house.

"Is it all right for him to be in your house by himself?" Tim asked.

"Unless he's a budding burglar. Not that I have much to steal."

"I wanted to look some more, Doc," Mike explained. "If we do find something bad, I didn't want the boy around."

"Thanks. What do we do? Quarter the area?"

"You got it. Work front to back. Nancy, you and Doc take the yard on the north side. We'll meet in the back."

Fifteen minutes later they had worked their way to the edge of the woods at the back of Tim's property without finding anything.

"I'll fill out a report and tell my boys to keep a lookout on patrol," Mike said. "Probably kids from town drunk on beer and stupid. You hear any hoo-rawing outside last night?"

Both Nancy and Tim shook their heads.

"Well, let's hope it's an isolated incident. Nice to meet you, Doc. Bye, Nancy. Come see us." He walked across the street to where his squad car sat behind Nancy's car. He gave no indication that he noticed Nancy's flat tire and dented bumper, although he must have seen the damage.

As he pulled away, a bright red tow truck turned the corner from the village common and pulled up in front of Nancy's house.

"Nuts," she whispered. "I haven't even brushed my teeth,

much less taken a shower. Can you see to getting the car onto the tow truck?" She started across the street. Tim followed.

"My bad. My responsibility. I talked to my insurance agent last night. He should have made arrangements with your dealer to have it fixed by now. He said they'd furnish a loaner."

"Fast work."

"He's an old friend." He grimaced. "Actually I told him the accident occurred on private property, and that I intended to pay the tab personally. I'm not making a claim."

Nancy's eyebrows went up.

"Cheaper than skyrocketing insurance rates."

"It's going to cost you."

"It's going to cost Jason in the long run," Tim said grimly. "By the time he finishes paying me back, he'll be the safest driver in Tennessee."

BECAUSE EDDY REFUSED to leave his puppy to go with Nancy and Tim to get her car fixed and pick up a rental, Nancy suggested they take the pup and Eddy with them.

"We can stop by the clinic," she said. "If you're going to keep him, then you really need a doctor to check him out. I'm good, but I'm a vet tech, not a veterinarian." She turned to Tim. "A dog, even a healthy one, is a big responsibility. He needs shots, heart worm tests and medication, the right sort of food, vitamins, toys and when he's better he'll need exercise and a safe place to play. Dogs run loose around here, but it's a bad idea, especially for a small one." She didn't want to add that despite her best efforts, the puppy might not make it.

Tim put his hand on Eddy's fair hair. "We can afford a little dog like this, can't we, son? He'll be mostly your responsibility, you know."

"I'll take good care of him," Eddy said, his pale eyes gleaming. He went into Nancy's bedroom and came back a moment later with the pup in his arms. After she settled child and dog in the back seat of Tim's SUV, she turned to Tim. "He's too little to take full responsibility for a pet, Dr. Wainwright. The responsibility will be yours. Are you willing to accept that?"

Tim grinned and shrugged. "My mission, should I choose to accept it? Yeah, I choose."

As they drove the twenty miles to Collierville, Tim said, "Jason and Angie are old enough to stay alone in the daytime. Frankly I doubt they'll wake up before we get home, but I left a note for them. On weekends they can sleep around the clock. They have my cell phone number. At your clinic last night, I found Jason staring at a ewe and a couple of lambs. He actually seemed interested. That young man—Kevin, I think he said his name was—took him to see a horse under treatment."

"It's Kenny. He's our very own rescue project," Nancy said. "He's a rich kid from the neighborhood. We caught him in the act of vandalizing and put him to work after school. Complete turnaround."

"Hmm."

At the car dealership, Nancy was horrified to learn the cost of her repairs. She was glad she wasn't paying for them. She had little enough extra money, and she was already culling some of her old growth trees to pay for a kitchen update on her cottage.

The good news was that the car didn't require as much work as she'd feared. She suspected the cost would be a shock to Tim as well. He couldn't be making much as a high school teacher at Maybree. She almost considered splitting the cost, but gave up the idea. Let Jason pay his father back.

"Should be done by Tuesday afternoon, Nancy," said Ralph Simmons, the service manager, who'd looked after her last three cars. "Here." He handed her a set of keys. "It's not what you're used to, but it's the only loaner they could get today. They brought it over first thing this morning." He pointed to a small, black two-door sedan. It looked as though it might hold two bags of groceries tops. Still, it was transportation. She wouldn't have to rely on Tim and his brood to get her around anymore.

"Follow me to Creature Comfort," she said to Tim. "One of the good things about being on staff is that we can go in the back door and not have to wait. Dr. Hazard's on duty this morning. He doesn't generally work Saturdays."

Later, as he went over the pup, Dr. Hazard said, "Nice job, Nancy."

"Can you stitch up his wound?" Tim asked.

Hazard shook his head. "Needs to heal from the inside out slowly. We'll treat it with antibiotic ointment, painkiller and, after it starts to heal, hydrocortisone ointment. I'd like to keep him here until Monday in our intensive care. The biggest threat at the moment is infection. And pups his age can simply fade." He glanced down at Eddy.

So did Nancy. From Eddy's narrow eyes and set jaw, she could tell he had no intention of relinquishing his charge without a fight.

"I can look after him," Eddy said. "He's my dog."

"Obviously you can," Dr. Hazard said. "He wouldn't have gotten this far without you. You can visit him tomorrow. By then he may actually feel like moving around a little. But doing the best for our animals is not always the happiest thing for us humans."

Nancy thought Eddy would keep fighting. Instead he deflated. Her heart went out to him. One look at the concern in Tim's face and her heart went out to him as well. "Tell you what. You and I will go settle him down in intensive care. I'll introduce you to the people who'll be looking after him. Your dad has to go fill out some papers anyway, so we can sit with him until he meets us. Okay?"

Eddy shrugged and turned away, all the fight gone out of him.

"Hey, you're forgetting somebody." Nancy pointed to the pup, who was scrabbling around on the slick table like a small brown seal.

Eddy looked at her. "Can I carry him?"

"Your dog, remember? Just because he's here doesn't mean

you can let other people take over completely." She handed him a clean towel. "Pick him up with this."

Eddy lifted the pup to his shoulder. He leaned his cheek against the little dog's silky head while the pup snuggled tight under his chin.

Nancy left Tim with Dr. Hazard as they walked down the hall toward the ICU area. "He's got to have a name. We can't just keep calling him pup."

At that moment Big Little opened the door to the ICU and stepped out into the hall. Eddy stopped so quickly that Nancy ran into him. He must also have gripped the pup, because the little dog let out a tiny yelp.

"Hey, Miss Nancy," Big said, flashing her and Eddy his brilliant smile. "Hey, young'un."

Eddy's gulp was audible.

"Hey, Big," Nancy said. "Eddy, Big here is our nursemaid. He'll take really good care of your pup."

"But…" Eddy looked back at Nancy over his shoulder. She could see the fear and consternation in his face.

"Y'all just come on in here," Big said. "Y'all can help ole—what's his name, boy?"

"Just Pup," Eddy whispered.

"Okay, now you give me JustPup here and we'll fix him up a nice soft bed."

"Can I pet him some?"

"Lordy, yes." Big opened the door to the ICU area and ushered Eddy, JustPup and Nancy through.

"He's shy," she whispered.

Big nodded. "Yes'm." He looked down at his gigantic feet a little sadly. "Guess he's sceert 'cause I'm so big."

Nancy patted his arm. "He won't be once he gets to know you."

Big set up the ICU cage, sat on the air mattress in the center of the room and invited Eddy and the pup to sit beside him. Big held the little dog as though it were a baby bird while Eddy stroked it. With each stroke he inched closer to Big until he was leaning against his massive thigh.

Nancy checked the large cages first. Wonder of wonders, the mastiff was sitting up on his own. In the small cages, the Jack Russell was already standing, wagging his tail and yapping. Bless Mac Thorn! He truly could work miracles.

"What say we put JustPup here in his house and let him have a nap?" Big asked Eddy. "I got to let out my dog, Daisy, for a little run. Can you throw a ball? Ole Daisy, she does love to chase her ball." He looked at Nancy and winked.

She backed out. "I'll come get you in a few minutes, Eddy."

He didn't raise his head.

She checked the charts for both the mastiff and terrier, saw that neither had a temperature and that they were receiving their antibiotics. She'd change dressings after she sent Eddy and Tim away.

She met Tim in the reception area where he was still filling out forms.

"Where's Eddy?" he asked.

"He's fine. Big's looking after him. If you'd like to get back to Williamston, I can bring Eddy home in a little while."

"You wouldn't mind?"

"It's hardly out of my way."

He handed the papers to Alva Jean, the day receptionist and Big's current girlfriend, then followed Nancy through the door to the examining rooms and down the hall toward the cavernous large animal area and the staff parking.

In the pasture behind the building, Nancy saw Big with his back to them and his hands on his hips. She realized that Eddy stood in front of him only when she saw his thin arm lob a yellow tennis ball down the pasture. A sturdy beige dog caught it in midair and trotted toward the pair in triumph. Eddy clapped as Daisy dropped the ball at his feet and sat waiting for him to throw it again.

"My God," Tim breathed. "Who's that? And isn't that a pit bull?"

"That's Mr. Bigelow Little, kennel man, security guard and general associate, and his dog, Daisy. Yes, she's a pit bull. She adores children. Don't worry, she won't attack Eddy."

"I—they have such a bad reputation."

"Any dog that's abused and not properly trained can get a bad reputation."

At that moment Eddy spotted his father and called to him, "Daddy! Watch, Daddy!" He threw the ball. Daisy chased it, retrieved it and deposited it once more at Eddy's feet. He dropped to his knees and cradled her head in his arms, then buried his face in her neck.

Nancy heard Tim catch his breath, but all he said was, "Great, son."

"Eddy looks like he's set for a while," Nancy said to him before calling out again. "Eddy, you want to ride home with me? You can feed your pup again before you leave."

"Can I, Big?" Eddy looked up at the big man with the same trust Nancy had seen in the eyes of everything from wild deer to newborn kittens.

"Sure. How 'bout we put Daisy back in my house and go do that little thing?"

"Okay." Eddy scooped up the ball, then did what Nancy was sure was a miraculous thing in Tim's eyes. He grabbed Big's huge hand and walked off toward the small bungalow at the back of the parking lot without a backward glance at his father.

CHAPTER EIGHT

IS THAT ALL it would have taken? Tim wondered. One puppy and Eddy was fixed?

Obviously not. But for the first time since Solange had been killed Eddy was showing signs of behaving like a normal boy. Once the novelty wore off the puppy, Eddy might well fall back into his silent misery. Tim prayed that wouldn't happen. He doubted the puppy would work the same magic with Angie and Jason, although they both loved animals. They wouldn't get to meet it until it came home anyway. If it survived.

Tim wasn't surprised they hadn't come downstairs earlier when they could have met the puppy. Like most teenagers, they could sleep through a riot. Even in their small Chicago apartment, nothing woke them on Saturdays before noon—not even police sirens.

Maybe Nancy Mayfield would find the key to unlock the normal parts of Jason and Angie. For the first time since he pulled away from his city apartment, he felt absolutely certain he'd done the right thing moving his family down to Williamston.

If he'd listened to Solange and gotten them out of Chicago earlier, she might still be alive.

His pigheadedness had destroyed their marriage and killed her. He'd live with his guilt for the rest of his life, not only for her death, but also for the life he'd forced on her, the choices she'd made.

No matter how much she'd demanded they all rely on her since Solange's death, he knew he'd been right to get his children and himself away from his mother-in-law, too. He'd certainly used her, but then she'd used him as well. She'd tried to submerge them all in permanent mourning. Solange would have been furious.

Tim had never called her anything except Madame, nor had she asked him to. The French term for mother-in-law was *Belle Mere*—Beautiful Mother.

And Madame *was* still a beautiful woman, small, reed-slim, with that innate chic that French women seemed to possess as a birthright. Solange had been even more beautiful than her mother. She was also clever and funny—at least in the old days.

Madame didn't hesitate to tell him she thought Solange could have done better for herself than a workaholic high school vice principal and adjunct professor. He might never even become a full principal or a full professor.

Solange had been three months pregnant with Jason when they'd married, so Madame considered her damaged goods. Madame had never forgiven Tim for that, either.

Actually Solange had seduced *him*, not that he needed much seducing. She saw him as an up-and-coming graduate assistant with a Ph.D. and a prestigious academic career ahead of him. He saw nothing except her beauty and charm.

"You never appreciated her," Madame railed at him. "You have no passion. You work all the time for no money and no prestige. Why else do you think she went back to graduate school? Why else did she take a lover?"

He'd endured her tirades and her guilt trips. The children needed her, and she had lost a beloved daughter.

Had he lost a beloved wife? He'd been furious when he let Solange out of the car to go to her French class, where her professor lover waited for her. She'd been just as furious with him.

Yet when the police came to tell him she was dead, he'd felt as though his heart had been torn out of his body. He grieved for what they had been to each other, for the love they had shared.

The love they might have found again had she lived. A marriage, even a marriage gone bad, must be grieved.

The children missed her, loved her, but they also hated her for abandoning them. Jason and Angie's rebellions were a form of acting out the unhappiness they felt. Didn't make them any easier to endure.

Nobody expected to be touched by sudden violence. No, not touched—struck, bashed, torn apart. His children had been secure in a stable environment. Then, suddenly, that security was ripped away.

Tim pulled into the parking lot of the Collierville supermarket, took a parking space, turned off his ignition and simply sat.

He'd been so certain his goals were Solange's goals, too. *Work long hours to gain a more prestigious position to make more money.*

Looking back, he saw that she needed him *then*, and not at some future date when he could afford to relax a little.

But he'd never had the chance to tell her.

He climbed out of the SUV, went into the grocery, took a cart and wandered through the unfamiliar aisles trying to remember what he said he'd buy for the house. What was the only kind of shampoo Angie would use? What kind of cereal did Eddy want? He should have made a list.

Tim picked up two dozen eggs. The kids were getting pretty sick of pizza, and he could make a great omelet.

His basket overflowed with microwave meals.

He checked his watch at the checkout line. He'd been gone three hours. It was after eleven. But in an unfamiliar house, Angie and Jason might be up and causing God-knows-what havoc.

He had remembered the extra half-gallon of orange juice for Nancy to replace the one he and Eddy had downed.

The orange juice gave him an excuse to see Nancy again. Among other things, he wanted to speak to her about those Halliburton people, to find out what he could do to make amends for kicking them out.

Before yesterday, when he'd literally run into her, he would have sworn he didn't have any libido left. He'd almost forgotten how soft a woman felt.

He turned into the driveway of his new house. From the outside, all seemed serene. The inside looked serene, too. Apparently Jason and Angie weren't even aware that he and Eddy had been gone, that the Sheriff had visited. His note lay untouched on the kitchen counter. He made half a dozen trips to carry in the groceries and found a place for them. He tried to recreate Solange's system, but this kitchen was gigantic compared to the galley kitchen in their Chicago apartment.

To get to the pantry, he had to edge between the boxes still to be unpacked. He'd tried to label each one, but after a while, he'd run out of steam, so at the moment he wasn't certain where the coffeemaker was hidden. He definitely needed caffeine.

He settled for a glass of milk.

He'd forgotten to pick up a Saturday newspaper. He'd have to call the subscription desk to arrange service, assuming they delivered this far out in the country. He took his milk into the empty living room—well, empty of everything except the randomly arranged furniture—and sank into the love seat in front of the bow window overlooking the porch.

He believed in writing To-Do lists, but at the moment his day-planner was buried somewhere among the boxes. He'd have to rely on his memory. Never a good idea, but he didn't even know where he could find a pen and a piece of scrap paper.

First, call his rental agent and find out about the Halliburtons. Then call them himself, and see if he could do anything to mend fences.

Next, check in at Maybree. With only a few weeks until school started, the office staff might be working on Saturday. His first staff meeting was scheduled for eight-thirty Monday morning, but it wouldn't hurt to seem eager.

He'd already sent the Maybree secretary a notice asking how

he should go about hiring a housekeeper. She'd posted it on the staff bulletin board, but he didn't know yet if she'd had any queries. He'd check on Monday.

If the school couldn't help, then he'd insert the ad he'd already written into the local papers. He wanted someone who knew the area. He also doubted anyone would be willing to make the commute from Memphis five days a week.

At some point, he'd wake his two older children and get them to help unpack.

He was reaching for the phone when out the window he saw a big crew cab pickup that had seen better days—much better days, as a matter of fact—roll up across the lane. It was towing a large open-sided stock trailer. Behind it another truck—this one a big professional hauler—pulled up towing a flatbed trailer.

One man climbed out of each truck. They moved so precisely in unison they seemed to be performing a well-rehearsed dance.

Each wore a pristine white T-shirt under equally pristine and well-pressed bib overalls. Each wore a broad-brimmed straw Stetson on top and a pair of shiny brown work boots on the bottom. Still in unison they pulled on heavy work gloves.

They were probably in their early sixties, although they might be anywhere from fifty to eighty. From the way their biceps stretched the cotton fabric of their T-shirts, he suspected they'd be able to handle a herd of buffalo.

As they turned their brown and craggy faces toward his house, he noticed they both wore perfectly trimmed white beards. Tim laughed. Twins. Tweedledum and Tweedledee grown middle-aged and transplanted from Wonderland to West Tennessee.

He wondered what they were doing across the street, so he kept watching.

One walked around to the back of the stock trailer, opened the double doors and stepped back.

Two immense gray draft horses backed out of the trailer and

stood quietly. Both wore heavy work harnesses. Even at this distance Tim could see each harness was shiny with fresh oil.

The twins each took a horse and attached some sort of pulling apparatus. Then they walked up Nancy's lawn and disappeared around her house. The horses followed without lead line or direction.

Tim had never seen horses that big. When he was a kid visiting in the summer, his grandfather had kept a couple of mules to plow his garden, but they looked like miniature donkeys compared to these big guys. The twins must be nearly as tall as he was, but their horses dwarfed them.

He was considering whether to trail along after them to find out what they were doing, when he heard a clatter from the staircase to the second floor.

"Daddy! Did you see?" Angie slid on the wood floor and caught herself on the back of the sofa. "Horses!" She raced to stand at his shoulder. "Where'd they go? Can we follow them?"

"Is your brother up?"

She grabbed his hand and pulled. "Jason? No way. Come on!"

He looked at the light in her eyes, a light he hadn't seen in much too long. Taking her outstretched hand, he let her pull him up from the window seat and followed her gallop at a more sedate pace.

Before he reached the lane, she was pelting across Nancy's lawn like an ordinary kid. "Angie, wait up!" he called after her. If she heard him, she didn't slow down to wait for him. He jogged after her and saw her reach the men and their rigs halfway across Nancy's back pasture.

"Hey, young'un," said one of the men. "Whoa-up, Henry, Herb." The two horses stopped and stood quietly.

Angie froze. He saw her mouth gape in awe as she realized for the first time that what she'd thought were ordinary horses were in reality gray giants larger than any she'd ever seen in her life.

Tim put his hand on her shoulder. "Hi," he said. "I'm Tim

Wainright and this is my daughter, Angie. Sorry to have bothered you, but Angie saw the horses and…"

The man nodded gravely at Angie. "Girls and horses." He pulled off his glove and stuck out his hand. "I'm Phil Cobb. This here's my brother, Phineas." He nodded over his shoulder. "Them's Henry and Herb. Best pair of loggin' horses in four states."

"Logging? With horses?"

"Yessiree." At that point Phineas stepped up, pulled off his glove and shook hands not only with Tim but with Angie. He nodded and stepped back without saying a word.

"Us Cobbs been logging with draft horses four generations I know about. You want to cut and sell a few hardwoods out of the middle of your woods to buy you some seed for spring, call on Cobbs. We'll bring in ole Henry and Herb here. Once we're finished cutting and moving the logs out, you won't never know we'd been in your woods, 'cept maybe the boys'll leave you some piles of fertilizer." He chortled. "Course you got to get in line. Me and Phineas, here, we're pretty well booked up into next spring."

"That's amazing. I had no idea people actually logged with horses anymore."

"No logging roads to cause erosion, no clear cutting. You won't lose so much as a rabbit, much less a deer."

"And you're logging in Nancy—Miss Mayfield's—woods?"

"Yep. We're moving the horses in this afternoon so we don't have to bring 'em here and back every morning."

"Moving them in?"

"Nancy's got a good barn back in her pasture. Needs some cleaning, but it's solid. Nobody's used it since she moved in. She used to ride, but she don't any longer. We're gonna clean it up for her and leave the boys here. Good pasture and room to store our gear."

At that point silent Phineas touched his brother's arm and nodded toward the forest behind them.

"Well, nice to meet you, Tim, Miss Angie. Time's a'wastin'.

Hot as it is, we don't like to work Henry and Herb more'n a couple of hours a day." He turned away and the big horses moved restively so that their harnesses jingled. Then he looked back at Angie. "Girl, you ever ride a horse?"

She shook her head. "Just pony rides at the zoo."

"Them's Percherons. Tell you what. How 'bout I put you up on ole Henry here and you can walk him to the woods."

Tim caught his breath, started to say no.

"Please, yes, oh, please," Angie said as she hopped on first one foot and then the other for all the world like a five-year-old.

"See them sticky-up things around old Henry's neck with them brass balls on top of 'em? Them's called hames. Now you sit right up there and hold on to them. I'll walk right beside you. If you start to slide off, I'll stop you, but you won't. Ole Henry's broad as a billiard table." Without another word, he swept Angie up and lifted her effortlessly over his head so that she could straddle the horse's withers. He hadn't asked Tim's permission, hadn't even glanced at him. These two could be anybody. Angie could fall, and from that height it would be dangerous.

"Come on, boys, let's git to work," said Phil. Harnesses jingling, the two horses marched off side by side dragging their logging chains behind them. Phil strolled along on Henry's left side with his hand on the horse's shoulder. Very casual, but Tim could see that he was in position to steady Angie or catch her.

Tim didn't relax. He longed to follow her, but Angie would never forgive him if he did. Whenever he refused her something, she howled that he'd never trust her again.

Pretty much right. He didn't dare trust her again. He'd come too close to losing her after that party. He couldn't endure that after losing Solange.

He watched the five of them meander off across the pasture and into the trees at the far end. He swore. Whatever Angie said afterward, he wouldn't let her go into the woods with strange—very strange—middle-aged men.

Perhaps sensing his unease, Phil slipped Angie off the horse, set her down, waved at Tim and sent her back to where he stood, while the men and their horses disappeared deeper into the trees.

Angie's skin glowed. She'd hadn't yet slathered on her white makeup and black eyeliner when she'd spotted the horses. She was probably close to hyperventilating. He'd never seen her eyes that wide. She was too stunned to smile.

She walked past him without acknowledging his presence, crossed the street and went into the house like a zombie. She'd always been horse crazy, but she'd had to make do with every model horse he could afford.

That was before she'd given up the mundane world and dedicated herself to the undead. She'd packed her horses, her stable, her miniature tack and all the other accessories she'd acquired in Chicago. The movers had put them in the attic along with the Christmas ornaments and boxes of books he had no room for yet. Angie said they were for babies.

If Angie could ride a horse, she'd be delighted to live in Antarctica or the Amazon rain forest. Williamston would seem like paradise to her. If he made looking like a normal kid part of the deal, he was willing to bet she'd agree.

He'd ask Nancy where Angie could take a few riding lessons. If she stayed interested, then eventually he might be able to give her a horse. He'd need a place to keep it, and an instructor to teach her how to ride.

More danger. Horses, Jason and his skateboards. He felt like that guy who handled the dangerous reptiles on television. He'd brought the kids down here to be safe in the bucolic country. All he'd done was replace one set of dangers with a whole other set.

CHAPTER NINE

WHEN NANCY WALKED into the reception area, Alva Jean, the daytime receptionist at Creature Comfort, handed her a list of clients to be seen and what they needed. No routine surgeries were performed on Saturday, and the clinic closed at noon. The other vets, Eleanor Chadwick and Sarah Scott, were both essentially large animal vets, although they rotated with Mac Thorn most Saturday mornings.

Eddy had been lucky that Rick Hazard, managing partner of Creature Comfort was on duty, so that he could look over JustPup before he left for his golf game. He only shared the rotation once every six weeks.

Nancy had already checked on Eddy. He was following Big around the large animal area while he mucked stalls and checked bandages. Big was comfortable not speaking. Eddy seemed comfortable as well.

"I'll be another hour, Eddy," she said. "Can you hold out that long? Big can get you a soda if you're thirsty, and there are peanut butter crackers in the machine."

Eddy shook his head.

"He's fine, Miss Nancy, aren't you, boy? He's helping with them lambs."

This time Eddy nodded.

She was leaning over the reception counter checking Alva Jean's schedule of patients when Sarah Scott ran in from the back.

"Hey," Alva Jean said as she and Nancy both noticed Sarah's expression.

"What's the matter? Somebody hurt?" Nancy asked and started toward the door that led to the examining rooms and the large animal area. *Please God, not Eddy.*

"I just had a call from Jack Renfro's wife." Sarah sounded breathless. "Jack's had a heart attack."

"What?"

"She was calling from CCU at St. Michael's."

"How bad?" Nancy asked.

"Don't know. Can we get Rick back? I want to go to the hospital right now. She's scared to death. We're the closest thing to family they have around here."

"He's turned off his cell phone by now," Nancy said. "Probably on the first tee."

"If you handle the routine stuff and feed me the things that absolutely, positively need a vet, maybe we can get out of here faster."

Nancy looked back at the waiting room and was met by a sea of avid faces. They knew something was up, they simply hadn't overheard what.

She went to the door and said, "Folks, there's been an emergency. Most of you know Jack Renfro. He's in serious condition in the hospital. Mrs. Renfro's with him, but she's all by herself, and Dr. Sarah would like to go to her as soon as she can."

There were sympathetic murmers. "Accident? Heart Attack? What?" asked a small balding man holding a cat carrier. "I've known Jack since he started working at the clinic."

"We don't know anything definite yet, Mr. Salomen," Nancy said. "Dr. Sarah won't leave until we've finished, but there may be some of you who don't actually need to see the vet. Is there anybody I can help?"

A hand went up. "Donny needs his rash medication. His hives are back."

"Sure. I can do that."

She felt Alva Jean at her shoulder. "Y'all, I've got a clip-board. Let me know if it's something Nancy can handle or if you need a doctor."

She started down the line.

"Karen," Nancy said, "didn't you say Walter needs his rabies shot? Come on."

A big, bulky woman with bright golden hair she hadn't been born with followed her with what Mac Thorn called a Plantation terrier, as he did every medium-size, short-haired country mongrel. Now most of the clients who owned them proclaimed them Plantation terriers as proudly as though they were purebred poodles. Alva Jean and Mabel even entered them that way under the line marked Breed in their records.

They were finished in thirty minutes. Nancy took a diet soda to Alva Jean and opened one for herself.

"Have you heard from the hospital?" she asked. She drank half her soda in one gulp.

Alva Jean finished locking the wide glass front doors and leaned over the counter to put the keys into her cash drawer. "Mrs. Renfro called a little while ago. They think Jack had a mild infarction. They're going to do an angioplasty tomorrow."

"On Sunday?"

"Don't dare wait, according to Mrs. Renfro. They think he may need a couple of bypasses."

Nancy came around the corner of the desk and sat on the second stool. "Jack is—what—in his mid-fifties? He may be short, but he's thin and tough. He's in great shape."

"Remember all those years he was a steeplechase jockey before he became a vet tech? He's been rode hard and put away wet all his life. He didn't give up smoking till four or five years ago, and you know he can knock back the beer when he wants to." Alva Jean walked around the counter and climbed on the other stool.

"But never that much. Besides, alcohol rots your liver, not

your heart." She rubbed the back of her neck and gently rotated her head. She could feel the knots along her spine. Tension invariably hurt her neck. Before her new neighbors moved in, she could count on easing the tension when she got home. No more.

"I notified our doctors and Mabel about his status," Alva Jean said. "Dr. Sarah told Big before she left to go to the hospital. Big's used to handling the chores alone." She dug her purse out of the supply closet behind the reception desk, pulled out a comb and dragged it through her curls. "Big and I are taking the kids to see that new cartoon tonight."

"Please. Go. I still have to check the small animals and collect Eddy. I'll lock up the back."

Big and Alva Jean had been seeing each another for some time, but neither of them ever mentioned marriage, although Alva Jean said her kids adored Big. What child wouldn't? Having Big around was like having your own personal grizzly bear to play with.

"Who's going to take Jack's place in surgery for the large animals?" Alva Jean asked.

"Jack will be back." Nancy crossed her fingers and said a silent prayer. "But not soon, if he has bypass surgery. I had an aunt who had a quadruple. She couldn't drive for a year, went through deep depression and endured six months of cardiac rehabilitation before she felt halfway decent."

"But she was all right eventually, wasn't she?"

Nancy nodded. "Better than she'd been in years, to hear her tell it. But not overnight. We're going to need a substitute tech to help with the large animal surgeries, if nothing else."

"For the next few days, that's going to be you."

Both Nancy and Alva Jean jumped. Rick Hazard stood in the doorway. Neither had heard him come in, although his clothes were loud enough they should've alerted them. He wore orange and red plaid Bermuda shorts that would have brought traffic to a standstill on an interstate and a yellow polo shirt with a fancy logo on the breast pocket. He still wore his golf hat—a wide-brimmed planter's straw boater. He had, however, removed his golf cleats before walking on the tile floors.

"I work with Mac, remember?" Nancy said.

"I'll take over your surgical duties with Mac as much as I can. He *can* work alone, you know."

"In a parallel universe, maybe," Alva Jean said.

"You two would kill each another halfway through spaying the first cat," Nancy pointed out.

"Liz can't do days until her hellions start school in a couple of weeks, and it's going to take at least that long to find a short-term replacement for Jack."

"I haven't assisted in large animal surgeries since…"

"Since last summer when Jack went on vacation to London for two weeks to see his cousins. Not that long."

"And Mac had a fit every morning when I wasn't there to hand him his scalpels."

"That's my problem. We can put off some of the routine procedures, large and small. We're not overburdened with surgeries this time of year anyway. It's not like the dead of winter when the horses get dehydration founder, or spring when they colic on the fresh grass. It'll mostly be prepurchase exams for horses, and working the cattle sale. Sarah can do those alone, or Big can help. Mac won't even notice you're handling two jobs."

"I will."

"But you're a trooper," Rick said. "Mac says you're the best in the business. I agree."

"Two jobs, two salaries."

"Come on, Nancy." The entire office knew that Rick was a notorious penny pincher. "You'll still be working the same hours."

"What if a horse colics at three in the morning on a farm halfway to Nashville, and Sarah needs help? In the past, Jack rolled out of bed. Then he slept late the next morning. I won't be able to."

Rick looked at Alva Jean.

"We can talk tomorrow."

"How about weekends? Am I going to be expected to work every Saturday morning?"

"You know I have to check with the money people before I can promise you anything."

"So check."

"Time and a half for any overtime you put in," Rick offered.

"Salary and a half, overtime or not."

Rick sighed. "Done."

Nancy grabbed his hand and shook it. "Alva Jean, you're a witness. Now I can pay for my new kitchen cabinets."

The telephone rang and Alva Jean picked it up, listened, then handed it to Nancy. "It's that guy—the one from Chicago."

"What now? If those crazy kids of his have done any more damage, I'll throttle them." She took the phone with a sigh. "Hey."

"Are you about ready to leave? I was getting a little worried about Eddy."

"He's fine. The last time I checked he was sitting with a couple of lambs. We're about to leave right now, as a matter of fact. Be home in half an hour."

"Could I come by this evening some time? I know it's an imposition, but I need some advice."

"From me? Whatever about?"

"I'll bring a bottle of wine."

"I've got errands to run this afternoon. Come by around seven."

"Fine. Thanks."

She hung up. She wanted to go home, lie down with the cats and pig, take a long nap and a long bath and spend the evening with a book in front of her television without speaking to a living soul, much less Tim. Still, the thought of seeing him gave her heart a jolt.

"Mabel says he's a hunk," Alva Jean said.

"Hunk-schmunk. I moved to Williamston for a quiet life. I feel as though I've landed in the middle of *Children of the Corn*."

CHAPTER TEN

TIM DECIDED not to ask Nancy about riding lessons for Angie right away. Transforming his daughter into a regular school girl seemed more pressing.

He and Nancy sat in the evening shadows on Nancy's front porch in a pair of matching rockers. Nancy had left the porch light off to discourage as many bugs as possible.

On small rattan tables beside each of their rockers burned two citronella candles. The tangy odor reminded Tim of evenings spent with his grandfather, long before air-conditioning, when people didn't watch television in the evenings, but came out after dark to call to one another from porch to porch in the darkness.

Nancy held a retractable leash that extended fifteen feet or so in her left hand and a goblet of chilled white wine in her right. At the end of his leash, Lancelot snuffled around the front yard, stopping every few feet to investigate. Whenever he found something of porcine interest, he oinked softly in delight and rooted at it. Nancy kept a wary eye on him even when she was speaking to Tim.

"If you want to get rid of that black hair without scalping the child, take Angie to a professional salon," Nancy said. "I can give you the name of the woman who cuts my hair in Collierville. If anybody can get the dye out, she can. She needs a shorter layered cut that doesn't half blind her every time she turns her head. At the moment she looks like one of those Hungarian sheepdogs—she has to peer through her dreadlocks to see." She leaned back and pulled her feet up under her, but kept the rocker moving gently with the motion of her body. "She needs somebody to teach her about makeup—"

"Whoa! She's barely thirteen! I'm trying to get *rid* of makeup, not add to it."

"At the moment she looks as if she died last Thursday." Nancy caught her breath. "Oh, Lord, I am so sorry. That was a stupid thing to say." She set her glass on the rattan table. The tiny candle flame danced with the breeze from her hand. In another half hour, the darkness would be complete except for the candles and the lightning bugs.

"A fact is a fact," Tim said. "From what I've heard, looking dead is the point of the Goth thing."

"It's working. She needs to know how to look after her skin, too. Lancelot, don't eat the azaleas. I think they're poison." She walked out into the yard to unwind Lancelot from the branches of one of the Gumpo azaleas under her oak tree.

She did have great legs. And when she bent over, her rear end was equally appetizing. Those short-shorts raised his blood pressure.

Tim had been crazy to think he could give up wanting beautiful women, or tamp down his hormones. He was still a young man—well, youngish. He didn't think she had any idea what she was doing to him. Probably thought of him as nothing but a father, and not very good at that.

He'd been a man long before he'd been a father, although lately he hadn't had time for both. Looking at Nancy made him want to take the time. Right. Fit courting Nancy in with his duties at school, his kids, shopping, cleaning and looking after Eddy's new puppy. How did working women manage?

Monday he'd have to leave Jason in charge while he reported to Maybree for his first staff meeting. Jason would spend whatever day was left, after he got out of bed, riding that damned skateboard all over Williamston.

He refused to send out a distress call to Madame. She'd

grumble, but she'd come if he begged her. And she'd make him pay every moment she was here.

God, he needed a housekeeper fast. He prayed the ad he'd put on the Maybree bulletin board would have brought in at least a couple of suitable candidates.

Nancy walked back and sat on the top step of the porch.

Lancelot trundled off to explore farther into the yard. Nancy let him reel himself out. "Then there's zits and chocolate—I assume she's menstruating?"

Tim gulped. He could not believe he was having this conversation with a relative stranger. Still, she was so matter-of-fact that he found himself less uncomfortable than he thought possible, and she was looking at Lancelot, not him.

"Yeah. Madame, their grandmother, got to deal with that."

"How about shaving her armpits? The right deodorant? How to keep her skin clean? Avoid blackheads? Use moisturizer? A tiny bit of makeup so that she looks thirteen going on fourteen, not thirty?" She clapped her other hand over the leash. "Come back here, pig. You're yanking my arm out of the socket."

Lancelot obligingly reversed directions, hurried back to the foot of the stairs and laid his snout on Nancy's thigh. She scratched his head, so he clambered up and tried to sit in her lap.

"Ow. Those trotters hurt. Down. Sit, stay."

Tim ran his hands through his hair. "Being a woman must be tough."

"The best thing about being a woman is that I'm not a man." She turned to grin at him.

"Hey."

He caught her gaze and held it a little too long. He saw Nancy's cheeks flush, the pulse at her throat throb. She looked away quickly and became extremely interested in the top of Lancelot's head.

His own reaction was less subtle. Maybe she didn't think of him as just somebody's father after all.

Without warning, a man and a woman chatting companionably on a porch on a summer evening had morphed into two people turned on by each other.

He moved over to sit beside her on the step and saw her shoulders tighten. "Will you do it?"

"I beg your pardon?"

"Teach her that stuff. Talk to your hair lady, buy her a razor—make up. Show her how to put it on. That stuff."

"I'm not her…"

"Her mother?"

She hunched her shoulders. "I can't keep my foot out of my mouth."

"If I work this right, can I make you feel guilty enough to help?"

"Even if I wanted to, she'd never let me."

"Yeah, she will. If you tell her where she can take riding lessons."

This time she did look at him. He could barely see her face now in the gathering darkness, but those big, beautiful eyes were still visible. And she didn't look very happy.

"How did we get from haircuts to riding lessons?"

"We met Phil and Phineas today. What's more to the point, Angie met Henry, the Percheron, and got to ride him back to the woods. Once she found out the horses would be staying at your place for a while, I had to put my foot down to keep her home at all. She wanted to take a sleeping bag back to your barn and spend the night on a hay bale just staring at them."

"Angie is horse crazy?"

"Until today, she'd only ridden ponies at the zoo. When Phil got her back down, she was too blown away to speak to me for ten minutes."

"From a pony to Henry is some jump."

"If I can promise her riding lessons with the faint possibility of maybe having her own horse someday, she'd probably dye her hair green. And you know everybody with horses."

Nancy felt the muscles in her neck spasm. At the sudden stab of pain, she dropped Lancelot's leash and reached up to dig her fingers into the pressure point at the left side of her neck. She took a deep breath and fought to keep her voice even. "I only know the horse people that use Creature Comfort for their vet work, and the neighbors that ride with the local hunt. I've been out of the loop since I stopped riding. I don't go to horse shows any longer." She caught her breath at another spasm. The very mention of horse shows and her neck rebelled.

Tim grabbed Lancelot's leash. "Hey, you okay?"

She could neither turn nor nod her head, only choke out, "I'll be fine in a minute."

Lancelot stared up at her in obvious concern and stuck his snout into her abdomen. The bristles on the top of his head dug in like needles. She shoved him away with her right hand while she kept the pressure on her neck with her left.

"You're not okay."

The pain began to ease, although her scalp had tightened so much that her jaw ached. "I will be in a minute." She managed to sound fairly normal.

What was it about the Wainwrights that tied her body into knots? Was it all of them? Or only one?

"Here, hold this," he said and put the leash in her lap. "Turn around, back to me."

"No, you don't understand. My neck…"

"I won't hurt you. My wife used to get muscle spasms."

"Just…"

He took her shoulders and moved her around so that her back was to him. Very gently he began to work the muscles of her neck. "Holy cow," he said. "You've got knots on your knots."

"I know what to do," she said just as he released one of the knotted muscles. The relief was instant. "Oh."

"Got it," Tim whispered. He kept working, gently at first, then deeper with his very educated fingers. She relaxed as she realized he did know what he was doing.

"Mmm."

He gently pushed her head forward. Lancelot apparently realized the crisis was over and sank onto his chest at her feet with his snout on her sneaker.

Every knot Tim loosened in her neck caused a corresponding tightness in her chest and a rise in her blood pressure. She wanted simply to lean back against him in silence. Instead, she began to talk—no, it was more like babbling than talking.

"Mac Thorn's daughter, Emma, is a year older than Angie. She shows her hunter locally."

"Where does Emma ride?" Tim said softly and continued gently kneading her neck.

Nancy started to shake her head then thought better of it. "Emma owns her own horse, but she may know an 'up-down' barn that has school horses for beginners."

"I assumed you'd know everybody in the business."

She didn't want to admit that she avoided knowing what was going on in the world of horse shows. She was no longer a colleague. She was an outsider, and it tore her up.

"Hey, you just tightened up again. Easy. Relax."

As if. "If Emma doesn't know, Sheriff O'Hara's daughter, Haley, may."

"Aren't there places that just rent horses?"

"And that would teach Angie what? She needs to *learn* to ride on a decent school horse that will forgive her mistakes but reward her when she does the correct thing."

"I had no idea this was all so complicated." He had moved from her neck to the tops of her shoulders.

"The past couple of years, I've given a few pointers to the hunters that leg up their horses on the green before opening hunt. They'll probably start to show up in a week or so. Maybe they know some place."

She felt a sudden pang of deep longing. Most of the time she managed to forget her old life, but occasionally she missed the feel of a horse beneath her so much, it was as though she'd been slugged.

"Let it go for now. Just sit quiet. We'll talk later."

Tim's fingers felt incredibly warm against her skin. When had they turned from kneading to caressing? She closed her eyes and felt them glide from her shoulder blades along the tops of her shoulders, then down over her collarbone. She longed for him to move lower, touch her swollen breasts….

Light spilled from Tim's front door.

"Daddy! Can I take Eddy and Jason to see the horses?"

A moment later his three children tumbled down their front steps. The door slammed behind them. "Daddy! You over there?" They raced across the street.

"Damn," he whispered. He dropped his hands and slid away to the far edge of the step. "I'm sitting on the porch with Miss Mayfield."

"Hey, Nancy," Eddy said. "How's JustPup?"

"Sleeping when I left the clinic. We're officially closed tomorrow, but I'll take you down to see him."

Lancelot stood and waddled over to Eddy, the only one of the Wainwrights he knew. The boy obligingly scratched behind his ears.

"Eddy told us you had a pig," Angie said. "Ooh, he's so cute." She dropped to her knees. "Does he bite?"

"Only if he considers you food."

"The property is Miss Mayfield's, the barn is hers and the horses don't belong to you," Tim said. "Besides, it's very dark back there now."

"But Daddy…" Angie wailed.

Nancy came to her feet. "Actually, they're not in their stalls. In the summer they stay inside during the heat of the day when they're not working in my woods, and then after their evening meal, they go out into the pasture. In the middle of September when it starts getting chilly, they switch—out all day and in all night."

"They stay out at night?" Eddy asked. "They could get hurt, or the coyotes could bite them."

"Jason," Tim warned. "What have you been telling Eddy?"

"Kenny at the clinic said we have coyotes," Jason protested but he wouldn't meet his father's eyes.

"We do, but you're unlikely ever to see one," Nancy explained. "They're very shy. In a battle between Henry and a coyote, Angie, who do you think would win?"

"Henry'd stomp it into a puddle."

"Poor coyote!" Eddy lamented.

"Never happen, Eddy, don't worry. They mostly eat mice. Plenty of them around," Nancy said. "Okay, come on in. I'll get a couple of battery-powered hand lanterns. More like a spotlight than a flashlight. We can walk out into the pasture and see if we can spot them."

"Nancy, you don't have to do this. I know you're tired."

Tired, maybe, but keyed-up as well. "I'm fine now. Thanks. Come on, Lancelot. Beddy-bye time."

In her kitchen, Lancelot immediately curled up in his basket as Nancy handed everyone a big lantern. "These are much stronger than flashlights and light up a wider area." There was no sign of Poddy and Otto. They'd seen more strangers in their house in the past few days than in the rest of their lives combined. Lancelot might trust them, but cats were warier than pigs.

As they walked out onto the enclosed back porch, Nancy called, "Wait, did you put any bug spray on?"

Blank looks.

She sighed and picked up an aerosol can of the strongest possible bug spray and went over all four Wainwrights carefully, then over her own body.

"Now, maybe you won't be eaten alive by chiggers or ticks or mosquitoes."

"Is that necessary?" Tim whispered. "We won't be out there long. My grandmother never worried much about bug spray."

"Your grandmother didn't have to deal with Rocky Mountain Spotted Fever or Lyme disease or West Nile virus. We do."

"Oh."

She'd brought a handful of carrots with her and passed them out to the children. She could tell Jason almost refused, but after a glare from his father, and he accepted them with ill grace. Too sophisticated to give a carrot to a horse.

"Come on. Follow me. Make plenty of noise." They walked across her backyard and through a wide metal gate into the pasture beyond. The air hummed with the songs of bullfrogs and cicadas. From somewhere nearby in the woods they heard an owl.

"Look, Daddy," Eddy whispered. "Little tiny lights."

"Lightning bugs," Nancy said. "You can capture them in a jar to light up your room at night, but you have to let them go in the morning or they die."

"Oh. I won't catch them then."

She'd forgotten Eddy's aversion to death.

She stopped and whistled softly. A moment later two gray shapes loomed out of the shadows.

"Oh, oh, oh," Eddy whispered. He moved behind his father.

"Man, they're humongous," Jason said. He, too, took a couple of paces back, putting Nancy and his father between them.

Angie, however, walked straight up to them.

"Hold the carrots flat in your palm," Nancy said. "In this darkness they can't tell what's carrot and what's finger."

The horses bent their huge heads and accepted the offering gently.

"Eddy, Jason, go on, give them yours."

"Nuh-uh," Eddy said. "You do it, Nancy." He handed her his.

Jason swaggered up to stand beside his sister, then took a quick step back when Henry, bumped him with his head. "Hey, man." He started to turn away, but Nancy put a hand on his shoulder.

"Henry, mind your manners," she said. She showed Jason how to hold the carrots, then passed hers to Angie, who was stroking

Herb's head and cooing to him. Horse crazy all right. If she could handle two eighteen-hand Percherons looming at her out of the darkness, she was well and truly bitten by the horse bug.

Yeah, all right. Nancy would have to check into riding lessons for Angie.

How many years ago had she been like this, looking forward to spending a lifetime on top of a horse? How she wished she could still be that wide-eyed child who lived for the smell of horse sweat and saddle leather.

As if in answer to her question, the left side of her neck spasmed.

SUNDAY MORNING dawned hotter than any day so far this summer. The sky was blindingly blue, and the heat index was predicted to hit a hundred and ten degrees before dark. No sign of rain in the foreseeable future.

Nancy fed the Percherons early and brought them inside to snooze in their cool stalls, each with its own electric fan. On workdays, Phil and Phineas would look after them, but Nancy had volunteered on Sunday to give the men a whole day off. They were both elders in their evangelical church and needed to be there for all three services.

By the time she walked back into her air-conditioned cottage, both her shorts and T-shirt were drenched. She took Lancelot out under the trees in her backyard so that he could play in the three inches of water in his kiddie pool for twenty minutes, then brought him back in for breakfast. He wasn't anxious to stay outside. He went immediately back to his bed, lay down and edged his blanket over his shoulders with his teeth so that only his snout stuck out.

Poddy and Otto were now so accustomed to his presence that they ignored him. Otto took up his normal position on top of the refrigerator, and Poddy dug his way under the duvet on Nancy's bed so that it looked as though she hadn't made it properly.

Nancy picked up the Sunday newspaper on her front porch and settled down to read it.

When her phone rang at ten, she was two clues away from finishing the Sunday crossword. She really should have caller ID.

Finally, guiltily, she answered it.

"Boy, do I ever hate to do this to you," Eleanor Chadwick, one of the two large animal vets, said.

"Whatever it is, I hate it worse. How's Jack?"

"Doing better. There's a possibility they caught it early enough to have prevented any damage to the heart muscle. He's a bit loopy from the lidocaine. Sarah called me from the hospital about eleven. I think she made it home by midnight."

"Are they still doing the angioplasty today?"

"This afternoon. Apparently Jack's surgeon doesn't take weekends off, either."

"Either? What either?"

"That's the thing. There's a major polo match this afternoon out at Charlie Crandall's place outside of Salter. We promised them a vet tech on site. Jack was all set up to do it—he used to play polo and always volunteers—obviously, he can't."

"What do they need somebody on site for?"

"It's one of the rules of their polo association. Besides, he's an old friend of Coy Buchanan's." Coy owned half of Creature Comfort. "He'd have a fit if Crandall had to go to another clinic."

Coy Buchanan, Rick Hazard's father-in-law and father of the redoubtable Margot, was the prototypical good ole boy. He exuded charm. He was also a multimillionaire who could skin his business rivals without ever losing his smile. Nancy liked him, but she never felt entirely comfortable when he was around.

"So what sort of injuries am I likely to encounter?"

"Cuts, scrapes, minor abrasions and sprains mostly. Of course if they need a vet for surgery for something dire like a broken leg, Sarah or I will have to come out, or they'll have to load up the horse and bring it in to the clinic. We've never had anything that bad before, and we've been doing this for a couple of years now."

Nancy picked up her giant-size ice tea off the kitchen counter and ran the glass across her forehead. The air-conditioning could barely keep ahead of the temperature outside. "They're playing polo in this heat? Are they crazy?"

"As a matter of fact, the polo players I know are generally insane, but that's another issue. Remember, my dear husband used to play polo before he got himself a family and good sense, not necessarily in that order. Didn't you ever play polo when you were riding?"

"Sure, when I was ten and still in Pony Club, but we weren't nuts. It was nice, slow polo on fat little ponies."

"These guys tend to play kamikaze polo, but they're careful of their horses, if not themselves. If you have played, you know how dangerous riding off another player can be. So, can you do it?"

There went peaceful Sunday. Cool Sunday. Quiet Sunday. "What do I take with me?"

"Jack had everything set up before he left. I'll call Big. Come by the clinic about two. He'll load you up. They're not playing until three-thirty."

"Just when the heat index hits a hundred and ten."

"Hey, pray for thunderstorms. They don't play when there's lightning. Seriously, I am sorry about this. I promise that by next week we'll have somebody else lined up or one of us will do it. Rick's calling around tomorrow to find a temporary replacement for Jack, but it may take a while."

Nancy sank onto one of the bar stools at her breakfast counter. Lancelot came out from under his blanket to trundle over and sit on her instep. "I'll do it, of course. But you owe me big time and don't you forget it."

After she hung up she glared down at Lancelot. "What else will I be stuck with while I'm doing Jack's job that I wasn't even aware we did in the first place? Rick put one over on me again. Time and a half. Huh."

Lancelot grunted at her, decided she wasn't going to give him a treat and went back to sulk in bed.

She'd have to leave to go to the clinic by one-thirty so Big could load up her Durango.

Damn! She no longer *had* a Durango to load up. She was driving a tiny little loaner sedan with a miniscule trunk. Nowhere to work, nowhere to store all the stuff she'd have to take. Rats!

She looked up Tim's number.

"Good morning," he said after she identified herself. He actually sounded glad to hear from her.

That wouldn't last. "I need your SUV this afternoon."

"I beg your pardon?"

She launched into chapter and verse about her afternoon's assignment at the polo grounds. "So you see, I can't get my supplies into that teeny little rental car and I can't lay them out in that trunk so I can work. I need an SUV."

"Isn't it going to be damned hot?"

"Right up there with Hades, but Eleanor swears they'll still play. I can pick the SUV up around one-thirty and probably have it back to you by six."

"And in the meantime, what if I need to go somewhere?"

"I'll leave you the sedan. I'll even fill the SUV up for you afterward and charge it to the clinic. With gas prices the way they are now, that should be incentive enough for you."

"Okay. So long as I can bring Angie over to pet the Percherons after lunch."

"Be my guest. Bring carrots or apples. They love both. But whatever you do, don't open their stall doors or let Angie go in with them. Anything they step on breaks."

"Right. Where is this polo match, by the way? Maybe I'll bring the kids to watch. None of us have ever seen polo."

Nancy told him how to reach Crandall's private polo grounds. "Load up with sunscreen and wear big hats."

"Does this mean taking Eddy to see JustPup is impossible?"

One more obligation. She *had* promised. "He can ride over

with me to pick up my supplies about one-thirty in your SUV. Maybe Big can drive him home after I leave."

"I wouldn't ask that. Doesn't Mr. Little have a cottage on the clinic grounds? He'd have to drive way out here and way back."

"The only thing Big likes better than animals is kids."

"Still, it is his day off."

Mine, too.

"I'll follow you over to pick up Eddy. Then, if it's all right, we'll follow you out to the polo grounds."

"It's your sunstroke."

She'd barely hung up the phone when it rang again.

"Nancy, it's Helen Halliburton. How's my sweet baby boy managing without me?"

Nancy looked over at Lancelot's bed. His little black nose was wobbling gently in a piggy dream, no doubt of food. "He seems happy, although I know he misses you and Bill."

"Poor baby."

"He's not getting enough playtime outside, I'm afraid. I haven't had time to give him a bath, either, and now I have to work this afternoon."

"Oh—you won't be home?"

Nancy laughed. "Come on out anyway. You know where the spare key is. He'll sleep sounder tonight knowing he hasn't been totally abandoned. Any luck on finding a house in this area?"

She could hear Helen's deep sigh. "Not so far. We've looked at everything from old house trailers with rotten floors to starter castles for half a million dollars. Doesn't seem to be much in between. Sometimes I think it's hopeless."

"Better not be. Lancelot would never forgive you." *Neither would I.*

CHAPTER ELEVEN

THE VISITING POLO TEAM had arrived at Charlie Crandall's place in a dozen large horse trailers. They were parked at the north end of the polo ground under a stand of large trees that provided the only natural shade from the searing afternoon heat.

Nancy pulled Tim's SUV in beside them and set up the bandages and medications she might have to use.

Her rental sedan drove past and down to the spectators' area alongside the field, but she didn't see where Tim had parked. She hoped they'd take shelter under one of the big tents.

She heard the whistle for the start of the first chukka and turned to watch.

Each chukka was seven and a half minutes of almost nonstop horse stampede. The eight players thundered up and down the field, stopping only when the ball was hit outside the playing area or a player committed a foul. Since she was on the same level as the field—more than three football fields in length—she couldn't really tell much about the action unless the players were riding at her end, and even then, she wasn't always certain when a goal had been scored.

She pulled a folding chair out of the back of Tim's SUV, took a diet soda out of her ice chest and settled down with a cold towel around the back of her neck and the latest bestseller in her lap.

Despite the thundering hooves, she was dozing when the whistle sounded for the end of the first chukka and the riders cantered to the trailers to change ponies. Both riders and horses were dripping with sweat, and there were thick lines of white foam on the thoroughbred ponies where their bridles had rubbed.

The players vaulted out of their saddles and handed their mounts to the grooms, who took them to cool down at the hoses setup behind the trailers. Several of the players took the hoses from their grooms and ran cold water over their own already wet hair and bodies.

It might look like minor chaos to an outsider, but everyone seemed to know his job. The care of the horses came first. The riders used the short break to guzzle water and electrolytes before they jumped onto their fresh mounts, already saddled for them, and cantered back onto the field to start the next chukka.

Nancy had about decided no one needed her this interval when a groom walked a sweating little bay mare to her.

"Señora." He nodded to Nancy and pointed at the mare's left hind pastern just above her hoof. "She got kicked a little I think. Is blood. Señor Crandall wants you take a look at it. Maybe need stitches?"

The mare showed no signs of lameness, but when Nancy knelt, she could see the dark blood against the sweat. "Not a bad cut," she said. "We'll clean it and wrap it and give her a shot of antibiotics."

"*Si, señora.*" He held the mare, which seemed too tired even to react when Nancy cleaned her cut and bandaged it.

"She have any deep tissue damage?"

Nancy looked up. She'd met Charlie Crandall several times, but couldn't really say she knew him. He was a real estate developer both in Tennessee and Florida, and had enough money to indulge himself and his family in their hobby. He was a big man with gray hair currently soaked almost black with sweat.

"A little cut," Nancy said. "Superficial. Keep it clean and wrapped. If you notice swelling or heat, call Dr. Chadwick or Dr. Scott at the clinic tomorrow morning, but I don't think you'll need to. Lay her off until it's healed. It's in a spot that could pull loose and bleed again."

"Thanks." He reached a hand down and pulled Nancy to her feet. "Do I know you? I'm used to seeing Jack Renfro, but you look familiar."

Nancy introduced herself and told him it was the first time she'd had this particular duty. She explained about Jack and assured Crandall he'd be back in no time. Not that he would, of course, but that wasn't Crandall's business.

He peered at her. "I could swear I know you from somewhere." He shook his head. "It'll come to me. I never forget a face. Got to get back. Next chukka's due to start in a couple of minutes."

He trotted back to the picket line, jumped on another horse and cantered back onto the field. The Mexican groom led the little mare back to her place in line with a smile and a wave.

Nancy sat down and hid her face in her book. Of course Crandall knew her. His kids had all showed hunters at the same time she was starting to ride jumpers for her husband Peter. Before she married him. Before she was hurt. She hated being reminded of those days.

She regretted that she'd had to stop riding, but not that she'd stopped showing. That had been a hard and sometimes brutal life. She'd spent more of her career and marriage camping out in the living quarters attached to her husband's big horse trailer than she ever had at their home training facility.

Owning a house that didn't change cities on her during the night, that stayed put on its own fifty acres in Williamston, was nearly worth giving up horses for.

Nearly. Not quite.

She prayed Crandall wouldn't remember her. Either he knew she'd stopped riding because of injury, or he'd demand to know why she had given up a brilliant career. In the end, he'd pity her. That she couldn't bear.

She sank back into her seat, discovered that her diet soda was now as warm as breakfast tea, dumped it and plucked a cold one out of her ice chest.

The riders were warming up their horses in the shade—not that they needed much warming. She heard Crandall say, "David'll never ride my ponies again. He hurts horses. Can't trust the little bastard."

Harsh words about somebody. Although they sometimes looked pretty cavalier in their treatment of their ponies, polo players were fanatic about the safety of their mounts. They might risk their own necks, but anyone that made a move that might injure a pony earned himself not only a heavy penalty and a dressing down by the umpire, but was in danger of being physically thrown out of a game.

The rest of the afternoon passed quietly. She checked out a couple of scrapes and a pulled shoe that had taken a hefty portion of hoof with it and would have to be wrapped until a farrier could look at it. None of the riders fell off, none of the horses crashed badly enough to injure itself or its rider.

She walked up to the edge of the grounds where she could see, but gave up after only a few minutes. The heat was stifling.

The final horn sounded, the riders turned to canter back to the trees as Tim, his family crammed into the little sedan, pulled up beside her. He lowered the window. "You're right. It's hotter than the worst circles of hell, but Angie wouldn't leave."

She started to answer when Crandall pulled his horse up beside her. "I remember you now. Nancy Mayfield. I saw you win the Grande Prix at Gladstone." He dropped to the ground and ran his gloved hand over his dripping gray hair. "You ate that course alive, girl. Way you ride, we ought to get you to come play polo with us. Make you a two goal player by the end of next season easy if you can hit as well as you ride."

"I—uh—I don't ride any longer." She was aware of Tim and his family staring at her.

"Hey, if it's ponies you need, I've got plenty. And gear, too. A little practice with a mallet is all you'd need. You've already got more guts than most of the riders I know."

She dropped her gaze. She hated this. She longed to say yes, she'd play and screw her neck and damn the pain. The thought of galloping the length of that field on a tough little thorough-bred even once made her heart soar. The knowledge that she couldn't was like a knife in her throat.

"No can do. Thanks for the offer." She pointed to Angie who was leaning out her father's window from the back seat. "There's a recruit you can have in three of four years." Why on earth had she said that? Tim was gaping at her. Angie was practically imploding.

Crandall grinned at Angie. "Hey, I'll hold you to that. We like to catch 'em young and fearless." He walked away with his horse, then turned back. "So if I can't convince you to play, how about training for me?"

"I know zip about training polo ponies."

"You sure as hell know about training hunters and jumpers. I've got a bunch of those, too. The Greens told me you do some training for them before hunt season starts. Good money. Think about it. Give me a call if you're interested, even part-time." He waved at Tim and walked away. His horse followed him quietly. Crandall didn't even have his hand on the horse's bridle.

"Wow," Angie breathed.

Jason rolled his eyes and made a vomit noise.

Eddy just stared.

NANCY PARKED Tim's Surburban in his driveway. He'd left the keys to her little rental on the driver's seat. He was learning.

She'd stopped to pick up a fast food chicken sandwich after she'd unpacked her equipment at the clinic. And now, in the kitchen Lancelot demanded her sandwich. When she refused, he squealed in frustration, so she gave him a couple of fries.

"Knock it off, that's all you get." He wasn't happy, but he finally gave up. She'd barely taken off her clothes when the tele-phone rang.

"Not tonight. I can't handle much more of this."

"Nancy? Pick up. It's Mac."

Rats. "What's up?" she said when she'd done what he demanded.

"Somebody just brought in their basset hound. He's been hit by a car."

"Bad?"

"Very bad. I'm going to need some help."

"Mac, I just got home from the polo matches. I'm worn-out."

"Tough. Want me to send Big to bring you in?"

"Is that a threat?"

"More like a kind offer. Get your buns in here before we lose this dog."

The basset hound was still alive when she arrived in surgery gloved, gowned, masked and ready to assist.

"About time."

"Hello to you, too."

"Somebody hit this dog on purpose." He picked up a scalpel. "I shaved and prepped while I was waiting."

"Knock it off, Doctor," she said gently. "Or you'll get one of those scalpels up your nose."

"Sorry. I am pissed off."

As usual, he took his fury out on the nearest human being—Nancy. She'd long since learned not to take offense. Well, not much offense. "Oh, my word," Nancy said. "This is Digger! He belongs to the Wilsons. They'd never let him roam."

"Look at that hip," Mac snarled. "We'll have to put it back together with spit and ceiling wax."

That "we" was one of the reasons Nancy put up with him. He truly considered them a team, not a star surgeon and a mere assistant.

They settled down to the surgery. Both Digger's hind legs were fractured. So was his right hip. Considering the basset's short legs, they didn't have much room to work.

"Surprise, surprise, not as much internal damage as I feared," Mac said. "I can pin the right leg and the hip, but his left leg's too smashed up. We'll have to amputate." Mac touched the dog's floppy ears. "Don't worry, Digger. In a month you won't even remember you used to have four instead of three."

Typical of Mac to know the name of the dog, but not of the owners.

Two hours later, Nancy rolled the now three-legged basset to ICU and settled him into a big cage. Liz Carlyle would check on him when she came in, give him antibiotics and pain meds, and Big would check him sometime before morning. At the moment, Digger slept peacefully.

"Will he live?" Nancy said as she and Mac walked out the back toward their cars.

"Barring infection or damage I didn't find."

"How can they possibly know somebody did this on purpose?"

"The owner—"

"Mr. Wilson."

"Yeah, well. He says somebody let Digger out of their fenced yard. The gate has a dog-proof clasp. The minute Digger was out, he put his nose to the ground and off he went."

"That's a basset hound for you."

"He didn't get far. His owners went out to call him in for the night, saw the gate open and were starting to hunt for him when they heard the thud from the road."

"But why does Mr. Wilson think it was intentional? People don't always stop when they hit animals."

"Driving without lights? Speeding out of nowhere? Digger was off the shoulder on the grass. The guy deliberately swerved to hit him. They found the tracks in the mud."

"What kind of car? Did they get the license plate?"

"Hell, you know people. Wilson said it was some kind of truck or SUV. The lights were off on the license plate."

"Who would do such a thing?"

Mac leaned against the hood of his car. "Who'd burn a puppy?"

"Oh, Mac. I can't believe it's the same person." She considered that for a moment, then said, "But the Wilsons live less than ten miles from my house."

"I'll ask Alva Jean to put out an alert to the other clinics tomorrow. If we've got somebody hurting animals on purpose, we need to alert the police." He stood and opened his car door. "So they can catch the son of a bitch before I kill him."

CHAPTER TWELVE

"As I TOLD YOU when we interviewed you, it is not outside the realm of possibility that you could inherit my job when I retire in a couple of years," Dr. Aycock said. He smoothed the few strands of hair that lay across his bald pate. "You are not without excellent credentials. Certainly if we decide that Maybree needs a vice principal, you might not be the last in line."

Why couldn't he simply say that Tim's credentials were excellent and his chances for the job good?

"One would not be lax in thinking that your descent from one of the old families in the area might be considered by some a plus."

Tim felt his eyes cross. Dr. Aycock might be the world's best administrator—something Tim seriously doubted—but he was about the most boring old fossil Tim had run across since his Greek professor.

On top of that, Dr. Aycock smoked. He had apparently decided that puffing on a Sherlock Holmes Meerschaum pipe gave him an academic air. What it gave his office was another kind of air— stale, sweet and eye-watering.

At least he didn't smoke in the halls of Maybree. Smoking on the grounds among students was grounds for suspension, and among faculty members grounds for reprimand.

Dr. Aycock, however, considered himself above the rules he rigidly enforced. Tim pulled out his handkerchief and blew his nose. His eyes would look as though he'd been on a weekend bender by the time he and Dr. Aycock walked down to the lounge for the first faculty meeting before school started. Tim would have to shower the minute he got home.

"You are not, I may say, the sole new hire this year. You are, however, the only new full-time teacher. We have several interns and teaching assistants working part-time as coaches and instructors in the arts. You will encounter them this morning. Hiring such part-timers is not without merit, and certainly not without value to our budget." Dr. Aycock raised an eyebrow archly, tamped out his pipe and pulled himself out of his plush leather desk chair. "Is it not the hour at which we are scheduled to meet?" He pulled an antique-gold watch from his vest pocket.

A vest and jacket in this heat. Tim wore chinos and a polo shirt and hoped the other faculty members were equally casual.

He hadn't precisely been promised a promotion, but at least the carrot had been held out to him. Now, he wondered, would he get the stick?

The school was small, the faculty smaller still. Tim already knew he'd be the only English teacher for grades ten through twelve, along with the advanced placement honors English class. One heck of a heavy load. He didn't mind, except that it would cut into the rest of his life. He'd spent his evenings working on administrative junk in Chicago. Here he'd be reading papers and making lesson plans, but at least he'd be at home available to his children.

"If we leave now, we will not be unduly late," Dr. Aycock said.

"I'll be right behind you, sir." Tim stopped at the desk of Dr. Aycock's formidable secretary, Mrs. Sagamore.

She peered over the top of her bifocals. "Yes, Dr. Wainwright?"

"I wondered whether you'd had any calls about my housekeeper problem?"

She sniffed. "Not a one. Our faculty members who have people they consider paragons don't easily pass along that information, even to colleagues. I would suggest you contact an agency. An ad is the paper in hardly likely to produce the quality of person you wish to also look after your children." She returned to her computer screen.

He was dismissed. He considered bowing out, but decided she might not take the joke in the spirit he intended. Worse, she might take it in *precisely* the spirit he intended. His first month as a lowly intern at his first school, he'd figured out that the head master's secretary was his most valuable ally.

True to her word, Nancy had spoken to Helen Halliburton about filling in as a part-time chauffeur and housekeeper at least until school started. He hoped she'd work out, because with no one else applying, he didn't have many options. He was meeting Helen and Bill at Nancy's house after the faculty meeting. He'd have to keep his fingers crossed. He pretty much had to let her write her own ticket—within reason, of course.

He got to the staff meeting just as Dr. Aycock was completing the introduction of the new faculty and everyone began to relax and chat.

He was surprised to find he wasn't the oldest person in the room. He expected Maybree would attract young teachers willing to forego city salaries for more academic freedom and fewer discipline problems.

The Latin teacher, Mrs. Martini, was probably nearing retirement age. She might already be past it. Tim had been delighted to find that Maybree still taught Latin, along with French, Spanish and German. Everyone had to take two years of Latin, then either continue for two years of advanced Latin or move to a modern language.

"I know all the pros and cons," Mrs. Martini said to Tim at the coffee machine. "Dead language and all that. But if you know Latin, you can think and you can write."

"Not to mention spell," Tim said with a grin.

"I try to make the classes amusing. We have toga parties and Roman feasts…"

"Orgies?"

Mrs. Martini raised her eyebrows and grinned. "Not recently, although several of the students have suggested that we have at least one a year."

"Are faculty invited?"

"Certain faculty, if I feel they would fit in," Mrs. Martini said. "You might be invited if you play your cards right."

He'd already learned that Mrs. Martini was married to a retired colonel, had several children and a dozen grandchildren. She looked more like Mother Hen than Messalina. Still, he leered back at her. She giggled.

"Dr. Wainwright?"

He turned to face the handsomest young man he'd seen not on a magazine. "Call me Tim."

The young man held out his hand. "I'm David Grantham. I'm coaching lacrosse this year." Grantham's grip was firm, but not bone-crushing.

"Our lacrosse coach died suddenly last spring," Mrs. Martini said. "Completely unexpected. Didn't smoke or drink. Nobody knew he had a bad heart." She patted David's arm. "David's in his senior year at the university, but he's stepped in to coach even though he's still in school himself."

David shrugged and ducked his head. "Don't make it sound like a big deal, Mrs. Martini. I only have two classes left, and they're both in the morning." He turned to Tim. "I'm scheduled to graduate in December, so after that I'll be coaching fulltime. Anyway, we practice in the afternoon after classes. No conflict. Dr. Aycock says you have a fifteen-year-old son. Does he play?"

He had steady blue eyes and naturally wavy blond hair cut long so that it fell across his forehead. He wore chinos and a blue polo shirt that precisely matched the periwinkle-blue of his eyes, but with the collar turned up in back. He was only about five-nine, but he gave off a bigger man's aura. Very sure of himself.

Tim wondered whether the color coordination was an

accident. Most men wouldn't bother to coordinate their eyes with their clothes.

"Jason rides a skateboard," Tim said. "Although it's been so hot he's cut back until it cools off."

"Can't ride a skateboard without athletic ability. Good balance, strong legs."

"He's something of a loner. Never been much for team sports. I tried to get him into Little League in Chicago, but it didn't take."

"Give me a shot at him," Grantham said. "We aren't big enough to field a football team or tall enough to be competitive at basketball, but we play killer lacrosse."

Dr. Aycock clapped David on the shoulder, "Won the regional championship David's last two years at Maybree."

"We're going to repeat this year, sir." Grantham smiled at the old man with genuine warmth and deference. "If I can assemble the kind of team I think I can." He looked over at Tim. "So, can I take a crack at getting Jason to play?"

"Why not? Although I doubt he's even heard of the game and certainly doesn't know how to play it."

"Just like field hockey, or ice hockey. Surely he went to ice hockey games in Chicago. Hit a ball down the field with a stick, except there's a basket on the end of the stick and you throw it overhand."

"He'll probably enjoy the hitting part," Tim said. "He's pretty strong for a fifteen-year-old, plus he's tall. Already over six feet."

"He'd make a good defenceman, then. Helps if you have long arms to extend your reach and long legs to keep ahead of your offensive opposite."

"David was a superb defenseman," Dr. Aycock said. "It would not be beyond the realm of possibility that he was the best player Maybree ever fielded." He kept his hand on David's shoulder. "One would be amazed at the size of some of the young players we face, particularly from Texas. One might consider them the size of college linemen."

"Tell you what, Tim," David said. "Can I drive by your house one evening this week to talk to your son? I don't want to wait until school starts. I recruit better on my prospects' home turfs."

"Just like the big college recruiters," Aycock said. "Except that we do not offer sports cars." He chortled. "Jesting, of course."

"Learned from Coach," David said. "Taught me everything I know about the game. I sure miss him."

"When does the season start?" Tim asked.

"Not until February 15, and they don't let us hold official practices until January 15." He shrugged. "But we hold optional practices pretty much all year. The players coming back after one or two seasons need to get up to speed again. The newbies have probably never held a stick before. They need all the practice they can get. Be a chance for him to meet some of the other guys before he gets thrown in at the deep end."

"And with David standing behind him, he will have no trouble becoming one of the 'in' crowd," Aycock said. "All the students look up to David's lacrosse players."

"Come on, sir, nobody remembers about when I played. We're certainly not a bunch of jock snobs."

"Of course, my boy, of course." He smiled at Tim. "He's also quite a scholar. Once he's finished his degree at the university, we already have a place for him on our full-time coaching staff. That is if he doesn't get a better offer, right, my boy?"

For an instant Grantham's face went still, his bright eyes flat. Tim didn't think this beautiful young man intended to spend his life teaching lacrosse at a penny-ante private school like Maybree.

A moment later that infectious grin was back. Tim wondered if he'd actually caught that other expression.

Oh, well, he didn't blame the guy. And he might be a good influence on Jason.

TIM WAS RUNNING LATE, so he assumed Helen and Bill were already waiting for him. When he got home, he found Eddy in his front yard with Lancelot, and Jason careening down the hill on his skateboard. Obviously he wasn't paying a heck of a lot of attention to his babysitting duties.

"Where's your helmet?" Tim said as he climbed out of his car.

"In the house. I don't need it."

"Go get it—and your knee and elbow pads."

"Sheesh, bogus!"

"Do it or the skateboard goes in the garage with a chain lock on it. Where's Angie?"

"Back in Nancy's woods with those guys," Jason said.

Tim's heart rate went up. "Jason, I told you to look after your brother and sister."

"She's fine. And Eddy's right there with that pig."

A bright red Volvo station wagon was parked in Nancy's driveway. "Angie's safe with Phil and Phineas," said a man from the shade of Nancy's front porch.

"I don't know either of them." Tim's imagination was beginning to make him lose it.

"We do. Known both of them and their families for years and years." A woman came out of the shadows of Nancy's front porch and down the front steps with her hand outstretched. "I'm Helen Halliburton and that's Bill on the swing back there." As she reached him, she said quietly, "They're trustworthy, if that's what's worrying you."

"Logging's dangerous," Tim stammered. Accusing two of the area's finest would certainly not endear him to the Halliburtons. He'd already dispossessed them.

"Of course it is." Bill came forward and shook Tim's hand. "They won't let her anywhere near danger. She said she'd be back in half an hour. The boys will send her home on time, don't you worry."

Eddy checked for traffic, then raced across the street with Lancelot trotting behind him. "Daddy, Nancy says JustPup can come home from the clinic tonight. She's going to bring him."

"She called," Helen said. "Oh, and she can pick up her Durango tonight."

He took his first good look at them. Nancy had told him that Bill was Mabel Halliburton's brother-in-law. Mabel was the night receptionist at Creature Comfort. No wonder she had been so annoyed at Tim. He had tossed her husband's brother.

Bill had a white beard and a fringe of white hair around his bald pate. He also had the beginnings of a paunch.

Helen was as spritely as a wren. Small, fine-boned, her hair was whiter than her husband's and fluffed around her head like a halo. They looked like Mr. and Mrs. Santa Claus on summer vacation.

"Come sit a spell," Helen said. "We can keep an eye on Eddy and Lancelot and make certain Jason's properly equipped. Bill and I thought he should be wearing a helmet, but we didn't like to say."

Tim sat on one of the rockers, while Bill and Helen sat back down side by side on the porch swing. They were holding hands.

"First, I want to tell you how sorry I am for kicking you out of your home," he said. "My real estate manager handled everything. I never even knew who was paying the rent."

"It was certainly a shock," Helen said. "But it was your right."

"Nothing lasts forever," Bill added. "Besides, now that our children are grown, we weren't using the upstairs at all except when the grandchildren came to visit."

"Although stairs aren't a problem for either of us," Helen said.

Bill squeezed her hand and grinned at her. "Yet."

"Still, we needed a smaller place without the big yard. I didn't think I'd enjoy living in an apartment, but it has its advantages. Are you still renting your pasture to Mike?"

"Mike O'Hara? I know I'm renting it to somebody. He didn't mention he was the one."

"Real estate agent again, huh?" Bill said. "Doesn't hurt to have the sheriff beholden to you, son."

"Mike's a good man. He keeps a real close eye on Williamston. His thirteen-year-old daughter, Haley, goes to Maybree. I assume you'll be teaching her this fall."

"Good to know." Tim sat on the top step. "I realize Williamston is small, but so far, the only neighbors I've met are Nancy and Mike. I never see anybody from the other houses." On his side three Victorian cottages, very much like Nancy's, sat way back from the road. On Nancy's side, a large four-square and another big white farmhouse sat behind white board fences.

"They all work in town during the day," Helen explained. "It's always the children outside playing who make the introductions to new people. In Williamston, most of the children are grown and either in college or raising families of their own someplace else."

"Besides, nobody much comes out until fall. The first cool fall Saturday, you'll see everybody in the yard mulching."

"Used to be we got together for picnics and such," Helen said, a little wistfully. "Now, everybody comes home exhausted, sits in front of the TV in the air-conditioning and never sticks a head into the yard."

"Lawn services," Bill said. "Killed neighborhood chats. I see your yard is looking a little ragged."

Tim looked across at his yard as Jason came out wearing his pads and helmet. He glared at his father, picked up his skateboard and trundled it up to the top of the hill.

"Nancy said you could recommend a lawn service."

"Me," Bill said with a laugh. "I have a big old riding mower that I sure can't use in the apartment. If I can bring it over and leave it in your garage, I can do your yard."

"How much?" Tim asked. He didn't think Bill was offering to cut his yard for free, and even if he were, Tim wouldn't let him.

Bill named a figure. "Once a week through October. Then you won't need to start again until middle of March. Next year I'll teach your boy."

"Done. Even if I had the time, I don't have the lawnmower or equipment. The plantings are lovely," Tim said. "I've never had much of an opportunity to garden. I've lived in apartments most of my life."

"I'll teach you. I like to garden," Helen offered. "Mostly bulbs. That means lots of spring flowers and day lilies in the summertime and less weeding."

"I hope you'll have your own garden before spring," Tim said quietly.

Helen sighed. "I wouldn't count on it. Marquette County is the fastest growing county in the state. Everybody's buying ten acres, putting a starter castle on it, then selling it for a million dollars."

"Which we don't have," Bill interjected. "And we don't want the ten acres even if we could afford it."

"Nancy says you need someone to look after the inside of your house, too," Helen waited.

He felt his face flush. This woman was hardly his idea of a maid.

"I need a housekeeper," he said. "In Chicago I didn't have either the room or the money for an au pair. Down here I have the room, but not the money."

Helen laughed. "Au pairs are not that easy to come by in Marquette County."

"Once school starts in two weeks—heck, right now even before school starts—I can't do my job and keep an eye on *them* at the same time." He flipped a hand toward Jason, currently rolling down the hill in front of them.

"Not to mention cooking, cleaning, washing, chauffeuring, fixing things, waiting for repairmen, etc., etc., etc.," Helen said with a laugh.

"You've got it. In Chicago my mother-in-law looked after them, and everything I needed was in my neighborhood. I could walk to the cleaners and the grocery store. The kids could walk to school. I don't know why I ever thought I could raise them alone out here where you can't pick up a bottle of milk without driving ten miles."

"You don't need a housekeeper, young man, you need a wife," Bill said. He squeezed his wife's hand and turned to beam on her.

"Now, Bill, the world has moved on. Men and women share the chores, or they should." She turned to Tim. "Would you believe with three children and half a dozen grandchildren this male chauvinist has never changed a single diaper?" She slapped his hand. "Wouldn't get away with that today."

"I don't know the going rate for housekeepers," Tim said. "I don't know what I need or when I need it."

"My dear, I married Bill for life but not for lunch, as the saying goes, so I'm looking for a way to get out of our little apartment before I throttle him. Besides, he needs to be searching for a house so we can move out of that apartment and get Lancelot back."

Across the street, Lancelot was chasing Eddy and squealing.

"Oh, I am so glad he has somebody young to play with. He can wear me out." She smiled at Tim. "I know that house of yours as well as I know my own name," Helen said. "And I drive a Volvo. Can't get much safer than that, can you?"

"Would you actually consider it? I can hire a service to clean. You wouldn't need to do anything except straighten up, and the kids should be doing that. It's the driving I can't handle. You wouldn't need to be there when they were in school, either. If I had someone picking them up after school and taking them where they need to go, then bringing them home and maybe even starting dinner… I'd pay for gas and your time from your home back to your home, of course, as well as a salary."

"Shall we see how it works out for the week?" Helen said. "I checked with my daughter about what I should be charging." She named a figure. "Can you afford that?"

"Barely." Tim laughed. "It doesn't seem nearly enough."

"It may not *be* enough, depending on what I wind up doing. We can adjust at the end of the week—up or down."

"The thing is, with meetings and setting up my classroom, I'll be gone most mornings until school starts. Jason's supposed to work three afternoons a week at Creature Comfort, although we haven't decided which days, and Nancy is trying to arrange riding lessons for Angie."

"And Eddy?"

"Eddy needs someone he can count on just to be there to keep him safe." Eddy had walked across the street and was now curled against the base of Nancy's big oak tree with Lancelot, all sixty pounds of him, flat on his back with four feet in the air while Eddy scratched his belly.

"Pigs don't generally show their bellies to anyone," Bill said. "It's a very vulnerable position. Eddy should be flattered."

"I'm discovering he has a real rapport with animals," Tim pointed out. "Although I never knew that until we moved down here. You've heard about the burned puppy he found?"

"Terrible thing," Bill said. "I guess there are bad elements everywhere."

Tim sighed. "I came down here to get my children *away* from people like that."

"My dear," Helen said, "you can't protect them from the world. If you have to drive ten miles for a gallon of milk, they have to drive their cars or motorcycles ten miles to get to your house."

"Or their ATVs," chimed in Bill. "We have quite a problem with them from time to time, but Mike usually runs them off."

"To the best of my knowledge, there are no *really* nasty characters actually living in Williamston."

Tim wondered if she was thinking "until you moved in."

"We used to have some real juvenile delinquents," Bill said. "Thank God they've all grown up and turned into responsible adults."

"Or taken their problems with them to college or apartments in midtown Memphis," Helen said with a laugh. "A good many of the ones that used to drive me craziest are now reaping the whirlwind."

"I beg your pardon?"

"Sow the wind, reap the whirlwind," Bill explained. "Helen means they're now raising children of their own, and all their rotten behavior when they were young is coming back to haunt them."

"The mother's curse," Helen added, "May you have children exactly like you."

"Now, that one I've heard," Tim said. "My mother used to dump that on me whenever I forgot to take out the garbage or missed curfew." He leaned back and rubbed the back of his neck. Was Nancy contagious? He had one hell of a crick. "I think Mom got her wish and then some."

"Nothing wrong with your children that time and being well occupied won't cure," Bill said. "You been down to the lake yet?"

"Not since I was a boy. I told the kids about it, but made them promise not to go hunting for it until I could go along."

"And that stopped them? Wouldn't have stopped my boy Andy when he was Jason's age. We had to be real strict about when they could be down there unless they were fishing from the dock. No swimming or boating without an adult present."

"So our Andy got his lifesaving certificate to spite us." Helen laughed. "Never had an accident down there." She knocked on the arm of the rocking chair.

"Mine aren't used to either the heat or the woods. Besides, Eddy can't swim and is deathly afraid of water. Jason, on the other hand, has made me promise to get him a canoe at the earliest possible opportunity."

"A canoe rather than a kayak?" Bill asked.

"Canoe. I think he visualizes taking girls for moonlight boat rides. Can't do that in a kayak. He went to camp for several summers until he decided he'd outgrown it, and he learned to canoe there. I promised I'd take him on a canoe trip in Canada, but well…"

"More broken promises, eh? Been there, done that. Don't get my children started on their litany of my broken promises. Life keeps getting in the way of living, doesn't it?"

"You got that right."

"So." Bill stood and pulled Helen to her feet. "Why don't we collect your kids and walk on down to the lake, see how it's fared this summer. Been more rain than usual. Suspect the path is pretty overgrown. May have to chop our way through."

"I can get Jason, but what about Angie?" Tim asked.

"Don't you worry, she's due any minute," Helen said. "As I said, Phil and Phineas will send her home on time."

As if in answer, Angie jogged around the corner of Nancy's house. Her face glowed bright red from the heat and was running with sweat, and her legs in their short shorts were all scratched from the underbrush. But her face shone as though she'd seen Paradise. In Angie's case, Tim guessed she had. Her black hair hung limp but if she'd bothered to put on her white makeup this morning, she'd sweated it off.

"Daddy! Phil let me ride Henry out to the woods." She pointed at the Halliburtons. "They said they'd tell you."

"Sure." He hadn't realized how uncomfortable he was when she was out of his sight. "But you can't bother Phil and his brother. They have work to do."

"I wasn't bothering them. I stayed way out of the way with the horses. They don't want trees falling on Henry and Herb, either." Now she sounded sulky, and started toward Eddy. Lancelot rolled onto his tummy, levered himself up and trotted over to be scratched.

"IT'S REAL BIG," Eddy whispered. He stood on shore a dozen feet behind his father and stared out at the dark water.

"Man, I'm going swimming right now," Jason announced. He pulled off his helmet, T-shirt and shoes, and stooped to unbuckle his knee and elbow pads..

"Me, too," Angie said.

"Not me," Eddy said. "Daddy, I don't have to, do I?"

"Not if you don't want to. Bill, how deep is it?"

"Twenty feet or so in the middle, but no more than five or six feet around the edges."

"So, no diving from the dock, you two."

"We used to have a float anchored in the middle," Bill said.

"We could dive in the middle. Can we build one?" Jason asked. He tossed his pads and his shoes on the dock.

"I won't have enough time before it's too cold to swim," Tim said. "Maybe next year."

"It's always next year," Jason whined. "Come on, Ange. Last one in…"

"Whoa!" Tim stopped them. "Lake rules. You're not to come down here to swim without adult supervision. Never, ever alone. No jackassing in the water, and you come out when you're told. You got that?"

Jason rolled his eyes. "I can swim."

"So can I," Angie said, and sneered at her little brother. "Eddy's the 'fraidy cat."

"Am not."

"Are, too."

"Angie, you sound like a three-year-old. Leave your brother alone. He'll learn when he's ready."

Angie rolled her eyes and heaved a cavernous sigh. "Yeah, when he's ninety."

Eddy stared at the ground.

"My grandfather seeded it with crappie and bream and cat-fish," Tim said.

"Oh, they're flourishing," Bill answered. "My Andy learned to fish right off this dock."

"*Eeew*. I'm not getting bit by fish," Angie said.

"Now, who's the 'fraidy cat?" Jason asked, and jumped off the end of the pier. "Man, it's great. Come on, Angie, I'll protect you from the *fishies*."

She looked back at her father, sat down on the end of the dock and gingerly lowered herself into the water. "It's warm."

"When our children were younger, we used to have picnics down here with the neighbors a couple of times a season," Helen said. "Then every fall we'd organize a clean-up-the-lakeshore afternoon."

"It's well enough hidden so most folks don't even know it's here," Bill continued.

"That's not true, Bill." Helen turned to Tim. "Two years ago, a bunch of ATVs drove in from Mike O'Hara's place after midnight every night for a week. He finally chased them off and had his deputies keep an eye out until they gave up and moved someplace else."

"That's when we put up the No Trespassing signs," Bill said.

"We haven't had a picnic over there the past three of four years," Helen said. "The kids have all grown up. Everybody would rather stay indoors in the air-conditioning anyway."

"It's still as beautiful as I remember." Tim shoved his hands in his pockets. "But smaller. The difference in the way a kid sees."

"How far back does it go around that bend?" Jason called. He was now treading water a dozen yards into the lake. "I can't see the end of it from here."

"It's shaped like a big kidney. As far back out of sight as this part here," Tim told his son. "Plenty of space to canoe."

"Spring fed, too," Helen continued. "So it stays fairly clear, but the bottom's silt and clay mud. Stir it up and you can't see your hand in front of your face till it settles down again."

"When times were hard, plenty of people lived on the fish they caught in this pond," Tim said. "Granddaddy never stopped them. Never mentioned it to them, either."

"You said we could get a canoe," Jason said. "Or is that one of those 'later' things that don't happen until next year?"

"Tomorrow after my meeting at school, we'll buy a canoe. But you'll stay out of it until I'm home to check you out in it, is that clear?"

"Bogus."

"And you'll wear a life jacket while you're on the water."

"Way bogus. How about water wings and a helmet?"

"You want the canoe? Then shut up." Helen and Bill Halliburton probably thought he was a jerk, but he was about one step from really snarling.

The sunshine glancing off the water was hurtfully bright. Tim shaded his eyes against the glare and to keep Jason and Angie in view.

"Sorry," he said to Bill and Helen. "I shouldn't have lost my cool."

"They'll goad you until you do," Bill said. "I never hit my son, but boy, there were times when I wanted to deck him."

"Yeah, but I'm not supposed to react."

"Really."

"Working with kids is my job. I'm good with them, or I thought I was."

Bill chuckled. "Hell, man, nobody's good with his own kids. You ever know a preacher's kid or a psychiatrist's kid who wasn't a hellion?

"Hey, you two," Bill called to Angie and Jason. "You interested in some lunch?"

"Can we come back to swim afterward?" Angie asked.

"For an hour or so, then I've got work to do in the house."

"Oh, Dad."

"An hour out here with no sunscreen on and y'all will be fried," Helen said. "Come on. Bill and I brought some fried chicken as a housewarming present."

"Yea!" Eddy rejoiced.

"Real food," Jason said and stroked toward the dock. "If you can't open a can or microwave it, Dad doesn't have a clue."

CHAPTER THIRTEEN

MONDAY MORNING Nancy and Mac pulled an abscessed tooth in a Great Dane, treated a nasty case of ear and eye canker in a French lop rabbit and trimmed the hooves on Moo Shu, one of their least favorite clients.

Moo Shu had been a client at the clinic since his owner first brought him in as a tiny potbellied piglet, and the staff and doctors had been known to draw lots as to which of them was stuck with him.

He was a very different proposition from Lancelot, who accepted all attention with good grace, so long as he could expect a treat at the end of the ordeal. Moo Shu knew he'd get a candy mint from the receptionist, but that had ceased to compensate him for the anguish.

Moo Shu didn't like to have his hooves trimmed, so his owner usually let them go long enough that the soft center overgrew the tough outer layer. No matter how they assured Moo Shu he wouldn't be hurt, they were pig-torturers, and that was the end of it.

Every time Nancy had to assist, she thanked God the treatment rooms were soundproofed.

"A jet plane taking off has been measured at a hundred and fifteen decibels," Mac remarked as he opened the door to Exam Room one where Moo Shu and his unhappy owner waited. "A pig can squeal at a hundred and eighteen."

"Bet you Moo Shu tops a hundred and fifty," Nancy whispered as she closed the door.

The moment he saw Nancy and Mac, Moo Shu let forth a blood-curdling squeal that made Nancy's teeth ache. Jane, his owner, looked apologetic.

"Let's get him on the table," Mac said, over the din.

"What?" Jane asked, then pointed to her ears. "I'm wearing earplugs."

Mac glared at her, grabbed Moo Shu's rear end while Nancy handled the front. Together they hoisted his hundred and twenty pounds up on the table and laid him on his side. He scrabbled frantically while Nancy tied his front and back feet.

Jane stepped over and begin offering him bits of carrot while Nancy leaned her weight across Moo Shu, handed Mac his tools and held first one foot, then each of the others.

The ordeal was over in less then ten minutes, but to hear Moo Shu tell it, he might as well have been barbecued over a fire.

When Jane finally hooked his leash on his harness and led him out, he glared over his shoulder, gave a disgusted grunt and marched out as though the governor had reprieved him.

Mac leaned both hands on the exam table. He was pouring sweat. "Next time it's Rick's turn."

Nancy elbowed him out of the way, tossed the hoof trimmings into the nonhazardous trash container, scrubbed the table down with disinfectant and dropped her gloves in the hazardous trash. Mac rolled his off his hands and tossed them as well.

"How come he counts as a small animal instead of livestock?" Nancy said as they moved on to the next room where a Yorkshire terrier with a torn ear awaited.

"Beats me," Mac said and as he opened the door and walked in. "Hey, Cagney, what'd you get into this time?"

Nancy was thankful his owner had already put on the muzzle. For a very small dog, he'd been known to remove a large chunk from anyone who tried to give him a shot. Shots were her job.

They worked steadily until nearly noon, then when they took

a break, she found a note asking her to go back into large animals to see Eleanor Chadwick.

"We have to do some planning right now," Eleanor said. "How would you feel about switching assignments with Jack?"

"I'm already doing both his job and mine."

"I don't mean that." Eleanor leaned forward and began to make concentric circles on her notepad without meeting Nancy's eyes. "I mean when he comes back."

"I beg your pardon?"

Eleanor looked up at her. "I know you and Mac are a team. The last thing I want to do is to steal you away from him." She took a deep breath. "No, that's not true. The thing I want to do is preserve a job for Jack. I'm not sure he'll ever be able to handle large animal surgery again."

Nancy opened her mouth to speak, but Eleanor raised a hand to stop her. "Hear me out. Even at a hundred and forty pounds and five foot six Jack could manhandle bad-mannered thorough-breds and give shots to full-grown bulls."

"I could probably handle the thoroughbreds, although my neck might be a problem. As for the bulls, forget it. They scare me half to death."

"That's why you and I are going to teach Big how to do the heavy stuff. He's already doing a good deal of it. With supervision, he can do it all. He may be a bit slow, but he's not stupid, and he's incredibly careful." She shrugged and grinned. "Bulls take one look at him and settle right down. They know they'd lose in a fair fight."

"I have no idea what he makes besides his rent-free cottage, but if he's going to do more, he should be paid more. Rick won't like it."

"Screw Rick. I mean that in the nicest possible way, of course."

Nancy laughed. "Okay. But as for leaving Mac—"

"I'm not saying leave him. He wouldn't stand for it. He'd put out a contract on me and Sarah if he even suspected you and I were having this little chat."

"So keep my mouth shut?"

"Right. For all our sakes. What I *am* saying is that we want Jack back at his job as soon as his doctor says he's up to it, not only for his sake, but for ours. I just think we ought to start him with small animals rather than the big guys. Then, once he's back up to speed, we ease him back into large animals if possible, but keep Big to do the heavy lifting."

Nancy leaned back in her chair. "I can't do the polo matches again," she said. "I wound up in surgery with Mac and didn't get home until after ten. I'm too old for that. I need my rest."

Eleanor hesitated. Then she nodded and said, "Okay. Done. Eleanor, Liz and I will take over when they play in town."

"So far we've been lucky. You haven't needed me to assist on an emergency at the same time Mac does. We can't stay lucky forever. How did Jack's angioplasty go?" she asked. She genuinely wanted to know, but she was also playing for time.

"Good, but he's scheduled for a triple bypass tomorrow morning. That means a week or so in the hospital, then home for recuperation, then to cardiac rehabilitation for a couple of months before he can even think of coming back to work. Then…" She shrugged. "He needs this job, Nancy. Not only for the money, but for his soul. He really would waste away if he couldn't work with animals any longer."

"Even if they're puppies and kittens instead of barrel-racers?"

"So long as we can hold out hope that he'll come back to large animals. That's why I don't want Rick to up and hire somebody to replace him forever. It's a darned sight easier to hire somebody full-time than for a few months with no hope of being hired permanently. If Jack could work with Mac for a few months, while you work with me and Sarah, Rick would be happy, even if he had to pay Big a larger salary to take up the slack. Does that make sense?"

Nancy closed her eyes. She and Mac knew each other so well that she understood what he wanted often before he did. His wife, Kit, who owned a kennel that trained helper dogs, said they reminded her of an old married couple. They didn't finish each other's sentences, but they often finished each other's actions.

She'd worked with Sarah and Eleanor a few times. They were superb veterinary surgeons, but they weren't Mac. She knew how Mac liked his trays set up and how many of each kind of instrument he was likely to need for each type of surgery. She knew how often he wanted to know vital signs on any animal, and how to regulate anesthesia and oxygen from Jack Russell terriers to Great Danes.

There would definitely be a learning curve when she went to work for Sarah and Eleanor, and not only for her, but for them as well. Jack undoubtedly knew them as well as she knew Mac. They weren't used to having to explain what they were doing or what they needed.

"I'm not getting in the middle of this," she said finally. "You doctors work it out. I'll do whatever you decide. But please don't expect me to know all your idiosyncrasies the way I do Mac's."

"Not at first. You'll catch on. Come on. I don't know about you, but I'm starved."

Nancy followed her to the staff break room. Eleanor pulled her own brown bag out of the refrigerator, then Nancy's, tossed it to her, pulled out a couple of diet sodas, and handed one to Nancy.

They began unwrapping their sandwiches. "How's your new neighbor?" Eleanor asked.

"He's okay."

Eleanor looked at her carefully. "If he's just okay, how come you're blushing?"

"I am not."

"Are, too. No wife? Divorced? Good-looking?"

Nancy leaned forward over her chicken sandwich. "He is incredible looking. Unfortunately he comes complete with three totally weird children and a dead wife."

"Whoops. How weird?"

"You'll meet Jason, the eldest, this afternoon. He bashed my car and Tim's making him pay for the repairs by working part-time here."

"Rick agreed to this? Paying actual money?"

"Yep. You know we always need help with the scut work. It's not fair to put so much on Big. Anyway, if you see a tall, scrawny kid with incredible eyelashes, the beginnings of dark curly hair, clothes that look too large for Big, and a sulky expression, that's Jason Wainwright."

"The beginnings of hair?"

"When he arrived from Chicago he was nearly as bald as the proverbial billiard ball. His father is making him grow it out. I take it Maybree Academy doesn't favor the cue ball look. Oh, and he rides a skateboard up and down the road in front of my house. I had no idea those things made so much noise. I'm considering stealing it."

"Why on earth are we allowing him to work at Creature Comfort? He sounds dreadful."

Nancy finished her sandwich, balled the paper bag into a wad and tossed it across the room into the trash can. She bit into her apple and wiped the juice off her chin before she answered. "Remember how Kenny Nichols was when he started working here after school? He only took the job because he and his buddies had vandalized the building supplies when we were finishing up this place. Now, there was a real J.D., and look at him now. Prevet."

"You think this kid could be another Kenny?"

Nancy stood and rubbed her neck. "A month or so with Big and he'll probably turn into St. Francis of Assisi. I've got to go check meds in the small animal section."

"And I'm off to do a prepurchase exam on a horse in north Mississippi." Eleanor tossed her wadded-up lunch bag, but missed the trash. "Damn. You never miss."

"I grew up shooting baskets with my brothers. You probably had a civilized childhood."

"You didn't tell me about the other weird children," Eleanor said as she bent over to pick her bag off the floor and deposit it where it belonged.

Nancy turned back from the door. "Eddy is seven, I think. He's the one that found JustPup—you know—the little dog with the burns. He seems to be coming out of his shell some, but he's scared of everything new. Plus he has a creepy stare. Angie, the thirteen-year-old, is a Goth. How would you like to have them for neighbors?"

She turned from the door to run head-on into Jason, who was standing in the hall looking lost. Oh God, he'd probably heard her.

"Um, they told me to find you. What am I supposed to do?"

She gulped. "Follow me. You'll be working for Big Little. Just do whatever he says."

She darted past him down the hall to the large animals. She could hear his gigantic feet in their huge white trainers clomping behind him.

She found Big with the exotic animals at the far end. He was sitting on the floor chatting with a big raccoon. He'd opened its cage, and it was now squatting on the floor in front of him while he fed it kibbles. "Now, you just let ole Big take a look at that foot."

"Oops, sorry," Nancy said.

Big turned his beatific smile on them. "Hey, Nancy, is this Jason?"

"I didn't mean to interrupt."

The raccoon had climbed into Big's lap and was sitting on his hind feet while he reared to threaten them.

"Hush up, you're all right," Big whispered. "You get on back in there now. Big'll come fix you up in a few minutes. Scat, now."

The raccoon gave a halfhearted hiss at the interlopers, then walked back into its cage. Big hooked the door, and rose.

Nancy was used to him, but for Jason, it must have been like Ahab spotting Moby Dick for the first time. She heard his sudden intake of breath as Nancy introduced them. "He's all yours until his father picks him up."

"Aren't raccoons dangerous?" Jason asked.

"Big raccoon'll eat your lunch," Big said with a grin. "And I don't mean no sandwich. You leave them cages alone, if they got something in 'em. Plenty to do with the empty ones. Come on, I'll show you."

Nancy left them to it. She'd never seen anyone who had the rapport with wild animals that Big did. She figured they understood that in some strange way he was one of them. They certainly realized they were safe around him. If he couldn't shape Jason up, nobody could.

But what must he think of her remarks about having the Wainwrights for neighbors?

CHAPTER FOURTEEN

Tim SAT ON THE FRONT window seat and waited for Nancy to drive in with her loaner. He could leave Jason with Angie and Eddy long enough to drive with her to the garage to pick up her Durango. Maybe stop at a Starbucks on the way home. Have what Jason called an FTF—a face-to-face.

His other expression was face time.

Tim badly wanted some face time with Nancy. A few minutes when they weren't under the gun either from her job or his, or from his family. They hadn't started off well, but once she'd gotten over being annoyed about the Halliburtons, she'd been kind and helpful toward Eddy and Angie.

If he were honest with himself, that wasn't the reason he longed for face time.

The woman was sexy as hell. He'd always been attracted to feisty, opinionated women—Nancy was feisty, all right, but she was also as luscious as a ripe peach.

It was about time he had a little success in his relationships. The only dates he'd had since Solange died had nearly convinced him to embrace lifelong celibacy. Nearly. Not quite.

Several of his colleagues had arranged dates for him a suitable time after Solange's death. He'd agreed to go. Big mistake.

Three dates. Three disasters. He was under the apparently old-fashioned impression that the man called and made the dinner reservations, the man paid and, if he was lucky, he got a good-night kiss on the first date.

He had to admit the three women had been physically attractive. But he wasn't looking for models. He was no beauty himself.

He couldn't remember any of their names. As a matter of fact, his subconscious had probably worked very hard to erase them.

The first one was a tall, leggy vegan who spent the evening damning anyone who ate a steak as a wanton murderer. He was in the middle of a rare T-bone at the time. When he attempted to offer another point of view, she got so mad he was afraid she'd grab his steak knife and slit his throat.

His next date spent the evening damning her ex, no, make that her *two* exes, and telling him in great detail that all men were cheaters and liars and should only be kept in harems as sperm donors.

The third had a laugh that made a donkey bray sound as sweet as a Maria Callas aria. She laughed at everything he said. Before they finished their entrées he had a blinding headache over his right eye.

He was certain they weren't any more attracted to him than he was to them, so he was amazed when he realized they all *expected* him to go to bed with them when he took them home.

He knew he'd be physically capable of performing. But the thought of facing any one of the three afterwards, even in the dark, appalled him.

He and Solange had loved to cuddle and whisper after they made love. He had adored caressing her, playing with her lovely dark hair, going to sleep with her slim leg thrown across his thigh. Waking in the morning to the scent of her warm body in his nostrils and her bottom fitted against his belly.

Good love. Hell, great love.

Until they pretty much stopped making love at all in the last few months before she died.

After she started her affair.

He couldn't settle for sex with a stranger simply because she had all the right parts in the proper places. One of his buddies called that kind of night committing orgasm.

He'd begun to feel that there would never be another woman who turned him on the way Solange had.

He'd decided not to accept any more blind dates.

He wanted a woman who raised his blood pressure, not just his erection. A woman who could laugh with him, fight with him, challenge him and come to his bed wanting him as much as he wanted her.

He had a feeling Nancy might be that woman.

He had to give them a chance to find out.

CHAPTER FIFTEEN

TIM GAVE NANCY a few minutes to relax and change her clothes before he called and offered to go with her to the dealership. It was open until 8:00 p.m. He'd already told the kids they could nuke some frozen dinners. He was too uptight to be hungry.

For food, at any rate. When Nancy swung her long legs out of her little loaner car, his other appetites increased logarithmetically. He'd suggest they grab a bite to eat on their way from the dealership.

He wouldn't give her time to fix herself dinner before he called. The timing had to be perfect.

As he reached for the phone, however, a black Hummer pulled to a stop in front of his house and David Grantham climbed out from behind the driver's seat.

Damn. He'd forgotten he'd told David he could talk to Jason, who was at the moment upstairs on his computer playing the latest video game. Tim could hear the violent sound effects.

He went to open the front door.

"Hey, Dr., er, Mr. Wainwright," the young man said as he extended his hand. "Is this a bad time? I probably should have called first."

"It's Tim, remember."

"Yeah. Right."

"It's not a bad time," Tim lied. "Forgive the mess. We're still unpacking."

The living room was fairly well organized, although there were no pictures on the wall and no books in the bookcases flanking the fireplace.

The dining room beyond, however, was stacked with unopened boxes.

"Great house." Grantham looked around. "Man, you got some *room*. I live in this little dinky town house in Collierville, and it's full of athletic equipment and my mountain bike."

"When I told Jason you wanted to recruit him to play lacrosse, he didn't seem too interested," Tim said. "But then he would probably act blasé if they asked him to captain the Olympic skateboard team."

"Hey, Tim, don't worry. I'll convince him to at least give it a try."

"Let me call him down."

"Great."

When Tim went upstairs to tell Jason, the kid rolled his eyes.

"At least listen to him," Tim said. "Close your private universe for a minute and come down."

"Yeah, yeah. But, you know, I mean, lacrosse? What's *that* about?"

Tim went back downstairs and found David staring out the front window. "He'll be down in a minute. I hope you're not expecting enthusiasm. Jason doesn't do enthusiastic these days."

"That's my problem."

"Do you mind if I leave you? I may have to go out for a while."

"Actually that works out better." David smiled that sunshine smile. "Thanks for the opportunity to convince him to play."

"I'm still not certain he has any talent for lacrosse."

"Hey, trust me. He's a blank slate. No bad habits to break."

Tim called Nancy from the kitchen. When she answered, he asked, "Hey, can I go with you to pick up your car? Just in case there's any problem with payment."

"Right now?" She didn't sound thrilled. "I just came in. I've got to take a shower and change clothes. I smell like the operating room."

"Dealer's open until eight. I checked. Maybe we could go somewhere afterward for a bite to eat." He waited for what seemed like hours as he listened to the silence at the end of the telephone. He was certain he'd get a "no."

"O-kay," she said. She sounded reluctant, but at least she'd agreed. "Nothing fancy. I'm putting on shorts."

"That's what I've got on."

"Meet you at your car."

She was obviously loath to come in his house. Maybe she didn't want to remember her last trip when he discovered her crawling on his bedroom floor. The memory made him grin. *That* would never have happened in Chicago.

Jason wandered downstairs. Tim introduced him to David. Watching Jason's face as he took in the preppy clothes and the haircut, he didn't give David good odds on recruiting Jason for the team.

He left them to it and sat on his back steps until he saw Nancy walk out her front door.

At the dealership, he waited while she returned her loaner and picked up her Durango. "All paid for," she said. "So, you still want to eat or what?"

"Absolutely. Any suggestions?"

"You like fried catfish?"

"Very much."

"Then get in. It's on the way to Williamston. It's Monday night, so we probably won't have to wait for a table. On Fridays and Saturdays the lines are out the door."

He'd seen the restaurant sign on the highway. It was a relatively small place advertising catfish and Memphis barbecue. If this turned out well, he could bring the kids over some time when he was sick of microwaves and pizza. So far they were still delighted to eat nuked food. In Chicago, Madame had cooked elaborate four- or five-course dinners every night. The food was superb.

Being fed that way as a general rule made his heathens long for cheeseburgers and fries.

He and Nancy were shown to a shadowy back booth and placed orders for the catfish dinner. When his beer and Nancy's iced tea had been delivered, he was suddenly struck tongue-tied worse than he'd been on his first date at fourteen. "Um…"

At the same moment, she said, "So…" then, "No, you first. Sorry."

"No, you go ahead." This was turning into a disaster.

"So, how was your first day at Maybree?" She peered at him over the rim of her glass, her eyes serious. Then she began to laugh. "And what did you learn at school today, dear?" She giggled. "My mother used to ask me that every afternoon. What do you say to that? The square of the hypotenuse of a right triangle is…whatever it is. I never can remember."

"You're speaking to an English major. When I had to take statistics to get my Ph.D., I pasted a note on the bathroom mirror that said, 'It is okay to make a B in statistics.' I was lucky to get that."

"But don't you have to do a bunch of math to run a school? I mean, you were a principal, weren't you?"

"Vice-principal, and that's why God gave you spreadsheet programs for the computer. Not to mention interns and secretaries who are dedicated to keeping you from making an idiot of yourself in front of school board members and parents."

The fish was good. The conversation was comfortable, the first steps in the oldest dance.

He knew he'd been right about her. He liked her laugh, he liked her eyes. He wanted much, much more.

After they drove home, she waved goodbye and disappeared inside her house before he could suggest they continue the evening. Her living room lights came on.

Damn. The one woman that he wanted to take to bed, and she didn't even offer a good-night kiss. At least she hadn't demanded they go Dutch. That would have been humiliating.

He thought he'd been pretty darned charming.

Apparently she didn't agree. Tim shrugged in resignation and went inside.

He dreaded looking at the state of his kitchen, expecting to find the remains of dinner and everything that had been used to serve it. Instead it was immaculate and the dishwasher was swishing quietly. "Wow," he whispered.

Jason called from upstairs, "Dad!"

When had that voice lowered from boy soprano to baritone?

Jason banged down the stairs. Either him or a visiting rhinoceros. The whole house shook.

When he reached the kitchen door, he languidly draped himself against the jam.

"You cleaned up," Tim said. "I hope you didn't make Angie do it alone."

"David made us. He stayed for frozen pizza. Said it wasn't fair to leave a mess for you to clean up."

"Good for David."

"I'm gonna play lacrosse," Jason said casually.

Tim knew enough to sound equally casual. "Oh?" He pulled a cold Sam Adams from the refrigerator and twisted off the top. He studiously avoided meeting Jason's eyes.

"Yeah. David said I'd make a great defenceman 'cause I'm tall. A lot of lacrosse players are short like him, but I got the reach."

"So do you still want the canoe?"

"What? Dad, you *promised.*"

"Just kidding." He began to add up the cost of a canoe, life jackets, paddles and all the equipment needed to equip a lacrosse goalie who might well grow out of his shoulder pads before the season started in February.

"Would you settle for a used canoe if we can find one in good condition?"

"A canoe's a canoe as long as it doesn't sink."

Tim knew he'd better learn to cook. They might be living on

peanut butter sandwiches after he paid the bills. "So, what kind of equipment does a defenceman require?" He'd have to find the money somewhere. He hadn't seen this much enthusiasm from Jason since his first afternoon on a skateboard.

Jason pulled a soda from the refrigerator, popped the top and poured it down his throat, then pulled out a kitchen chair. "Hey, Pops, it's okay. Kids who graduate and don't plan to play in college leave their stuff to the school. You have to buy new gloves and the uniform and a mouth guard thing, but that's all. I've already got a cup. David told me they've got plenty of pads and sticks and helmets and stuff, and he's got more in his apartment. No sweat."

Tim heaved a sigh of relief. Now all he had to worry about was riding lessons, and paying off JustPup's vet bills.

JustPup.

"I thought Nancy was bringing JustPup home this afternoon. What happened? Is he worse?"

"Nah. Bill ran over and got him this afternoon. He's upstairs with Eddy. Little guy's not quite housebroken. Eddy left him in his room during dinner. He's got newspapers all over his room."

"I'd better go up and see him." Tim tossed his empty bottle into the trash. "Coming?"

"In a minute. I'm hungry. I'm gonna fix a couple of sandwiches or something."

Tim nodded. Jason was a bottomless pit.

"Hey, Pops," Jason said. "Go easy on Eddy, okay? He's scared you'll get rid of the puppy if he makes a mess."

Did Eddy really think he might do that? What had he done to terrify his son? Or did Eddy simply not trust that anything he loved would endure?

When he opened Eddy's door, he saw the floor *was* completely covered with newspapers. Eddy was curled tight on his bed with his light and his clothes still on. He hadn't even taken off his shoes. JustPup's new leash lay across the foot of the single bed as though Eddy wanted it close by if he had to take the little dog outside in a hurry.

Eddy didn't wake. JustPup, however, who lay curled in the crook of Eddy's knees, lifted his head, pricked his burned and bandaged ears, and stared at Tim. Tim was afraid he'd bark and wake Eddy, but he remained silent. After a moment, he dropped his head back onto his paws, although he continued to watch Tim warily. A small water dish and an empty food dish sat beside the door to Eddy's small bathroom.

Tim backed out and pulled the door shut.

He knocked softly on Angie's door. When she didn't reply, he opened it enough to peek in. She sat on the floor with her headphones on, her back to him, her black hair bobbing.

At her feet sat her old stable and several of the miniature horses she hadn't played with in over a year. She was happily building a jump course out of pencils.

He shut the door without bothering her.

Tomorrow he'd make an appointment for her hair and makeup redo. Helen Halliburton could shepherd her through that little experience, and take any flack Angie might deliver. He was a coward when it came to confrontation with his kids. They'd had enough problems.

He already had their school uniforms. He planned to wait to buy other clothes for them until they found out what was in at Maybree. They'd want the same brands and the same styles, no matter how bizarre.

He came downstairs and checked that the doors were locked and Lancelot's pet door was safely barred.

The light in Nancy's living room was still on. He wanted to go knock on her front door, and when she opened it, grab her and kiss the heck out of her.

And progress from there.

To what? Spend the night over there while his children slept over here? What if they needed him in the night? Bring her home to his bed? Nope.

He would definitely have to work out the logistics of a relationship with Nancy.

Hell, a man who could reorganize an entire school so that every student had a desk and every class enough time and space to work should be able to handle an illicit liaison with one neighbor. People did it all the time.

CHAPTER SIXTEEN

"THAT JASON don't much like working," Big said to Nancy the following afternoon after Jason left the clinic for the day. "Got plenty of muscle, though. Big for his age. Likes the animals, too, but said he didn't plan no career scrubbing dog poop out of cages." Big grinned. "Told him he might like scrubbing horse poo off'a walls better. He shut up after that."

Big held the halter of a Guernsey cow that had lost an altercation with a barbed wire fence and had torn a long gash in her udder. She was healing nicely and would probably go home in two or three days, but Eleanor wanted to make sure the cow wouldn't develop an infection in the suture site and that the cut was healing. Since she was a milk cow, Big was milking her every three hours to keep pressure off the stitches.

"Keeps trying to kick my head off my shoulders," Big said, still grinning. He stroked her shoulder. "She's gonna be okay to milk once she's cured, ain't she, Nancy? Hate to see nothing happen to her from pure dumbness."

"She's too valuable a milker to send to slaughter. Once the cut heals, she should be able to hold milk without rupturing her udder," Nancy replied. "Keeping her from straining the cut in the meantime is the key."

"Gonna teach that Jason boy how to milk her tomorrow afternoon." Big chortled. "He may just decide he likes dog doo better'n he thought."

Nancy glanced at Big. If she could figure out some way to

bottle the gentle essence of the big man, she could probably bring about world peace.

Hard to believe he'd been in prison for nearly killing a man. Of course, the man had been torturing an animal. Big was slower than an arctic glacier to wrath, but once he was riled about protecting either his people or his animals, he could be an awesome force. She didn't think she needed to warn Jason. He liked animals. She'd seen him cuddling the French lop with the ear mites when he thought nobody was looking.

No, Jason wasn't guilty of animal cruelty. JustPup would've recognized him. Animals never forgot the hands that caused them pain. That's why they often regarded the vets as enemies. When the vet showed up, pain followed.

Besides, Jason didn't have a driver's license and hadn't had time to learn where Digger lived.

JustPup hadn't carried his animosity over from the person who hurt him to Nancy. Good thing, since he lived across the street.

If Big ever had a run-in with whatever juvenile delinquents had run over Digger and burned JustPup, he might wind up back in jail for murder.

After injecting the cow with antibiotics and checking her over, Nancy decided to take a break. She'd been running nonstop since eight in the morning, barely taking time to wolf down a packet of peanut butter crackers from the snack machine in the staff room.

Mac demanded that her work with him in surgery was first priority. So far, she'd been able to schedule assisting at the few large animal surgeries to comply. Well, let the big dogs fight it out. She planned to stay on the porch.

That morning Rick had stuck his head in the surgery door. "Hey, guys, need a little help?"

Mac snarled. Rick withdrew without another word.

Mac *had* agreed to handle his nonsurgical patients alone.

Nancy got him organized, then checked the patients in the

small animal cages and withdrew afternoon meds for the large animals. Digger was beginning to get his three-legged balance. He was still unsteady and a bit puzzled, but he'd be fine.

She found Big in the large animal area waiting beside the biggest ram she'd ever seen. Its horns had grown so long they curled around and threatened to penetrate his skull from behind.

"Funniest looking sheep I ever seen," Big said. "Man owns him says his hair don't never get no longer'n that."

Nancy took the chart from Big. "He's a Katahdin. Raised for meat, not wool. I've heard of them, but I've never seen one before." She patted the ram between his huge horns. He butted her hand.

"Dr. Sarah says if we don't get them horns cut out, they'll kill him." Big shook his head. "Shouldn't never have waited this long, them folks. Dr. Sarah says he's probably got him one heck of a headache night and day. Ain't no wonder he's ornery." He shrugged. "Course, rams generally are."

"Are she and Eleanor out?"

"Yep. Dr. Sarah got some semen shipped in this morning. She's getting some mare pregnant. Dr. Eleanor's giving a bunch of horses West Nile vaccinations. Won't be back."

Nancy took a deep breath. "Okay, we've got a short list to handle. If we work fast, maybe we can get out of here early for once."

Big wasn't long on chatter, so they worked silently from animal to animal, giving shots, changing bandages and recording vital signs.

All the while her mind ran in a different direction.

Maybe Tim hadn't noticed she'd darned near sprinted for home last night. Every time she remembered how easy she'd felt in his company, how he made her laugh, she dreaded their next meeting.

The man was pure poison. Everything she planned at all costs to avoid.

Certainly nobody over thirty came without baggage, but three dysfunctional children and a murdered wife were too heavy a load for Nancy to carry. Not to mention the domineering French mother-in-law, who would undoubtedly shout with joy at the thought of her son-in-law's involvement with a physically challenged vet tech who never even graduated from college.

And she would fit in so perfectly at the Maybree faculty teas!

She could see the fashion magazine headlines. "Dog blood is the new black."

She'd been smart to insinuate Helen into the life of the Wainwrights. Now Helen could take Angie to the beauty salon. No need to bring Nancy in. She could hide from Tim in her house and her barn, just as she'd hidden from him when he came to pick up Jason after his shift.

Hide from her own feelings. The needs she'd denied for far too long.

While she was dragging her scrubs off in preparation for leaving the clinic, her cell phone rang. She said a silent prayer that neither Sarah nor Eleanor had run into a snag that required her assistance.

She caught her breath when she heard Tim's voice.

"We need to talk," he said without preamble as soon as she answered. "About Jason's job and Angie's riding lessons."

"Is there a problem?"

"Not really."

She sighed. Nobody ever said "we need to talk" about good stuff. Oh, well. Might as well get it over with. "I should be home about five-thirty if we don't have any emergencies. Come over then. I'll give you a beer or a glass of wine."

"Um, the thing is, I bought a canoe for Jason this afternoon. He can't wait to try it out down at the lake. Could we meet there? I don't want to leave him alone the first time he tries it out."

A canoe was quiet and might keep Jason from riding his skateboard in front of her house. Nancy was happy to do what she could to get him into the water as soon as possible. "Sure. I'll change my clothes and meet you at the dock. Incidentally I'd suggest both of you cover yourselves with bug spray. The mosquitoes down there have been known to drain a body of blood within minutes, not to mention the chiggers and ticks."

Tim chortled. "Thanks."

Actually, Nancy didn't mind walking down to Tim's lake. During the years the Halliburtons lived in Tim's house, Williamston had considered it the community lake. Nancy hoped it would continue to be used that way.

The adults were careful not to let the children go unattended, although after dark no doubt some virginities had been lost down there, especially on the far side where there was an area of picnic tables and benches. The kids were smart enough to know that so long as they didn't leave any evidence of alcohol or pot or worse, they were fairly safe.

Nancy didn't intend to discuss the lake's future with Tim. Let Bill and Helen or the other neighbors approach him. No one had ever worried about the liability of having nonfamily members swimming and kayaking and canoeing down there. Tim might feel he had to restrict usage.

Not that it had been much used in recent years since a lot of the kids grew up and moved away.

Nancy wondered whether it had ever had a name. As long as she'd lived in Williamston, it had been known merely as the lake.

Nancy waved to Eddy, who was throwing a small ball for JustPup in Tim's front yard. She was surprised Tim had left him alone, until she saw that Angie was curled up in the swing on the front porch reading a book. She didn't look up and Nancy didn't speak.

A good thing Eddy had learned to stay out of the street. Angie probably wouldn't have noticed if aliens abducted him. Even in the shadows, she could see a white horse on the cover of the book.

Eddy tossed the ball again. JustPup chased it to Nancy's feet and sank on his tiny brown bottom with his short tail thumping while he waited for her to toss it for him. The little dog was moving almost normally now, although the scabs and scars on his back and ears remained hairless.

Nancy obliged him and tossed the ball. He ran after it like a small clockwork tank, but he didn't bark. Had he learned that silence protected him? Or had the fire somehow damaged his vocal chords?

"You didn't want to go down to the lake with Jason?" Nancy asked Eddy. "I'm sure Jason would take you for a ride in his new canoe."

Eddy drew his arms against his body and lowered his eyes. "Nuh-uh." JustPup looked up at him, then sidled over and shoved against his leg. Obviously the dog had more empathy than Nancy did.

By now she should be used to Eddy's worries when faced with a new experience and his habit of shutting himself down like a clam closing its shell against predators.

"I don't know how to swim," he whispered. "I don't like it down there."

"Oh." She'd suggest to Tim that he enroll Eddy in classes at the Y. Maybe Maybree Academy had a pool. If so, it would probably be indoor, so it could be used all the school year. With the lake so close, Eddy would be safer if he could swim.

And it was her business because…?

Because she was a nosy neighbor? Because she didn't trust Tim to think about it?

Because she was entirely too involved with Tim for her *heart's* own good.

And now she was involved with Jason as well at the clinic. Nuts. She didn't even like children all that well.

She smiled at Eddy and walked into the trees at the back of Tim's property.

The sun above the horizon cut a swath of molten bronze across the still water of the lake, while under the trees the shadows had convinced the frogs and cicadas it was time to tune up for their evening serenade. As she strolled along the path, sweat trickled down the back of her neck and between her shoulder blades. Even her shorts and T-shirt felt as heavy as wool. Next time, she'd insist Tim come to her house to discuss in air-conditioned comfort whatever he wanted. If there was a next time.

From somewhere on the other side of the pond and beyond the trees, a tractor growled. Probably Sheriff Mike cutting hay for his cattle.

Before she left the trees, she saw Tim standing at the end of the old dock. He was staring out across the lake with his hands on his hips. He was shirtless and wore only a pair of khaki shorts and sneakers.

What on earth did he do to keep that body looking so fine when he stood behind a desk all day? She gulped and felt her heart speed up. The heat in her center shot up way out of proportion to the ambient temperature.

The man was sexy, dammit.

His brown hair curled damply at his nape and his body was burnished from the sunset.

She cleared her throat and called to him, but he didn't hear her because of the noise from the tractor. He had his eye on Jason, who paddled his red and gold canoe on the far side of the pond.

Jason was apparently no novice. He slid the canoe through the water smoothly. As she watched he passed the turn on the far side and moved around the bend.

Tim watched him out of sight, then bent over the edge of the dock, probably checking to see that the pilings were still solidly stuck into the mud at the bottom. He'd brought a hammer and what looked like a box of nails.

The man had great legs. She'd always liked men with good legs. Peter had wonderful legs. All that riding gave him muscles on his muscles. Tim's were every bit as good. How did *he* manage?

She'd seen him nearly naked when Lancelot invaded his bedroom, and had wondered even in the midst of her embarrassment how those strong arms would feel wrapped around her. Nothing felt as delightful as a sleek, taut male body. "I am turning into a dirty old woman," she whispered and walked out of the trees.

That's when she saw it.

Lying stretched in the lengthening shadows on the dock, soaking up the last of the board's warmth, lay six feet of gold and brown snake.

Its tail stretched toward her. From her angle she couldn't see its head, couldn't tell whether it was narrow and neckless, or broad and triangular. She certainly couldn't see its eyes, and had no way of knowing whether the pupils were round or straight up and down.

She froze.

Water moccasins generally didn't grow that long—they went for girth. Brown and gold and thick as a man's bicep usually meant moccasin. Seldom over five feet long. However, in the lake with plentiful prey, they might grow humongous.

So might copperheads. Particularly the females.

There were no rattles on the tail. She'd almost have preferred a rattler. At least they generally avoided trouble.

Copperheads and water moccasins, however, didn't back off when threatened. Water moccasins seemed to enjoy confrontation. Once, when a snake threatened her in her old barn, Phil Pritchard told her to poke it with a stick. "If it rears up, hisses and the inside of its mouth is white, it's a moccasin all right."

She ran like the devil in the other direction and never did check out the inside of that snake's mouth. She'd never regretted that decision.

Unfortunately, with the snake between Tim and the bank, that was not an option.

She prayed this was a king snake, but from the markings, she couldn't be sure. It was thin, so the odds were in her favor. A full-grown water moccasin could weigh twenty pounds. This one looked skinny.

It wasn't coiled, but she knew from past experience that snakes could coil and strike like greased lightning. It was well within striking distance of Tim's ankle as it was and, despite lore to the contrary, snakes didn't have to be coiled to strike. They simply couldn't strike as high or as far from a prone position.

She didn't dare alert Tim. If he stepped back, he'd practically stand on the snake's head. At the very least, he'd disturb its nap. Nancy preferred to keep Tim calm and the snake asleep until she could figure out what to do.

She'd handled snakes, of course, even a couple of poisonous ones, but never alone. Once she'd helped Mac remove dead skin from a python's eyes, and they'd stitched a gash on a boa's abdomen and treated it for fungus. Handling snakes was not her favorite pastime, even with Big Little holding the snakes down.

And she'd never do it by choice.

The bow of Jason's canoe reappeared across the lake. He wasn't headed toward them, and seemed to be taking his time.

Still, she had to act fast.

She found a sturdy four-foot pin oak branch devoid of leaves. It felt stiff and strong enough to pick up the snake without bending or snapping.

Then she eased down to the edge of the dock and prayed that the tractor would keep up its covering racket. She'd have preferred a stick with a fork in the end, but she didn't see one. This would have to do.

At the edge of the dock, she leaned down carefully toward the snake's tail. It dozed on.

She picked up its tail gently, and even more gently slid the stick under its belly as close to its head as she could reach while keeping her body out of striking distance.

Tim must have caught her movement out of the corner of his eye. He straightened and turned.

He started to smile at her, then he looked down and saw the snake.

The sound he made was like the sound he made when he saw Lancelot beside him in bed, only louder. He stepped back, caught his heel on the edge of the dock and fell full length into the pond.

She grabbed the snake's tail, yanked it toward her with all her strength, grasped the end of her stick and sailed the snake as hard as she could toward the trees. The horrified snake flew through the air in a series of curves, plopped on the edge of the bank, and slithered unhurt into the trees at breakneck speed.

She reached the end of the dock as Tim surfaced, soaked and sputtering, and leaned over to reach a hand down to him. "You okay?"

"Hell, no!" He grabbed her hand and yanked.

She fell on top of him.

The muddy water closed over her head and filled her nose and mouth. She kicked and pulled herself up Tim's body until she could lock her arms around his neck.

"You…" She spat out the water and shook her wet hair. It whipped across his face.

"Hey, stop that!" He wrapped his arms around her waist.

The only thing between her breasts and his chest was one very thin wet T-shirt.

She tried to struggle away from him, but he held her hard against him. And hard was the appropriate word. She could always say her raised nipples were the result of the cool water. What was his excuse?

"I'm standing on the bottom," he said. "Relax. I've got you."

She blinked and opened her lips to speak just as his lips met hers. Hard, demanding. Hot. His tongue probed her mouth and hers met it with the same fierceness and need to explore. If she tasted like lake and silt, so did he. She wouldn't have thought that could be appealing, but on Tim's hot, educated tongue it was like rare French champagne. She prayed it was a magnum.

The water around them ought to be boiling like lava. Her body sure was. Her hips moved against him as his hands slid down to cup her against his groin. He felt so good, so male. She wrapped her legs around him and dug her nails into his neck. *Don't stop, don't stop, don't stop.*

"Hey, Pops, Nancy, you okay?"

Jason.

She broke the kiss and unwound her arms.

"Hell," Tim whispered, but he let her go.

Jason drove the canoe against the side of the dock in three smooth strokes. He couldn't have missed that kiss.

When she glanced at him, however, there wasn't even the hint of a smirk. He was being very, very cool. She'd have to thank him for that somehow—maybe a big platter of cookies or some other kind of empty calories.

"Hey, Nancy, you okay? What happened? How'd you guys fall in?" Jason held the canoe against the edge of the dock with one hand.

"Is there a snake on the dock?" Tim asked.

Jason yanked his hand away and checked. "Nope. Was there one?" He grabbed the dock again to keep the canoe in close.

Nancy turned around in the water. "Help me out," she said. Amazing how calm her voice sounded when her heart was pounding and her blood pressure was off the top of the charts.

She rested her forearms on the dock and felt Tim's strong hands under her bottom. He nearly catapulted her out of the water onto her knees, but made no attempt to follow her.

"Where'd it go?" Tim asked.

"Into the trees. Long gone. It's safe to come out now."

He gave her a long look. "Safe maybe. Appropriate? Maybe not quite yet." He cut his eyes at Jason.

"Oh."

Jason was staring at her chest. She had no doubt he was in the same state his father was, and in those spandex trunks he'd be less able to conceal the fact. No wonder he made no attempt to get out of the canoe and kept his life jacket in his lap.

She wrapped her arms across her swollen nipples.

"What was it?" Tim asked. "Water moccasin? Copperhead? Rattler?"

"I think," Nancy said, "it was just a big old king snake soaking up some rays."

"Wow," Jason exclaimed. "How big?"

"Big." His father shuddered. "Very big."

"As tall as your father at any rate," Nancy added.

"They get that long?" Jason asked. His eyes were wide.

Tim levitated out of the water and onto the dock in one smooth motion. His shorts clung to him, and his groin was precisely at Nancy's eye level. She gulped and looked away, feeling that same heat in her midsection and below.

"How'd you kill it?" Jason demanded. "Where'd you put it? Can I have the skin?"

"I didn't kill it," Nancy said. "King snakes are *good* snakes."

"Thought you didn't know for sure."

"I didn't take the time to check him out thoroughly."

"What'd you do with it?"

"I threw it into the trees back there. Poor old thing. Scared it half to death."

"Who are you calling a poor old thing? Me or the snake?" Tim asked.

"The snake, of course." Nancy's lips, still hot from Tim's kiss, curled into a smile. "Was the big old man scared of the little bitty ole snake?"

"Cut that out. Snake is snake." Tim shuddered again. "I hate snakes."

"Me, too," Jason said. "Couldn't you just sort of shoo it away? I thought snakes tried to get away from people."

"I was afraid your father was going to step on it."

"But king snakes aren't poisonous," Jason said.

"No, they aren't poisonous, but a king snake that size can deliver a nasty bite that can get badly infected. And if you step on their heads, they tend to lose their tempers, bite first and ask questions later. Do you blame them?"

"So he's back there someplace in the trees waiting for us?" Jason climbed out of the canoe. "I am never going home. You guys can bring my food down here."

"He's probably left the county—hell, the continental United States—after what Nancy did to him," Tim said. He was trying hard to sound flippant, but Nancy could tell he was shaken, whether by the snake or the kiss or the dunking she couldn't tell.

"Come on, son, let's get the canoe tied down. Nancy can guard us up to the house."

"Yeah. Okay."

Nancy moved aside and watched the two working side by side, laying the life jackets on the dock, turning over the canoe, securing it and the paddles to the cleats.

Jason was almost as tall as his dad and might eventually be taller. At the moment every bit of nourishment he took in must be going straight up into his scrawny frame. The testosterone had kicked in and was already providing him with long teenage muscles that would turn him into a handsome young man, once he got past the zits stage. His baritone voice might eventually deepen to bass. Now that his hair was growing out, she could see it was darker than Tim's and curly.

He smelled like a goat. Her brothers used to take at least two showers a day when they were teenagers, but their bedrooms still smelled of adolescent hormones.

He must have gotten those killer eyelashes from his French mother. Once his skin cleared and he learned not to scowl all the time, he'd be a heartbreaker.

His father, on the other hand, was a *man*. He looked like a heavyweight boxer. No extra weight around that middle. Just a flat belly with a line of dark hair that started on his chest and disappeared beneath his wet shorts. Be nice to follow it down, curl her fingers in it.

She felt her nipples doing their thing again, while her groin followed suit.

"Come on," she said when she saw they had finished fastening the canoe. "Aunty Nancy will protect the big old men from the mean snake."

Jason snickered. His father snarled. "After you, *Aunty* Nancy. That thing's out there somewhere and it's not mad at *me*."

CHAPTER SEVENTEEN

AS THEY WALKED UP the path, Nancy asked Tim, "What did you want to talk to me about?"

"Have you had a chance to find a stable where Angie can take some beginner lessons?"

She stopped. "I'm so sorry, Tim. I've just been swamped at the clinic. I haven't had a chance."

He ducked his head. "No, I'm sorry. That was stupid. I know you're doing double-duty. But if you can give me some ideas, I can make the calls myself. I looked in the telephone book, but I have no way of knowing which stables would be better or even where they're located."

She sighed. "And I did promise. Okay. I'll make you a list tonight and leave it inside your storm door tomorrow morning. I'll ask Mac to talk to his daughter, Emma, to see if she has any ideas."

"Thanks."

Jason loped ahead. He kept a wary eye on his feet in case the snake should be waiting for him.

"Now, what's Jason's problem?"

"He's agreed to play defense with the Maybree lacrosse team. They start practice three afternoons a week starting next week. Jason won't be able to work more than two days week, and only from three to five, if you think it's worth having him."

"I do if he does. I'll tell Rick. Actually, after the fuss he made about scrubbing cages, I'm surprised he's not quitting entirely."

"Fuss?" He stopped and took her arm. "He behaved badly?"

She disengaged her arm gently. "Just teenage bitching." She walked on. "Big straightened him out. Says he's fine with the animals. Just a little lazy."

"Bitchy and lazy. The perfect employee." Tim sounded disgusted.

"Hey, lighten up. He is coming back tomorrow afternoon, isn't he?"

"I'll swing by here, pick him up and drop him off at the clinic after my morning meeting."

"Unless I run into an emergency, he can ride home with me at five."

"I don't like to impose."

"Puh-leeze. I live across the street."

"Wait." They'd reached the line of old oak trees that surrounded Tim's backyard. The westering sun left the yard in deep shadow, and under the trees it was twilight. "I enjoyed last night." He grinned. "I *really* enjoyed this afternoon."

She could feel the blush suffuse her entire body. Even in the shadows she'd be willing to bet Tim could see her change color. He could certainly see her nipples under her wet T-shirt. "Me, too."

"Then why run away?"

"I didn't. I was tired."

"Bull. You ran. You're running now."

"I'm standing in one place."

"Your body is in one place, but inside you're halfway to your front porch."

"How do *you* know?" He was starting to annoy her.

He took her face between his palms and kissed her gently.

Whoo, boy.

A moment later he dropped his hands to her waist and pulled her close. His hands slid down to cup her near his hips.

Without conscious thought she moved against him, pressing her hips to his erection. She slid her arms beneath his and around his waist to hold him tight.

All the while they kissed. Tongue answered tongue.

She wanted to open to him right there against an oak tree with one leg locked around his waist to hold him inside.

"Daddy," Eddy wailed, "Jason's got my ball and he won't give it back!"

Nancy and Tim sprang apart like guilty teenagers.

"Jason." Tim yelled without taking his eyes or his hands off Nancy. "Stop being a jerk and give your brother back his ball."

"Hey, it's *my* ball. Eddy, you little creep, you stole it out of my room."

Tim roared, "Give it back anyway!"

"Yeah, all right. Little creep."

"And don't call your brother names." Tim let Nancy go and lifted his hands in a gesture of defeat as Eddy and JustPup ran toward them. Jason was already disappearing around the corner of the house.

"Can I come over later?" Tim whispered.

Nancy slipped past him. "I've got to clean the barn. Not a good idea."

JustPup dropped his ball at her feet. She picked it up and tossed it for him. She could hear Tim behind her, but she kept walking across the street and into her house.

EITHER JASON HADN'T HEARD her remark to Eleanor at lunch about his family, or he chose to ignore it. At least in public. He'd probably tell his siblings and maybe his father. Now how would that play with the patriarch of the Wainwright clan?

Nancy didn't really need to do chores in her barn. Phil and Phineas were looking after Henry and Herb, feeding, watering, turning them out, grooming them and cleaning their stalls. The two Percherons might be at her place for another six months the way the weather refused to cool down. Nobody could work for long in the heat.

After the hours spent cutting and dragging trees in her woodland, the brothers brought the horses in to cool off and, without being asked, began replacing rotten boards in the barn walls.

She'd asked them to bill her, but they just grinned and shook their heads. Phil, the talkative one, said they were using leftover boards from their last job that might otherwise go to waste.

She didn't ask again.

A stable had been her refuge as long as she could remember. No matter how bad the situation was at home when she was a child, no matter how her parents screamed at one another, she could find quiet and harmony at the boarding stable a mile down the road from her house. Happiness had always been a warm horse.

She began riding her bike to the stable after school as soon as her mother allowed her to ride alone. She mucked stalls, cleaned tack and would have driven the tractor if the owner had let her, all to pay for her first lessons on a school horse that wouldn't break into a trot if he was hit with a rocket. She didn't care. He was a live horse.

Not that her mother would have noticed if she disappeared totally. Not unless she didn't show up for at least a couple of days. Mom was too taken up in her charities and her luncheon parties and her shopping. When she was up.

When she was down, she wouldn't notice because she was probably in bed.

Nancy often wondered how different her life would have been if doctors had diagnosed her mother as bi-polar and ADD when she and her siblings were young. The last five years of her life, with appropriate medication, her mother had become a different woman. Better living through chemistry, all right.

She and her mother had actually come to an understanding. For so many years, she'd wanted her mother to pay for the emotional hell she'd put them all through. Only in the last few months of her life had her mother come to terms with the damage she'd done, and by that time Nancy understood and no longer needed closure.

Nancy hadn't bothered to explain to Eleanor that it took one weird kid to recognize weirdness in other kids. She'd have been a whole bunch weirder if she hadn't discovered horses and taken refuge in hay bales and the saddle. She hoped horses would be Angie's salvation as well.

As for her own siblings, her older sister Charlotte had been in therapy for years, but was still a neat freak who scrubbed her kitchen floor with disinfectant at least once a day and refused to allow her children to have so much as a gerbil because animals were messy. Having Nancy around drove her nuts.

Her eldest brother James, never Jim, lived in a mansion, drove a Mercedes 450 SL and sported a trophy wife younger than Nancy. The new wife had agreed not to have children, so that she'd be available to travel and entertain at a moment's notice. James had largely abandoned his first family except for the monthly alimony and child support. Like father, like son.

She remembered James's rages when they were growing up and wondered when he had grown so cold. How did his wife warm her feet at night when her husband was sculpted of ice?

Her other brother, Mickey—never Michael—only a couple of years older than Nancy, was probably the happiest of all of them. He rebuilt antique motorcycles, made an adequate living, wore his hair in a slightly graying ponytail, owned three Labrador retrievers and refused to take on any work during duck hunting season so he could stay in his duck blind up to his armpits in ice water. His wife was overweight, dowdy and gentle and raised their two children in an atmosphere of peace and tranquility. They seemed to love one another.

Peace and tranquility. Nancy had ached for that when she was growing up.

Her alcoholic father walked out on them on Christmas morning when she was eight. She hadn't really blamed him. She *had* blamed him for knocking over the Christmas tree and breaking half the lights the night before in a drunken stupor, but that was just Daddy. He was always falling over things when he was sloshed.

He stopped drinking the day he left. The last time she'd had dinner with him after a horse show, he'd said, "The day I left your mother, I didn't need vodka to sleep." He never apologized for leaving the four of them to cope with her mood swings.

No wonder Nancy had escaped into marriage at eighteen. To a man fourteen years her senior, the man whose horses she'd ridden. Peter Lombardi. Her boss, her trainer, her mentor and finally, her betrayer. The father figure she'd never had.

A really bad substitute.

Then she was divorced at twenty-three with a mangled neck, a high school diploma and no skills other than riding horses over fences—which was denied her for the rest of her life.

Mac Thorn had helped her repair her life. Finally she had a job she loved and was good at, friends who cared about her, a house she was slowly turning into her dream house, land of her own where she could see horses and touch them even if she couldn't ride them, and blessed, blessed peace and tranquility.

She refused to allow her raging hormones to drag her back into the wild swings and emotional roller coaster of a relationship. And a relationship with a man, however attractive, with three children? *Get real.*

CHAPTER EIGHTEEN

NANCY MADE A LIST of three horse trainers who were clients of Creature Comfort and left it inside Tim's storm door. She decided not to get Haley O'Hara's recommendations until she heard what luck Tim had with these trainers.

She didn't see or hear from him, however. No doubt he was busy organizing the school year. She was busy at work doing two jobs and often came home late, so their paths didn't cross.

"That boy Jason's shaping up right well," Big told her on Thursday. "Shame he ain't gonna be with us more'n a couple of hours a week from here on in."

"He's probably made enough money to at least give his father a token payment toward fixing my car," Nancy said. "Once school starts and he's involved in after-school activities, he's likely to quit altogether."

"Be a right shame. The boy likes working with the cows and sheep." He snickered. "You know that big ole ram? The one with no hair?"

"The Katahdin ram."

"There you go. Jason watched us poll that ole ram. Blood didn't bother him one bit. After we was done, he asked could he have the horns to hang on his wall." Big rumbled with laughter. "Told him he'd have to boil 'em up pretty good or they'd stink up the whole house."

"I'll bet he wanted them for school," Nancy said. "The team is called the Maybree Rams."

"Oh. Well, that makes sense then."

She'd ask Tim the next time she saw him.

If she saw him. She saw the lights on in his kitchen and living room, and then in his bedroom. They were usually still on when she went to bed.

She still saw Eddy regularly. He came over to her cottage so she could check JustPup's burns. The dead skin had sloughed off, and the burns were healing over. In places the new skin was already covered with soft fur—white, not brown as it had been originally.

"We ought to call him Ole Paint," Nancy said one evening as she watched him run circles around Lancelot in the front yard.

"Nope," Eddy said. "JustPup's his name forever and ever."

Both boy and dog loved roughhousing with Lancelot, although the cats were still wary of the puppy. Now that he was being fed regularly, JustPup was growing fast. He was about the size of a half-grown miniature dachshund and could race off with Lancelot's small ball held precariously in his jaws. The three had developed a kind of interspecies soccer that kept them all occupied for long periods at a time.

Lancelot always slept better after a session with Eddy and JustPup.

She glimpsed Jason occasionally, scrubbing floors or mucking stalls at the clinic, but they didn't speak.

She even saw Angie on her front porch one evening when Sheriff Mike's daughter, Haley, and her friend Meghan rode down to the common on their hunters.

Wonder of wonders, Angie had brown hair in a short and very becoming layered cut and wore a red polo shirt and khaki shorts. Even from this distance Nancy could see that her skin was a normal pink.

She also seemed to have shot up two inches in a month, although that was impossible. Some of the baby fat seemed to be coming off, and she was developing both a waistline and a tidy little bosom. Helen had done a marvelous job transforming her from Undead to fairly normal teen almost overnight.

If she quit sulking, she'd be very pretty. Who would have thought?

But then Tim was handsome, and Solange was probably a real beauty. The kid had pretty genes.

The two girls on their horses waved to Nancy as they passed. "Hey, Miss Nancy," Haley called. "Almost hunt time. Mrs. Green says she and Mr. Green are going to try to start coming down next week."

"Hey, Meghan, Haley."

From across the street she could tell that Angie longed to speak, to go up to them, touch their horses, but she hung back.

"You girls know when paint day is?" Nancy asked. "The jumps on the green are looking pretty ratty."

"Daddy said maybe the last Saturday in September," Haley said. "He's getting folks together. He says the town can buy the paint. You going to coach us some this year?"

"You want me to?"

"Yes'm. Please."

"Shoot, I don't want to fall off on opening hunt," Meghan said, laughing. "Strutt hasn't been over a fence in six months." She patted her little bay gelding's neck. "He's a tub of lard." She looked down at herself. "Me, too."

"Tell your daddy to call me. I'll help clean and paint, and I'm sure the new people will, too."

"Yes, ma'am."

"Angie?" she called. "Come meet a couple of your neighbors."

Angie came off the porch and walked toward them. Nancy could see that her natural shyness warred with her desperate desire to meet girls her own age that actually sat atop horses.

"Hey," Meghan said. "Your daddy's teaching at Maybree, isn't he?"

"Uh-huh."

Nancy backed off, waved, and left them to it. She was delighted to see that when the girls walked their horses off toward the green, Angie walked with them.

Mike O'Hara had never ridden a horse over a fence in his life, but his daughter Haley had been riding hunters since she was old enough to sit her Shetland pony, so every year Mike organized the neighborhood with paint, brushes, weed trimmers and leaf blowers to tidy up the common. After that there would be horses and riders on the green every evening and most weekends until opening hunt the second week in November, and sporadically after that.

The first year she lived in Williamston, Nancy drove an extra two miles so she could reach her house from the west without seeing the riders. The second year, she'd driven home as usual, but didn't look at them.

The third year, Bill Halliburton called her a dimwit. "You might as well stroll on down there, hang over the fence and maybe give those old farts some pointers so they don't break their fool necks on opening hunt."

When she protested, he said, "You might just have a little fun yourself, sugar. You can't ride 'em any longer, but you sure can teach them that can."

She'd figured the hunters would speak politely to her, simply because she was a neighbor, then just as politely ignore her.

She was surprised to discover that they were looking for someone to train them and their horses after a long spring and hot summer. Now, once the jumps were cleaned up and the common all spiffy for fall, she'd probably be down there most evenings. Bill had been right. It wasn't riding, but it was better than nothing.

Last year Milton and Charlotte Green from a mile down the road, Peachtree and Starnes Wilson and Jerry Tamblin, who boarded their horses with the Greens, offered to pay her to teach them. "You're worth it," Charlotte said. "Without you to shape him up, Milton would probably have broken his neck by now."

"Thanks, but no thanks," Nancy had said. "If you pay me, we have to schedule sessions. I have to be there and so do you. I'd rather do it this way."

"Whatever you say."

They'd given her a new dishwasher for Christmas.

She'd missed meeting and training them after hunt season was over, and they turned their horses out for the hot weather.

She was actually looking forward to the first cool evening. Meghan and Haley were the advance contingent. Probably trying to get in as many trail rides as they could before school started and the days got shorter.

Somebody ought to warn Angie. In a couple of weeks, riders would be exercising their horses nights and weekends on the common. Angie would be able to watch them from Tim's end of their front porch.

Nancy hoped Haley and Meghan would tell Angie what to expect. Watching without riding would be torture for the girl, as it had been for Nancy. Tim had to get that child up on a horse.

She considered calling to ask if he'd called those trainers yet, but decided she should leave him alone until school started.

And alone was how she felt. Henry and Herb were pleasant companions, but they didn't talk a bit more than Phineas did.

Lancelot loved to come with her to the barn, but he was more a hindrance than a help. The first time she took him along, he completely dismembered a bale of hay, spread it around and burrowed into it so that only his nose showed.

The next time, he knocked over a full bucket of water in the aisle.

When she went after him with the push broom, she'd slipped and fell flat on her rump.

He butted her to be sure she wasn't dead, then shoved her out of the way and settled down in the muddy patch with an oink of contentment.

She spent twenty minutes hosing him off outside on the grass.

Although she took her cordless phone with her and tested it

every night, Tim didn't call. Wasn't that what she said she wanted? No further involvement with Tim and his brood?

For the first time in nine years, her house seemed *too* peaceful and a darned sight too quiet.

She even missed the whir and clatter of Jason's skateboard on the road.

Big told her he was being picked up after his two hours by a bunch of boys in a green Land Rover. He never rode his skateboard now.

She saw the Land Rover, all right. How could she avoid looking out her front window when it screeched to a halt across the street with its woofers thudding at such volume that her house shook?

She dug her manure fork into a pile of moldy hay with a vengeance. Tim had kissed her, groped her and she'd groped right back. Had he decided getting involved with a neighbor was a bad idea?

Well, good for him. They were in agreement. Very sensible.

Darn him, too.

CHAPTER NINETEEN

HER PHONE RANG very early in the morning. "Mayfield," she said, instantly awake. She didn't bother to look at the clock. Didn't matter what time it was.

"Nancy? Sorry. We've got a bad colic. I'm operating as soon as you get here." Sarah Chadwick.

"Thirty minutes."

"Make it twenty. I'll start the prep."

Neither woman bothered to say goodbye. Nancy didn't even brush her teeth. Lancelot grumbled to be let out. She shoved him, basket and all, into her laundry room and dropped the pet gate in place. If he messed, at least he'd do it in one spot.

The dashboard clock read 2:52. As she pulled out of her driveway, she saw that the light was on in Tim's bedroom. She thought she saw the curtains at his window move.

What was he doing up at this hour? And watching her?

The colic surgery took four hours. No way to tell, once the horse was propped up against bales of hay to come out of anesthesia, whether they'd been successful, whether the horse would live or die.

"Go on home, Nancy," Sarah said as she stripped off her scrubs. "Thanks. You did well."

Nancy yawned. It was seven-thirty. She was due back at eight-thirty. Half hour home, half hour back…no time to take a shower and let Lancelot out.

Nuts. She called Helen at home. Bill answered. "Nancy?"

"How'd you know it was me?"

"Caller ID. You'd be the only one calling from the clinic. Is it Lancelot?"

She heard Helen's panicky voice in the background.

"Whoa! Nothing's wrong. I've been here all night and I don't have time to go home to let Lancelot out. Can you and Helen take care of him for me?"

"He's ours, isn't he? Can we bring you anything?"

"I keep a change of clothes and makeup and stuff in my locker here for nights like this. Don't worry about it."

Nancy heard Helen's voice in the background, and a moment later, she came on the line. "You'd think with me working across the street, we'd see each other the way we used to. I miss you."

"I miss you, too, but since Jack's heart attack, I seem to get home late nearly every night."

"I seldom see Tim, either. He leaves for faculty meetings before I get to the house, then the minute he comes home, he shuts himself in his study to work on his computer." Helen took a deep breath, then blurted, "Nancy, I am worried to death about Eddy."

Nancy went cold. "I—I thought he was doing so well since he got JustPup."

"I don't know what to do. Tim's got so much on his plate what with school opening Monday. Besides, you can't tell a child he can't speak to his grandmother."

"What's his grandmother got to do with it?"

"Some days Eddy's just an average boy. He's a truly sweet child. But let that French woman talk to him for five minutes, and he shuts himself in his closet with JustPup and won't come out for hours. He just sits and stares at his mother's picture and sobs. Nancy, it breaks my heart. He misses her so much… I've a good mind to listen in on the extension. Lord knows what she says to upset him. I wish she'd shut up."

"Helen, you have to tell Tim."

"I keep hoping once school starts, Eddy will be too busy with second grade to let that woman get to him."

"Busy or not, Tim needs to deal with her."

"I know." Helen still didn't sound convinced.

"How are the other two?"

"They're starting to shape up, although…" Another heavy sigh.

"Has Tim found a place for Angie to take riding lessons?"

Big sigh. "That's another thing. He keeps putting off taking her to look at stables. He swears he'll do it next week, but what with the first week of school, he'll have even less time than he does now."

"Jason seems to be doing all right, though."

"Well, I suppose you could call it that. He has fallen in love with lacrosse. He has this basket on a stick thing. The minute he finishes eating everything in the house that doesn't fight back, he goes outside to the garage and hits that ball against the wall. Thud, thud, thud until I think I'm going to lose my mind."

She laughed. "I'm too old for this. If I didn't have Bill helping me, I don't think I could take it."

Please don't quit. Tim needs you.

"He's paying us well, and Lord knows we can use the money."

"Any news on the real estate front?"

"Not so far."

Nancy heard Bill rumble in the background.

"Bill says to get off the phone so we can get breakfast and go play with Lancelot. Honestly, that man."

After Nancy hung up, she went to her locker to find clean clothes, makeup and shower stuff. She made one last call to Alva Jean.

"Could you pick up breakfast on the way in? I was here most of the night."

"Sure. Doughnuts okay?"

"Oh, why not."

She stood in the shower they kept for the staff and let the hot water sluice down her body. Tim had brought his family to Williamston to spend time with them. Old habits were hard to break.

He was obviously falling into the same pattern—long hours working with other people's children.

She might not be able to do anything about Eddy's withdrawal or Jason's lacrosse. She could, however, see that Angie got her riding lessons even if she had to pay for them herself.

CHAPTER TWENTY

MAC TOOK ONE LOOK at her and snarled, "How long do you think you can keep this up?"

Nancy pulled herself up from the sofa. "Come on, Mac. Last night was the first time I've been called out after midnight. Don't forget, you dragged me out Sunday after the polo matches."

Mac poured himself a double cup of coffee. "If Rick doesn't bring in a substitute tech by Monday, he can start coming in himself after hours. You look like hell."

"Thank you so much. I needed that." She handed him her cup. "More caffeine please. Preferably intravenous. You think Margot would let Rick disrupt her social calendar?"

"That woman runs the society circuit like a marathon. Sometimes I think even he forgets he's one hell of a good vet." Mac handed Nancy their schedule of appointments.

Thank God. An easy day. Barring emergencies.

"Come on. We've got a full waiting room out there. That blasted python's here again."

"That python was over ten feet long the last time we saw it. Don't they keep growing until they die?" Even with Big and its owner holding it down, they'd had trouble treating its fungus before. Now it should really be fun.

Three hours later, nursing an aching shoulder the python had bruised while he was preparing to eat her, she collapsed in the staff room and reached for the telephone book. If Tim wouldn't take the time to find a place for Angie to take riding lessons, she would.

Forty-five minutes later she was ready to give up. She'd started with the three trainers she'd recommended to Tim. No dice.

She hadn't ridden in so long that she didn't know the players anymore, but the business had definitely gone upscale, at least in this area.

A half dozen times, she heard a variation of, "We do not train beginners. We do not keep school horses. We are not an up-down barn."

As though up-down was a dirty phrase.

Where did kids like Angie start? Did they go out and buy or lease a horse before they even knew whether they liked to ride? Did they buy their own tack—quite an expense in itself—and britches and boots and hardhats and gloves and halters and lead lines and brushes and the host of other necessities, when in six months they might prefer to go out for gymnastics or cheerleading?

Crazy. Even used, tack and clothes cost a bunch. If she'd had to learn on a horse she owned, Nancy would never have had a career at all.

She'd never actually been owner-of-record on the horses she rode. She began by taking lessons on school horses, progressed to catch riding for other people, then Peter spotted her and made her his professional rider.

Even Panache, the Grande Prix jumper that had ruined her neck, had not actually belonged to her, but to a wealthy client who couldn't ride, but liked to win. Apparently that was no longer possible, at least in this area.

At last she found one place. The people sounded nice, they did teach beginners. It was thirty miles south of the Mississippi line in Marshall County. Way too far.

If Angie was ever going to learn to ride, she'd have to beg, borrow or steal a horse.

With the horse came monthly board bills, even at the barns that allowed clients to look after their own horses. At a self-run barn, the horse would have to be fed, watered, stall cleaned, turned out and brought back inside every day whether Angie took a riding lesson or not.

And farrier bills. Horses needed to be trimmed and reshod every six weeks. Nancy could trim hooves, but she couldn't put shoes on.

And vet bills. Nancy could handle most of those for the cost of the inoculations, but anything requiring veterinary assistance, even with the employee discount she could probably slip by Rick, would cost.

Even if the horse was relatively close to home, the logistics would be impossible.

Helen would have to pick the kids up at school, drop Jason at Creature Comfort, drop Angie at the stable, run errands with Eddy, return to Creature Comfort for Jason, drive back to the stable for Angie, then take them home and start dinner. If Jason was practicing lacrosse at school until six or seven, Helen would have a completely different schedule.

How did people manage to have children and stay sane?

No wonder Tim hesitated to put Angie into riding classes.

Nuts. She wasn't Nancy's problem.

Well, of course she was. Nancy understood Angie's almost physical need to feel a horse under her.

There had to be a solution. Herb and Henry wouldn't work as school horses. Not only did they both disapprove of any gait faster than a walk, they were both so tall that if Angie fell she could be hurt.

Nope. Angie needed access to a fifteen-hand schoolmaster that knew everything and forgave a beginning rider every transgression. She also needed a teacher. And a bunch of tack. And boots. And a hard hat. And gloves.

If Nancy could present Tim with a total package that he could afford and fit into Helen's frenetic schedule, he couldn't say no, could he?

Nancy vowed to put that child on a horse if she had to steal one.

CHAPTER TWENTY-ONE

HALF A DOZEN TIMES a night Tim picked up his phone to call Nancy and put it down without dialing. He knew she frequently came in late and was probably as tired as he was. After their last meeting, she needed to make the first move. He wouldn't crowd her.

If she wanted to see him, she could call as easily as he could call her.

Nancy was definitely a problem. He couldn't stop thinking about her. They clicked. They laughed together. Their bodies fit like a key into a lock.

Men were supposed to be commitment-phobic.

He wasn't asking for a commitment. Just a relationship that would give each of them pleasure and companionship.

Damn straight he wanted to sleep with her.

But that wasn't all he wanted to do.

Maybe Nancy might enjoy a moonlight paddle around the lake and a glass of cold champagne some evening. With plenty of bug spray, of course.

He'd even be willing to brave the snakes.

He didn't know when he'd fit a moonlight canoe ride into his schedule at the moment, even if Nancy did call.

He might not have the title or salary of assistant principal, but Dr. Aycock was already treating him as though he had the job. He wondered what Dr. Aycock actually did all day in that fancy office.

Tim not only had his own lesson plans to write, his lectures to rewrite and beef up, his goals for his classes to work out. He also had budgets and student records and every other kind of record that the private school system of Tennessee required.

He couldn't complain without sounding whiny. He was becoming trapped in the same old rat race, but without the perks or the money.

He didn't seem to have any more time to devote to his children.

Jason didn't mind. David Grantham had integrated him seamlessly into the lacrosse team. School didn't start until Monday, but Jason already had what he called buds. With the time he spent at Creature Comfort and then at the lake and cruising, he was seldom home until after dark.

Fine with Tim. He knew Grantham wouldn't let his boys get into trouble.

Angie *looked* wholesome enough now since Helen had taken her to Nancy's beauty salon and to buy a few new outfits, but inside, who really knew?

Eddy? Eddy went from a normal, raucous, feisty kid to mopey, lonely and grief-stricken in a heartbeat.

Madame's damnable telephone calls didn't help. Helen spoke of her with her lips pressed into a thin, angry line and her eyes narrowed.

He couldn't very well forbid Eddy to talk to his grandmother.

The last time she'd called, he'd got to the phone before Eddy. "Madame? *S'il vous plait*, don't make Eddy miserable with your calls."

She'd been furious. "Never would I do such a thing. Is it so terrible to tell my *pauvre* grandchild that I miss him with great despair as I miss his beloved mother? As he misses her? That he grieves as I grieve?"

"Madame, please be more careful not to upset him."

"I upset him? Is it not you that have upset the entire apple basket?"

"Applecart."

"Poh. Basket, cart. Do you wish to keep me even from speaking to my own dear grandchildren? It is I who have cared for them."

Tim was dying to tell her to knock it the hell off, but he knew he'd only make things worse.

Jason was never there to speak to her, and Angie lit out for her room whenever she discovered who was on the other end of the line.

But Eddy hungered for her calls, even if his grief after he hung up was palpable.

Tim didn't know what to do.

And he hadn't even made the first call to the training barns on Nancy's list.

CHAPTER TWENTY-TWO

"I DON'T CARE whether it's a one-room schoolhouse in Appalachia or the finest prep school in Philadelphia, the first week of school is chaos," Mrs. Martini said. She sank onto one of the shabby couches in the faculty lounge and blew a strand of gray hair out of her eyes. "Plus the air-conditioning can't handle all these hot teenage bodies pressed together."

Tim handed her a bottle of water from the refrigerator and perched on the edge of the library table in the center of the room.

"This is bliss compared to my old school," Tim said. "No air-conditioning, and thirty-five to forty students in every class. The largest class I have here is fifteen."

"Fifteen hormonally challenged, blasé, uninterested rich kids."

"But no gang colors, do-rags or backward baseball caps. No oversize high-tops without socks. No dangly earrings on either the boys or the girls. No underwear hanging over droopy shorts."

"Dangly earrings on the boys?" Mrs. Martini asked. "I am way out of the loop."

"No purple or green Mohawks, shaved heads—on the boys and girls...."

"You're making this up, Tim, just to josh the little old lady from the boonies."

Tim raised a hand. "Swear to God. I didn't even notice the barbed wire tattoos around their biceps and necks after a couple of years."

Mrs. Martini drained her water, lobbed the bottle into the

trash can and heaved herself to her feet. "Before you get too cosy, Mr. Big City, our problems may be different, but they're just as dangerous, and these kids are every bit as much at risk. It's just that our drug of choice is alcohol."

She picked her briefcase off the table and headed for the door. "Our parents miss conferences because they're too busy with their careers and their charities. Thank heavens for good role models like David Grantham." She pinched Tim's cheek. "Sweetie, this ain't hog heaven and don't you forget it. Don't be fooled by the scenery and the costumes." She waved to him as she shut the door.

Tim watched her go. She shook herself like a cat preparing to pounce on a rat. Or a warrior preparing for battle.

"At Maybree," Dr. Aycock said at his morning staff meeting. "We pride ourselves in not being an enclave of the wealthy and privileged."

He was on a roll. "We provide full scholarships and complete support to gifted students from all races, colors and creeds, and from all economic backgrounds. We give as many scholarships as we can afford, and would give many more if we had the money."

After he dismissed them with a wave that resembled a benediction, they trailed out into the hall. Greg Benjamin, the social studies teacher, snickered, "Bet he's speaking to a bunch of possible corporate sponsors at lunch. We just got his speech rehearsal."

Tim went to the staff lounge, opened his locker, took out his briefcase and his notes.

"Maybree's only in business to get kids into top colleges and into med school and law school and corporate management, so they can donate megabucks back to the school." Greg opened his own locker. Half a dozen books and a snowstorm of paper cascaded onto the floor. "Damn." He bent over to pick them up. "Wish they gave teachers more of that money."

"It's a damn sight easier to force-feed information into their bored little domes if you aren't wondering whether the two rival gang chieftains sitting next to one another in the back row have managed to smuggle Tech 9s into your classroom. That's why I brought my kids down here."

Greg slammed his locker and leaned against it. "No middle-class guilt because you gave up the battle for the hearts and minds of the kids you left?"

"I don't think I saved a single kid."

"Not exactly the Mr. Chips of Chicago, huh."

He hadn't saved the two kids who had blown his wife away and presently sat in an adult prison for twenty-five years to life without the possibility of parole. "Don't bright kids deserve a chance to excel? I got sick of pandering to the lowest common denominator."

"Ooh. Not politically correct."

Tim shrugged and left him leaning against his locker with his arms full of books and papers, which threatened to land back on the floor at any moment.

As Tim walked to his tenth grade class, he decided that if Dr. Aycock thought his little Eden had no serpents, it was better for everyone concerned if he stayed in his office and let the rest of the faculty deal with reality.

CHAPTER TWENTY-THREE

TIM DIVED FOR THE TELEPHONE. The kids were all upstairs after eating a superb pot roast Helen had left for them.

Tonight they'd dashed upstairs and left the mess in the kitchen for him to clean up. He knew they didn't have homework on the first day of school, but he let them get away with it. They were probably as tired as he was. "Hello," he said as he cradled the phone between his shoulder and his ear to avoid covering it with soapsuds.

"I've found Angie a horse."

"Nancy? You've what?"

"You were doing damn all solving her problem, so I took it out of your hands."

"Wait a minute. You can't…I can't…"

"It's the perfect solution. If you don't agree, then you explain it to Angie."

"But…"

"I'm going out to my barn. Come over."

He put the phone down as though it was filled with nitroglycerin. Had the woman lost her mind? He called upstairs, "I'm going across the street. If you need me, call me on my cell." No response. "Jason!"

"Yeah, yeah."

He followed the light spilling out of the barn door. On the other side of the fence, the two mammoth shapes of Henry and Herb materialized, probably looking for treats. "No carrots tonight, guys. Sorry."

He didn't see her at once. Then she stuck her head out of the end stall. She had hay in her hair and wore a pair of cutoffs and a very skimpy T-shirt. He couldn't swear to it, but he thought she wasn't wearing anything under the shirt.

Even that made his body tighten.

"What's this all about?"

She came toward him.

Definitely nothing under the shirt.

"You bought Jason a canoe and lacrosse stuff. Eddy has JustPup. Angie is still spinning her wheels. Or you are. Same thing."

"I've been so damn busy."

He nearly lost his train of thought watching her hips move in those shorts as she walked back to the far stall. He wanted to reach out to her, pull her back against his body, drown in the scent of her, the feel of her skin.

He shook himself back to reality. If he was dealing with a nutcase, he'd better keep his wits about him.

"Here." The stall was packed with bales of hay. She grabbed a horse blanket off a hook and tossed it over a stack. "Sit. There's nowhere else."

He sat. She stood.

"Okay. I know it's none of my business and she's your daughter and blah, blah, blah."

He nodded.

"I also know you've been busy, so I made some calls to find a place to give her riding lessons."

"And?"

She shook her head. "The only barn I could find that has school horses is way down in north Mississippi, much too far for Helen to drive after school."

"Damn. She'll have to wait until next summer."

"So I found her a horse."

"Nancy, I know you mean well, but…"

"Will you just up and listen? Late this afternoon Charlie

Crandall, the man who owns the polo team, came in to have one of his ponies ultrasounded, and we got to talking about where kids can start today if they don't have their own horses. I told him about Angie—remember, I pointed her out to him at the polo match?"

"Told him she was going to be a polo star for him in a few years. I remember."

"He said it was a pity she didn't have a barn or fencing on your place because he had the perfect horse."

"A polo pony? Is he crazy? Are you?"

"Not a polo pony. His mother's old hunter. His mother's eighty-five. After last season, her doctor said she couldn't hunt any longer. Her horse, Cloud, is a real packer. She's half quarter-horse, half Arabian. She's fourteen years old, but Crandall says she's never been lame a day in her life. She's big enough so that Angie wouldn't outgrow her in a year, but not so big she couldn't handle her."

"Nancy, I can't afford to buy a horse right now."

Nancy threw up her hands. "You don't have to buy her. Crandall is willing to lease her to you. You only have to pay her expenses."

He put his hands on his knees and stood. "I'm sorry you've been to all this trouble. I can't even afford to pay board for a horse, much less the cost of lessons and all the other expenses I don't even know about."

She shoved him back into the hay, leaning over him with her hands on her hips. "You can afford an extra hundred bucks a month, can't you? Give up pizza. Heck, feed Jason only three meals a day, you'll save three times that much."

"Nobody is going to board a horse for a hundred bucks a month."

"That's not board. That's feed and hay and shavings for her stall and having her feet trimmed. Crandall says she doesn't need shoes. You'll have to budget another hundred a month for shots and vet care, but you probably won't need half that."

"Where can I get that kind of deal?"

Nancy lifted her arms. "Here."

"I beg your pardon?"

"Crandall will bring her here. She'll have Herb and Henry for company until at least Thanksgiving. Heck, after that Lancelot can keep her company. No, that won't work. Horses don't generally like pigs. We'll get her a goat."

"Nancy, that's kind, but…"

"If you keep running your mouth, I swear I'm going to slug you. Angie will have to feed her before she goes to school in the morning and turn her out. She'll have to get up a lot earlier. She'll have to groom her before and after she rides her, muck her stall every day, feed and hay her in the evenings and clean her tack after she rides. She's going to have to agree to a lot of extra work."

"What tack? The tack I am going to take out a loan to pay for?"

Nancy grabbed his hand. "Come with me."

She pulled him out of the barn, up her back steps and into her bedroom. He realized where they were and reached for her, but she ducked him. "That's not why we're here."

She opened the door Tim had believed led to the second bedroom, the one in the front.

When she turned on the light, however, he realized the whole bedroom had been turned into a closet.

"When I have guests, they sleep on the sofa," Nancy said. "They don't stay long. Come."

He followed her to the far end of the closet where she moved aside a hanging bag. "That tack."

Two saddles perched side by side on identical steel saddle racks. The oiled and polished leather gleamed like bronze. Above them hung three bridles, and a pair of leather halters with lead lines carefully coiled around them. It all looked as though it had been polished only hours before.

Nancy pointed above her head. Three black hard hats with chinstraps were ranged on the top shelf—one was covered in velvet so old it had turned green. The hats sat on a stack of clean saddle pads.

She shoved the canvas bag farther out of the way. Beneath it sat a pair of shining black tall boots and a pair of equally shiny paddock boots.

Next she unzipped the canvas bag. It held half a dozen pairs of riding britches, several white shirts and three black riding coats. She reached out to caress the sleeve of one of the jackets.

"These are yours," he whispered, deeply touched.

She shrugged. "Couldn't bear to part with them. Other southern women polish the silver when they get depressed. I polish my saddle. This smaller one may be a little big for Angie, but it should fit Cloud. I don't think Angie can wear my boots, but paddock boots and half chaps don't cost that much. You can probably find them used at one of the local tack shops anyway."

"You can't just give these things away."

"Damn right I can't." She grinned. "But I can lend them to a neighbor."

She was acting casual, but he knew how much these things meant to her. One hell of a gesture. "That only leaves the cost of a trainer, assuming I can find someone who will drive out to Williamston once a week to teach one kid."

"I'll train her if she'll have me."

"You?"

"Can we get out of the closet now? I'm not in the habit of sharing the secrets of my limited wardrobe with strange men."

She followed him out, clicked off the lights and closed the door behind her. "I train the hunters down at the common a couple of days a week this time of year. No reason why Angie can't join us. They're more advanced, of course, but they won't mind having a beginner around. They're all from this area. You probably haven't met them yet, but you will at the Thanksgiving and Christmas parties, if not before."

He sat on the foot of her bed. Poddy hissed at him and disappeared into the kitchen to burrow under the covers with Lancelot, who hadn't bothered to wake up. "This is all going too fast. I know Angie wants to ride, and I've come to terms with the theory, but when I'm faced with it actually happening…"

Nancy sat beside him. "Isn't this what she wants?"

"Why are you doing this?"

"I'm a nosy neighbor?"

He shook his head. "Not good enough."

She went into the kitchen and got out a beer. "Want one?" He nodded. She took a diet soda for herself, and leaned against the refrigerator. "She reminds me of me. I know that ache, that sheer physical longing to be on the back of a horse. When I was her age, people gave me chances. I'm just passing it on."

She leaned over Lancelot's bed and scratched his ears. He rumbled and turned over. Poddy flattened his ears, but stayed with Lancelot, although he eyed Tim warily when he followed Nancy into the kitchen.

"What's your problem?" Nancy asked. "Don't like being beholden?"

He opened his beer and sat on a stool at the breakfast bar. "Last March I almost lost her."

"Good grief! What happened? Car wreck? She ran away?"

"Little more complicated." He took a swig. "You've probably done it yourself. Told your parents you're spending the night with a friend while she tells her parents she's spending the night with you?"

"Who? Moi?" Nancy grimaced. "Maybe once or twice."

"She was twelve, Nancy. Her thirteenth birthday wasn't until June. She and her good buddy Denise met in the women's bathroom at our branch library, of all places. They went in as twelve-year-olds and came out looking like a pair of sixteen-year-old hotties in Solange's clothes, jewelry, high heels and makeup. Denise is two years older than Angie, but dressed up, Angie looked older than she did. She had the black hair then, too, which helped the illusion."

"Where did they go in all this finery?"

"Denise had scored some fake IDs. I don't know how they managed, but they got into a rave in a warehouse a couple of miles from our apartment."

"Good grief," Nancy breathed.

"You know what a Ruffie is?"

"Somebody gave her a Ruffie?"

"That or Ecstasy. She didn't know you can't take your eyes off your drink at a party, and you'd better open your own soda can. It's dumb luck that Denise's parents called our place to talk to Denise. I called another friend of theirs. She spilled the beans, told me where they were holding the rave. She swore they were just dancing. They were all under eighteen. No alcohol, no drugs. Right."

"You went after her?"

"Damn right. Denise's father and I. We came into that place like a contingent of Marines. It was so packed we didn't find them at first. Hell, half the kids there were from my school." He laughed. "Here they were having a little orgy and the assistant principal descends on them like an avenging angel. Talk about scatter!"

"But you did find her?"

"Staggering, half blotto. Denise's father thought they were drunk, but I recognized the signs. She and Denise spent the night in the emergency room, had to have their stomachs pumped out." He closed his eyes. "They could have died, Nancy. They could have been taken out of there, raped, murdered."

He didn't need to remind her that his wife had been murdered. He knew about violent death.

"No wonder you got them out of Chicago."

"I hope she learned her lesson. She was one scared girl. But I'm afraid to let her out of my sight. Scared something will happen to her. If she rides horses, she could fall off."

"If she rides long enough, she *will* fall off, but she probably won't hurt anything but her dignity."

"You did."

Nancy caught her breath. "Low blow."

"I'm a father. I play dirty." A thump against Tim's calf nearly knocked him off his bar stool.

Nancy laughed. "So you decided to join the party, huh, pig?" She reached into the refrigerator and found a bag of carrots on the top shelf. "If I keep the treats any lower, he climbs into the refrigerator and gets them himself." She handed Tim a carrot. "Let me put his leash and harness on. We can sit on the front porch while I tell you story of my life, assuming you want to hear it."

"I want everything about you."

She stiffened for a moment, then acted as though she hadn't heard him.

Lancelot snuffled and wriggled, but Nancy fastened his harness around his fat shoulders, clipped on the extension leash and went to the front door. "Coming?"

He followed her to the front porch. For the first time, he felt autumn might eventually come to relieve this heat. The breeze carried the merest scent of dry leaves. Hell, maybe that was the drought. School should start in cool weather, not in this heat.

Nancy sat on the top step and let Lancelot trundle around the yard like a clockwork toy.

This time Tim stood beside her where he wouldn't have to see anything except the top of her head. And those long legs. Damn. "So, tell me the story of your life."

"You really want the story of my accident, right? Okay. Short version. I was riding a Grande Prix jumper named Panache in a big show with top prize money. Peter, my husband and trainer, had been pushing us since the show started. Panache and I were both worn-out. We should have scratched, but Peter and Panache's owner insisted we ride."

"He wasn't your horse?"

"I've never owned a horse outright. Peter and I owned a couple together, but mostly they belonged to clients who were willing to foot the bills to watch a professional ride their horses to victory while they sat in their boxes and drank champagne."

"You sound bitter."

"I'm not, really. I am bitter that Peter let me ride when he knew I shouldn't have."

"So what happened?"

"Grande Prix fences are tall and wide and full of traps that require not just a horse with incredible athletic ability, but a clever rider as well. I wasn't feeling too clever and Panache was exhausted. He jumped into a big vertical a stride too early, hit the rails, demolished the jump…and threw me straight through the jump standard. He was bruised and scraped, but I broke half a dozen ribs, my collarbone and a vertebra. End of story. End of career. End of marriage."

"Why would that end your marriage? You'd been doing it for your husband. He should have carried you around on a pillow."

She leaned back against the porch column. "I don't know why I'm telling you this. It doesn't put the horse show business in a very good light."

"It doesn't put your *husband* in a very good light."

She reeled Lancelot in. "Pig, I told you, don't eat the azaleas."

Tim hunkered down on the stair beside her. He saw the glint of tears on her cheeks in the pale light of the moon. "There's more to it, isn't there?"

"I was two months pregnant. Peter knew, but nobody else did, not even my mother. I lost the baby. I'll never have another."

He closed his hand over hers. There didn't seem to be anything to say. "I'm sorry."

"Me, too, although I probably would've been a rotten mother. I was a rotten stepmother."

"I don't believe that."

"Believe it. Anyway, Peter had me back up on a horse six weeks after I crashed, although the doctors said to wait at least four months. That time I fell in the practice arena. I didn't break my neck, but I screwed up the disk below the one I'd cracked."

"Bastard."

"I was a rider first, a bed partner next, and not much else. This time the doctors said no riding for a year. I went home to our farm in Florida while Peter carried on with the show circuit. He came back six weeks later with an eighteen-year-old blond rider and bed partner." She stared into the night and whispered. "He gave her Panache to ride."

She shrugged. "I filed for divorce the next day. A very nasty divorce it was, too. I walked away with my tack and my clothes."

Tim realized that had hurt as much, possibly more, than the breakup of her marriage. She'd been stripped of everything that had circumscribed her life, and betrayed by the man she'd loved and trusted.

No wonder she wanted some space.

"So, unless Angie intends to canter down on five-foot fences, the chances of winding up like me are slim." Nancy ran her hand under her eyes to wipe away the tears.

"But possible."

"She could be hit by a car or fall in gym class. You don't worry about Jason. You let him swim and canoe and run with teenagers in big cars."

"Of course I worry, but he's nearly sixteen. Besides, he's a boy."

She stood up. "Well, whoop-de-doo. Why don't you and Lancelot stay out here and oink at each other?"

He caught her by the ankle. "Do you want Angie to ride or don't you?"

"I went to a heck of a lot of trouble. Of course I do." She shook her foot loose and reeled in a rebellious Lancelot.

"Then no jumping."

"Shoot. She's your kid. She wouldn't be jumping for six months or so even if she's talented. In six months she may be taking karate or ballet or gymnastics, and I may be stuck with Cloud Shadow."

"Never. Promise me."

"She might want to go out with the hunt next season or go to a schooling show."

"Tell her she's not ready to jump and keep telling her."

"Even after she is?"

"Promise or call Crandall and tell him thanks but no thanks."

"You'd do that?"

"If that's what it takes to keep her safe, you bet."

"She could fall off her bicycle."

"I have to play the odds."

Nancy sighed. "All right. So, do you want to talk to Crandall?"

"I suppose I'd better. I don't want to mention this to Angie yet."

"Of course not. You tell her. She may not want to have anything to do with me."

"Frankly, Nancy, if you can get her on a horse, I doubt she'd care if you were Frankenstein's monster."

CHAPTER TWENTY-FOUR

DAVID GRANTHAM groaned, rolled over and slammed his fist onto the top of his alarm clock, silencing it. He hated when anyone tried to control him. Even an inanimate object.

In this case, however, he had stuff to do. He pulled the covers off and sat on the edge of the bed.

A slim hand snaked around his hip and brushed his naked belly. "Um."

Damn. Who said, "A man should remember in the morning who he took to bed last night"? He couldn't keep the cheerleaders straight. Was this one Taylor or Tiffany or Tammie?

"Come back to bed."

"No can do. Up, up and away."

"Ooh, that's what I was hoping." She found him with that educated little paw. Infuriating that his body responded to what he didn't have time for. Her tousled blond head appeared at his waist, and her little pink tongue—everything about this girl was little except her boobs—lapped at him like a thirsty puppy.

Okay, so maybe he could be a few minutes late to lacrosse practice.

Twenty minutes later he kissed her goodbye in the parking lot of his townhouse and waved her off in her red convertible, then climbed into his Hummer. He had no idea how a sixteen-year-old girl could spend an entire night in his bed without causing some consternation at home, and so long as he was the beneficiary, he didn't plan to ask.

Mentally he checked her off his list. He hadn't precisely followed the alphabet, but close enough. He still had Wendy and Vickie and Zelda to go. Then he could start all over again with the "A's." But maybe not cheerleaders. He liked initiation ceremonies. So far most of these girls knew more about sex than he did, and that was saying a lot. Be nice to find a virgin.

He chortled. He'd have to start younger. Much younger.

That might present problems. He'd been careful never to screw a girl under sixteen, although the chances one of them would yell rape were slim. They were too grateful, too *honored*, he'd chosen them. They wouldn't have cared if he'd organized a threesome or even a sixsome. The mind boggled. His private harem.

He didn't consider himself a chicken hawk, but a virgin, even if she was only twelve or thirteen, would be an interesting experience.

He pulled into a parking space beside the gym. It was still damned hot, but he never let his team know that he felt physical discomfort. Gods didn't. That's what he was to them. A god. They worshipped him.

Why not? He showed them how to beat the system, how to play their parents and their teachers. How to fly under the radar. He'd already begun training them in the doctrine, "Do what thou wilt." But he added his own corollary. Don't get caught at it.

He didn't know how old he'd been when he discovered that if you act perfect, adults pretty much left you alone. Maybe four? He'd just scared the au pair with a violent temper tantrum, and had bashed his cousin Jessica with a block. He hated the bitch. He didn't know the word or what it meant, but he understood the concept, all right. Mealymouthed, smiling little Jessica got the attention *he* wanted.

Of course he got a giant time-out. He could hear Jessica and the au pair singing nursery rhymes behind him. They should be listening to *him*. He knew the words better than stupid old Jessica.

He wasn't certain whether four-year-olds were capable of blinding flashes of insight, but that's what it felt like in his memory. Jessica sang rhymes and ate cake and got fancy toys because she was perfect, while he was, according to his father, "a vicious little bastard."

So, could it be that if he was perfect, he'd get what Jessica got? Worth a try. Hard to do, though. He really had to practice. And he had to figure out what *they* considered perfection. *Not* hard to do. Obey their dumb rules. Take a nap, go to bed when they said, eat his green beans. He still loathed green beans and sleeping in the daytime.

Every time he wanted to kill Jessica or the au pair or his mother and father, or the family dog, for that matter, he tamped down his rage and hid it behind perfection.

It worked. Not right away, of course. And right away is much too long for a kid his age. Still, everybody started telling him what a good boy he was and giving him seconds of ice cream and buying him stuff. And leaving him alone to do as he liked when they weren't watching, so long as he didn't leave any evidence to show he was still a vicious little bastard.

The first time he realized he wasn't the same creature as the rest of the world was when he fell off his bicycle at age twelve and got a concussion that kept him in the hospital overnight. His parents hung over his bed. His mother sobbed and held his hand.

They actually felt something. What they called love. They'd feel something bad if he died. Not that he would, of course.

He didn't feel anything but surprise. They weren't acting. The doctors weren't acting. Other people actually felt love and compassion and pity and grief. The only emotion he'd ever felt was rage, and he'd learned a long time ago not to feel that.

He was left with no feeling at all. Was that normal? He didn't think so. Obviously it was better not to feel. His mother's tears were proof of that.

That meant that if he didn't feel, he was *better* as well as different. He was the next evolutionary step. To the Neanderthal, the Cro-Magnon must have seemed like a god, just as he was to these people. He'd seen on some science TV show that chimpanzees share 99.9 percent of their DNA with human. It was that one-tenth of a percent that made the difference.

He must have some sort of genetic mutation that raised him above them another one-tenth of a percent. A higher being.

They must never know. They'd want to test him or put him in a cage. No, he would continue to be perfect to be left alone. Everybody adored him, of course. He was flawless.

Most of the time.

Occasionally, and very carefully, he would give his rage free rein. He liked causing pain to things that couldn't fight back. He was a trifle bothered that lately he'd felt the need to let his rage out more often than once every couple of years. He was having trouble holding his libido in check as well.

He did feel orgasm, of course. He could produce it as well. He knew how to make love as perfectly as he did everything else. He would watch his lovers to learn all that he could about counterfeiting love. He'd gotten pretty good at it.

Now, in his final year of college, he'd decided to move onto the next step, the next plateau in his life's career.

The lacrosse team and the cheerleaders already adored him. But they were a relatively small group.

If he could make *them* his disciples, his worshippers, lead them into doing things they'd never have before in their safe middle-class lives, then he'd be ready to move on to bigger and better things.

He was on a tight schedule. He'd given himself until Halloween. After that night he'd own them all, body and soul.

Hail, Caesar. Well, anyway, hail David. He giggled. That didn't sound nearly as good.

CHAPTER TWENTY-FIVE

CRANDALL BROUGHT CLOUD over to Nancy's at six-thirty Sunday morning. When he pulled into Nancy's driveway, Angie exploded out her front door and ran across the street without looking left or right.

Nancy doubted she'd slept for the past two days, not since she and Tim had driven her out to Crandall's, introduced her to Cloud and laid out the parameters.

Not quite her very own horse, but close.

Cloud had no doubt been born gray, but at fourteen, she was white. She backed out of the trailer with the ease of long practice and stood beside the trailer waiting for Crandall to pick up her lead line.

Angie stopped dead on the sidewalk.

Nancy came out of her house, took the lead line from Crandall and caressed the mare's neck. "Who's a good girl?"

"Mother is so glad she'll be teaching someone to ride." Crandall turned and saw Angie, who still stood transfixed. "Hey, Angie. Come get your horse."

Angie walked hesitantly up Nancy's front yard. Nancy could see her chest heaving.

"Oh, oh, oh," she whispered. She reached a tentative hand out and touched the mare's shoulder. The mare turned and looked down at her.

Angie burst into tears.

"Hey," Crandall said, surprised by her reaction.

"It's okay," Nancy whispered. "Come on, Angie. Let's get her settled. Mr. Crandall has to get home. He's playing polo this afternoon."

The mare followed Nancy around the house. Angie trailed both of them without a backward glance.

Nancy grinned. At some point the girl might remember to thank Crandall, but it wasn't necessary. She knew he'd seen that look before. That horse-stunned look was thanks enough. Yeah, Crandall knew Cloud would have a good home.

By 7:00 a.m. the sky was overcast. By eight the first cool front of autumn moved through. The temperature dropped twenty degrees in an hour, and two inches of rain in thirty minutes broke the drought.

Nancy and Angie sat on bales in front of Cloud's stall while she munched hay.

"Why did it have to rain *today*? It hasn't rained since we've been here," Angie wailed. "I'll never get to ride her." Thunder rumbled and a second later a crack of thunder shook the building. Angie jumped.

Cloud didn't raise her head.

"Close," Nancy said. "Should pass in another couple of hours. The common will be a lake until tomorrow."

"Oh."

"I didn't say you couldn't get on her. Of course you can. How could you wait? We'll have to walk her down to the common, then I'll give you a leg up. I'll keep you on a lead line after you're in the saddle."

"But…"

"Remember, you agreed."

"But…"

"Everybody starts on a lunge line. I did. You come off of it when I say and not before. Got it?"

"Yeah. Okay." Angie's shoulders sank.

"When you're on this property or in this barn or anywhere near Cloud, when I say frog-jump, you say how high? Got it?"

"I guess. But she's my horse."

"Actually, she's Mrs. Crandall's horse. You have the use of her, but I have the control of her and you, too. Otherwise, I'll turn her out with Herb and Henry to be yard art."

"But when can I…"

"There's plenty to do while we wait for the rain to stop." Nancy stood. "Time you learned to muck a stall."

"But she just got here."

"Henry and Herb were in yesterday. I told Phil and Phineas we'd muck for them today. You need the experience." She handed Angie a manure fork. "Now, here's what you do."

CHAPTER TWENTY-SIX

TIM STOOD at his bedroom window and watched his only daughter, Solange's child, climb onto a white horse in a driving rainstorm. He had never thought she looked like Solange. She was already taller than her mother, and a good deal heftier.

But without the vampire hair and makeup, there were hints of Solange in her daughter's unformed countenance, and Solange's lovely autumn eyes met his over the breakfast table. God help him, she was going to be beautiful. He hoped she would also be happy.

Having a beautiful daughter invited problems. He knew boys. Their brains turned to turnips around beautiful girls. They were ravening pits of amoral lust. Race cars without brakes.

He tore his eyes from Angie to look at Nancy, who stood in the center of a large circle while Angie and Cloud walked around the outside on some sort of long tether.

Oblivious to the rain that sluiced over her head and down her face and body, Nancy kept up a running commentary while Angie adjusted her hands, her body, her legs.

Boys weren't the only ravening pits of amoral lust, not the only ones whose brains turned to turnips when they looked at a beautiful woman.

Not merely beautiful. Kind, caring. For all her tough exterior, Nancy had gone to a great deal of trouble for his family.

He wanted her badly. If he could have figured out some way to manage it without Angie seeing, he'd have run out into the rain and dragged Nancy down in the mud.

But, hey, the horse might spook. It was always something.

Since school had started three weeks ago, he couldn't leave campus for a romantic bed-and-breakfast tryst, even if Nancy could have left the clinic. She was a slave to that place.

But he was as much a slave as she was, only in thrall to different masters.

Amazing how his thoughts revolved around her since he'd first seen her in mid-July.

On weekends, Nancy would be teaching Angie, while he'd be running the errands he didn't have time for during the week.

And there was Eddy. Jason was always off with the Lacrosse team even when they didn't have a practice scheduled. Today they said they were hitting the new sci-fi film, then grabbing burgers. He didn't think he could trust Angie until she came down off of Cloud nine, no pun intended.

He needed a babysitter, but Angie would have a fit. She had friends the same age that babysat all the time.

Did he trust her? She was thirteen. She'd already made one dumb decision that could have killed her. He hoped she wouldn't make any more, but he couldn't be sure she wouldn't.

TIM WAITED until Angie and Eddy were upstairs, the kitchen was tidy and he knew Jason was at his friend Daryl's with the rest of the team before he walked across the street and knocked on Nancy's front door. He knew she was home. Her car was there, the lights were on. It was barely nine o'clock, although darker than usual because of the rain.

She didn't answer, although he heard Lancelot's little hooves click on the hardwood floor inside.

His trainers sank into the mud as he walked around the house and out to the barn. The lights were on.

"Hey," she said when she saw him. "Don't just hang around outside and get wet."

Cloud stood in the aisle cross-tied between two lines. The two Percherons dozed in their stalls, in because of the rain.

Nancy was picking manure out of Cloud's stall and tossing it into a rolling cart. She'd put on jeans, a long-sleeved cotton shirt, and wore heavy leather work gloves.

He really missed those shorts.

"Cleaning her stall is Angie's job," Tim said. "Part of the deal."

Nancy dropped a forkful of manure into her cart. "She did her job. She picked the stall this morning after we rode and groomed the mare. I come down here when I want to think and relax. Might as well get a head start on tomorrow."

"You have a weird way of relaxing."

"So I've been told. There's a bucket of horse brushes over there. Make yourself useful. Curry the mare. She'll enjoy it and you should get to know something about horses. You don't know anything, do you?"

He reached into the bucket and came up with a tough-bristled brush. "This?"

Nancy shook her head. "No. That's a dandy brush. The curry is that round rubber thing with the nodules on it."

Tim picked it up and raised his eyebrows.

Nancy nodded. "Start just behind her ears and rub in circles. Hard. She likes it hard."

"How about the Percherons? They like it hard, too? Or is it just mares?"

Nancy turned away, her face flaming. "Them, too. Want to start on them next?"

He took a step toward her, but she swung the forkful of manure between them. "Better step back if you don't want this all over your clean jeans." She pointed. "White horses need a lot of attention. The dirt shows more."

He went to work.

"So, what did you want to talk about?" she asked after some time had passed in silence. She set the fork down beside the mare's stall, pulled off her leather gloves and ran her fingers through her damp hair. "I assume you watched Angie while she was riding. I can tell already she's going to push herself and me."

"Don't let her run over you." The curry stopped in midcircle, then Tim started again on the mare's shoulder. She sighed and leaned against him. "I wanted to thank you."

"You're welcome."

"That's it." He flung the curry across the aisle and into the bucket with so much force that both Nancy and Cloud jumped. Then he unhooked the horse, led her back into her stall and shut the door on her.

"Hey, I wasn't finished."

"I am. Finished acting as though you and I are casual acquaintances who speak across the picket fence."

"There isn't a picket fence."

"There's a wall. And I'm about to tear it down." He pulled her into his arms. "Kiss me."

"I don't…"

"You, me, lips. You know. We've done it before. This time you start."

Her eyes narrowed. She slapped her hands against his cheeks, stood on her toes and kissed him. Hard and fast.

"There, satisfied?"

"Are you kidding?" When he bent to kiss her again, he felt her strain away for a nanosecond before she came to him, really came to him, suddenly soft, arms twining around his neck, body pressed against his.

He kissed her ear, moved to the hollow at the base of her throat and the vee of her blouse. She gave a small whimper, pulled his shirt out of his shorts and slid her fingers into the muscles of his back.

He cupped her against him and she slid her leg behind his.

"We can't," she whispered against his mouth. "The lights…"

He took her hand and led her to the stall where they'd talked earlier that day. The horse blanket was still spread over the bales, bigger than a king-size bed. The stall lay in deep shadow, well away from the lights at the front of the barn.

"You're not serious," she whispered.

"Want to bet?"

She threw back her head and laughed.

And began to unbutton her shirt.

He caught her hands. "My pleasure."

He hadn't undressed a woman since Solange died. His hands were trembling and felt like sausages.

The first button came apart easily. The second refused. "Hell," he said and pulled. Buttons flew.

"You want to play rough?" She yanked his shirt over his head before he'd had more than a glimpse of her. "You got it, cowboy."

She toppled them both onto the makeshift bed.

Muddy shoes flew, zippers snagged and came open. It became a race to see which one could get naked first.

Dead heat.

She lay beneath him, her eyes wide, pupils dilated. No longer smiling, but sighing through lips swollen with his kisses.

She felt so damned soft. He was so damned hard.

He ran his tongue over her nipples and heard her quick intake of breath as she wound her fingers through his hair. His hand needed no guide. When he touched her, she arched her back, gasped and encircled him, caressing him.

"Now," she sobbed. "Now. Don't wait."

He positioned himself above her. She took him and guided him. Her hips rose to meet him, her legs locked around him and drew him deeper until he was drowning in the sweet, soft depth of her body.

He held himself so that he could watch her face, hear her.

He wanted her with him or ahead of him. Slow and easy. Let her set the pace. Give her joy as she was giving him joy.

Except she didn't want slow and easy. She wanted wild.

Thrusting, biting her lip, her head tossing from side to side as she drove them both higher, battering him with pleasure.

Suddenly her body went rigid, her back arched, her mouth opened in a silent sob. He felt her spasm, drove into her harder and felt her come.

That did it. He exploded.

He wasn't certain he'd ever breathe again. He moved beside her, cradled her in his arms and kissed her hair.

She snuggled into him, her arm and leg across his body. "Um," she said. "This is the best part."

"I beg your pardon?" He lifted his head to stare down at her.

"Well, maybe not the *best* part." He felt her chuckle. "But nice. At least I'm in my right mind to appreciate it."

"So that was insanity?"

She raised herself on her elbow. "It wasn't smart."

"'Tis folly to be wise, my girl, and don't you forget it."

She snuggled against him once more. "You know, I've never actually rolled in the hay before."

"In your misspent youth?"

"Nope. Hay prickles."

"Then thank heaven for this blanket." His eyes were growing heavy. They couldn't fall asleep here. If he didn't come home soon, they'd start looking for him.

Just a few moments longer to hold Nancy, caress her lovely breast, slide his hand over the curve of her hip.

A flash of lightning lit the barn. A moment later thunder rolled.

A moment after the thunder, the lights went out.

CHAPTER TWENTY-SEVEN

TIM SLID OFF THE BALES and began frantically searching the stall floor in the dark. "I've got to get home. Eddy will freak out in the dark. They won't know where I am."

"Of course. Wait a minute. I've got one of the hand lanterns up front." She slipped past him and ran naked and barefoot to get the light and bring it back to him.

He'd already put his shorts on, and was pulling his shirt over his head.

Nancy directed the light around. "There's one," she said and handed him his left shoe.

"Where's the other one? No, that's yours."

"Here." She picked up his right shoe.

He grabbed it, pulled it on and tied it hurriedly. He took a step toward the door of the stall, then turned and touched her cheek. "I'm sorry."

"Oh?"

"Don't be silly. Not about this. This was fantastic. Sorry that I have to leave. You have any idea how hard it is to walk away from a beautiful naked lady on a bale of hay?"

"Nope."

"Trust me, it's brutal." He leaned over and kissed her.

"Go. Before they come over here and catch you with a naked lady on a bale of hay." She handed him the light. "Take this so you don't fall in the mud. I have others."

She followed the light until it passed out of sight around the corner of her house. She scrambled into her own clothes in the dark and walked across the lawn in the drizzle. She dropped her muddy shoes inside her back door.

The whole neighborhood was without power. The lightning must have taken out a generator at the substation. If the power company ran true to form, power might not be restored until daylight.

No power meant no air-conditioning. More important, the pump for the well wouldn't operate. If the power didn't come on in an hour, she'd crank up the generator. It ran lights, air-conditioning, the refrigerator and the well.

Did Tim have a generator? If so, did it work? Generators were notoriously difficult. He had a total of four people to get clean, dressed, fed and off to school tomorrow morning.

Should she call and offer her bathroom? She had to go to work at the same time they went to school. She decided to wait. She wouldn't be surprised if Tim pulled back after tonight. Men did, usually, although she didn't think Tim was the usual kind of guy.

She sank onto the sofa. Poddy and Otto materialized from one of their hiding places, climbed into her lap. They didn't like lightning and thunder.

Lancelot nuzzled her foot.

"You've been outside already. I'm not taking you out just because you want to roll in the mud."

The bottom third of her jeans was soaked. Her open shirt felt damp. She hadn't been wearing a bra, but her underpants were somewhere in the hay. In the mad scramble after the lights went out, she hadn't been able to find them.

She sat up. Oh, Lord! Phil and Phineas would be back early tomorrow to look after Henry and Herb. What would they think if they discovered a bright red thong? With luck they'd be hidden behind one of the bales of hay that was not being fed to Henry and Herb.

No way was she going back out there tonight. Phil and Phineas would simply have to be shocked.

Well, she'd done it. Literally. Her heart and her body had wanted Tim, but until he forced the issue tonight, she'd kept her libido under control. Now the horse was out of the stable. Heck, she could rattle off clichés all night without even approaching the cataclysmic experience of making love with Tim.

She'd thought Peter was good, but then she had no frame of reference when she married him. She'd been a virgin. She'd had a few lovers since her divorce, but nobody long-term.

Nobody like Tim. She ached. Nice ache. She swung her legs onto the sofa, and Poddy and Otto reassembled themselves. She pulled her grandmother's knitted afghan off the back and snuggled under it. In a minute she'd get up and go to bed.

In a minute.

She woke when the lights came on at one forty-five. The cats hadn't moved, but Lancelot had retired to his basket. The lights in Tim's living room were on, so he had power, too, but apparently he'd gone to bed.

As she started to turn away, she saw an SUV turn the corner by the common. It was running slowly without lights. It eased to the shoulder in front of Tim's house, and a moment later Jason climbed out of the front seat, closed the door gently. A moment later the car glided over the hill.

He walked none too steadily in the back door.

Did Tim know he was coming home so late on a school night?

After what they'd done in the barn tonight, Tim was probably very, very, sound asleep.

Had Jason been drinking?

She'd thought that coach—what was his name? Chatham? No. Grantham—kept them all straight. Had they gotten away from him tonight?

Maybe he didn't have quite the total control over his team that Tim thought he did.

DAVID GRANTHAM had much more of a hold over his players than even Tim guessed. He was always the designated driver. He abhorred alcohol. His body truly was a temple. He kept it free of drugs, cigarettes, fatty foods.

Since he was teaching his young disciples the doctrine of "do as thou wilt," however, he had to allow them a taste of vice occasionally.

So far they had never been stopped and questioned by either cops or parents. If he ever was, he could say he'd found them drunk and had brought them safely home. Good Samaritan. St. David, patron of lacrosse.

Jason knew how to sneak into his house without getting caught. He told David he'd perfected his technique after raves in Chicago. If he could sneak into an apartment, he could certainly sneak into a big house.

David knew he was taking a chance when he enlisted the son of a teacher that dumbass Aycock was dumping all his work on. Taking over the hearts and minds of lemmings like Daryl and Scott had been too easy. Jason, on the other hand, vacillated between his need to be a part of the group—or mob, as David thought of them—and righteous morality.

The other members of the team had all been students at Maybree since at least middle school. Some of them had started in kindergarten. Daryl, for instance. They had grown up mesmerized by the mystique of the Maybree lacrosse team.

They had watched David lead his team to the division championship in his junior and senior years. They were ready to do anything to maintain that mystique. They were his soldiers. He was their general.

Jason was new. He had talent as a defenceman, although he wouldn't really be efficient and deadly with his stick until he'd been working at his technique for at least a year.

Unfortunately he didn't have the years of watching the team, basking in their glory, didn't need desperately to be one of them at all costs. He'd said his father didn't drink anything except the occasional beer or glass of wine. He wasn't used to seeing his parents half-sloshed before the evening news was over.

Tim would never have considered hosting a safe keg party for the team as Daryl's father had last May. Better the kids should drink where they had adult supervision and no access to their car keys.

Made a sort of lunatic sense, but David didn't think Tim would agree.

Jason had a latent Goody-Two-shoes streak that annoyed David. Take tonight, for instance. He'd pretended to drink much more than he actually had. A couple of beers was all. None of the others paid attention. David did. When Jason staggered up his walk, David knew he was exaggerating to prove he was part of the gang.

David was enjoying the challenge.

He already knew the right button to push. Jason's guilt.

Jason had finally broken down and told David what even his father didn't know. He'd been the one who scored the fake IDs for Baby Sister Angie and her friend in Chicago. He told them where the rave was.

"They threatened to tell Dad I was going and about the IDs if I didn't," Jason said miserably.

David, always the good psychologist, listened and nodded, ready to grant absolution.

But there was more.

"There were about a million people in that warehouse," Jason continued. "I didn't even see Angie and Denise come in. I figured they got cold feet. Hell, I probably saw them and didn't recognize them. When Dad brought Angie home from the E.R. the next morning, she looked like some twenty-year-old bimbo."

"You had no way of knowing they would actually come," David said soothingly. "Not your fault."

"They got Ruffied," Jason said. "When my Dad and Denise's dad raided the place looking for them, I hid in the men's room."

"Wise."

"Don't you see, man, I should'a looked after her? I mean, like, you know, she could've been raped or kidnapped."

"They chose to be there. The entire episode was not your responsibility. You did the right thing."

Jason dropped his head in his hands. "She's my little sister. I should've looked after her."

Jason had actually cried. David spent twenty minutes absolving him. He wasn't certain the absolution had taken fully. The kid did have an overwrought sense of responsibility to others. He needed to lose that if he were to be responsible to David alone.

Well, David was working on it. By Halloween he and Baby Sister should be ripe for plucking.

CHAPTER TWENTY-EIGHT

"WHEN CAN I SEE you again?"

Nancy put her toothbrush down on the side of the sink and turned her back to the bathroom mirror. She didn't want to watch herself blush. Her heart had set up a samba beat the instant she heard Tim's voice on the telephone.

"When do you want to?"

"Today and tomorrow and tomorrow and tomorrow."

"That brings us up to Friday."

"You are a insatiable, you know that?"

"So I've been told." She longed to ask whether Tim knew what time his son had come in and in what state. She kept her mouth shut. It was his problem.

"Tonight? Nice romantic candlelight dinner? White table-cloths? Good wine?"

"Not too nice. I don't own a pair of panty hose without runs."

Silence. Then he asked, "Why do you keep panty hose with runs?"

"They're great tail wraps. You can slide them over bandages on a horse's leg to keep the bandages clean. Other stuff."

"I should have guessed. How about knee-highs without runs?"

She laughed. "Only a man who's been married would know about knee highs. Yes, I have a brand-new pair. I even have a couple of decent pairs of slacks. Real shoes. Maybe earrings."

"Don't go overboard."

I already have. "What time?"

"Seven? Jason can take charge of the others. They hate the term babysit."

"Unless something comes up at work, I'll be here."

ON AVERAGE mules beat horses out in the brains department hands down, so Nancy was surprised when Elroy Morrison brought his white pony mule Jennet into the clinic at four-thirty covered with blood and shivering in pain.

"Darn fool mule knows that culvert is there. It's always been there. So today she falls into it upside down, gets herself stuck, and if I hadn't seen her wheel mule standing at the edge looking down at her, I might not have found her till she was dead."

While she was waiting for Eleanor Chadwick, Nancy checked the mule's gums. Nearly white. On the verge of shock.

Eleanor took one look and ordered saline, glucose and radiographs.

The mule didn't want to move her hind end, but she was so miserable that when Big managed to inch her along, she didn't try to bite his head off. She was too lame to kick him.

"Damn," Eleanor said when she checked the radiographs. "She cracked her stifle bad. What do you want to do, Elroy? It'll cost a lot to put a pin in it, and she'll have to stay up for at least six weeks."

"She's a good ole girl, and she'n Jackson done won me a lot of trophies at the mule shows. Not but six years old." When he heard the possible figure for the surgery and after care, he whistled. "Any other way to do it?"

Eleanor shook her head. "We could put her in a sling and hope the bone knits in the right place, but it probably wouldn't." Eleanor took a deep breath. "Or we could put her down."

"Woman, you do not give a man a lot of options. Good thing I ain't poor as Job's turkey. Made a fine crop last year. Do it."

"Nancy?" Eleanor asked. "Can you assist? And I'd like to get Mac in on this, too. He's had more experience pinning joints than I have."

There went dinner with Tim. The surgery might take three or four hours, then someone would have to stay until Jennet was conscious and standing without fighting her sling.

"Sure. I need to make a call first." She got the answering message on Tim's cell phone, and the machine at his house. No doubt Eddy and Angie were in Nancy's barn with Cloud, while Jason was at school or with one of his friends practicing lacrosse. She left messages.

"Get a move on," Mac said. "She needs scrubbing and shaving."

"Aye, aye, Admiral."

ON HER WAY HOME at eleven, she munched a couple of packs of peanut butter crackers out of the machine. A far cry from a romantic dinner for two with wine.

She saw Tim on his front porch when she pulled into her driveway. Another problem with living across the street. He knew when she arrived and when she left. A short step to asking where she'd been when she wasn't on schedule. She hadn't reported to anyone since Peter and didn't plan to start again now.

She was tired, dirty, hungry and grumpy. Definitely not in the mood for a repeat of last night's wild ride. She would love to cuddle, to be held and petted. But men expected cuddling to lead to foreplay and foreplay to sex.

He rang her doorbell before she could get Lancelot's harness on to take him outside.

Her heart was too tired to walk, much less samba. She didn't have enough circulation left to blush. Her neck hurt, her feet hurt. She wanted a hot bath, a glass of wine and sleep.

"Come in," she said without much enthusiasm.

He looked at her, standing beside Lancelot. "I'll do that."

She hesitated, then relinquished the leash. "Thanks. I must smell like a slaughterhouse."

"Something go wrong?"

"No." She rubbed her aching neck. "The mule's going to be fine if we can keep her quiet. Big's handling that. But there was a lot of blood. They can lose a couple of quarts without adverse effect."

"Okay. I'll do pig duty while you get out of those clothes."

"Tim, I…"

"And put something comfortable on. Helen put my bottle of wine in your refrigerator when she and Eddy came over to play with Lancelot. You curl up on the sofa. If you ply me with wine, I may be persuaded to work on your neck."

"It's my feet that are killing me. The floor in the surgical theater is concrete."

"Then I'll do your feet, too. Go."

She burst into tears.

"Hey!" He pulled her into his arms. Lancelot wrapped his leash around both of them. "I do something wrong?"

"No," she wailed.

"Unwind then, and let me get this hog outside. I'll massage your feet, but I'll be darned if I'll clean up hog poop."

When he came back and unharnessed Lancelot, then gave him his carrot, Nancy was lying on the sofa in the ugliest gray sweats she had. Her hair was wet from the shower, her face devoid of makeup. Not exactly a hot item. Tim would probably take one look at her and renege.

Without asking her, he opened the chilled wine and poured them both a glass. He picked her feet up from the sofa, sat and dropped them into his lap.

"You're not really going to do that, are you?" she asked. "You don't have to."

"Shut up and drink your wine."

Talk about educated fingers! She felt like a cat that had gorged on cream and catnip. If anyone heard the sounds she was making, they'd think she and Tim were making love.

In a way they were. Or he was. She laid her head back on the arm of the sofa and groaned.

He chuckled. "Did you know that the Romans kept masseurs specifically trained to massage feet?"

"I want one."

"Won't I do?"

"In a pinch. God, that feels so good. Hey, don't stop."

"Time to work on your neck."

She made a distressed moue. "I feel bad that I'm not doing something for you."

"Sit up."

He moved to the other end of the couch. "Bend your head over."

The foot massage had been unalloyed ecstasy. This hurt. As he worked his fingers deeper and deeper into the knots, she could feel the tension release, the pressure on her vertebrae ease. When he stopped, she leaned back against his chest.

He wrapped his arms around her and rested his chin on the top of her head.

Now that he'd relaxed her, petted her, stroked her, would he demand that she reciprocate?

Peter always had. No matter how long and hard she'd ridden or how stiff and bruised she was, his gentle touch was always followed by a demand for her to get his rocks off. He didn't much care about hers.

She waited for Tim's hand to cup her breast, his fingers to move to her belly and below.

Minutes passed. Her eyelids began to droop. Still he didn't move.

Finally he put his hand on her arm. "Come on, sleepyhead. Let's get you into bed."

She came awake instantly. He hauled her to her feet and guided her into her bedroom. He pulled back the quilt and pushed her gently onto the bed, then reached down, picked up her feet and swung her around.

He lifted the quilt to her chin and bent to kiss her.

She wrapped her arms around his neck and started to pull him down to her.

"Oh, no, you don't."

"But…" He *didn't* want her. She forgot whatever she'd said about demanding men. She wanted him to stay, to ravish her.

He sat on the bed. "Go to sleep. You're worn-out, and I'm not about to lose all that time I spent getting you to relax."

"But…"

He took her hand. "Of course I want to make love to you. But tonight isn't right for you. There'll be plenty of other nights. For tonight it's enough just to hold you." He lay down beside her. She cuddled into his arms.

Suddenly she began to chuckle.

"What?"

"The euphemism for 'I want to boff your brains out' in the South is 'Honey, I just want to hold you a little.'"

"I do want to boff your brains out, as a matter of fact," he said to the top of her head. "But I'd prefer that you were at least semi-conscious when I do it."

"I am semiconscious."

"Okay. So I really prefer my women totally conscious."

"Picky, picky, picky."

He kissed her forehead. "I still have dibs on a romantic dinner. Tomorrow night?"

"Uh-huh." She took his hand and tucked it under her chin.

He must have gone home at some point because he wasn't there at six-thirty in the morning when Poddy and Otto landed in the middle of her chest and woke her up from the best, the deepest, the most contented sleep she'd had in years

What a man. No wonder she was falling in love with him.

CHAPTER TWENTY-NINE

THE HEAVY BEAT of Zulu drums rocked out of the CD player in the corner of the lacrosse locker room. David's fifteen players were the elite of Maybree Academy and knew it. David hadn't had to create the myth or the fellowship. The former coach, the man who had coached him and his team to three consecutive tournament victories, the man who had died of a massive heart attack a year before, had done it for him.

All David had to do was add his own touches. He stuck out his hand and snapped his fingers. Jason Wainwright jumped to bring him a bottle of ice water from the cooler.

Strict hierarchy. No hazing. None of that paddling nonsense. No towel snapping in the shower. The freshmen who were serving their first year on the team knew they were in charge of fetching and carrying. If a starting defenseman needed a new stick, a freshman would tear back into the locker room to bring it to him.

A senior starter never carried his own gear. Never. If David was a god, the starters were demigods.

The team had a separate locker room from the rest of the grunts who attempted to play competitive basketball or baseball. Separate and anything but equal. The lacrosse team got all the new equipment, new paint, new lockers.

In the east, lacrosse was already big. Down here in the south, it was growing faster than any other sport among the small schools and private academies, perhaps because it rewarded speed and strategy instead of sheer size.

Maybree didn't even have a football team. Lacrosse was their only claim to fame in athletics.

Jason would make a great defenseman once he got his ball-handling skills down. Add the length of a defenseman's stick to those gorilla arms of his and he'd be able to pick the ball off an offenseman's stick halfway across the middle.

And he was big enough to bash heads and bodies and sticks with anybody—just in case speed and stategy needed a boost. He didn't back off, either, the way some of them did at the beginning. He loved the contact. As a matter of fact, David had to tone down his aggressiveness. He wasn't skilled enough not to hurt somebody when he bashed them.

David surveyed his kingdom and stood. "Okay, let's do it."

By the rules of the lacrosse organization, teams couldn't hold official practices or games until February. Nobody said anything about optional practices, however. They took place year-round, and were anything but optional if you expected to play for Maybree.

His guys ran out on the field. The seniors wore less protection than the freshman. The better a man was, the less padding he was willing to wear.

In exchange for greater speed and mobility, an expert player preferred to wear his bruises and scrapes and even the occasional broken bone as badges of honor.

A freshman brought out the portable CD player. David popped in a Native American war chant from Canada's Northwest Territories. His men, his worshippers, lined up in front of him. At a hand signal, they began their warm-up routine.

Every school team created its own warm-up routine. Each was as perfectly choreographed as a ballet and performed to the team's special music. David had built their warm-up from scratch when he took over in June.

At a game, the two teams would face off and attempt to intimidate each other. David had spent a month in New Zealand when he was twelve and had never forgotten the Maori greeting ceremony with its stamping and brandishing of spears. He'd even liked the popping eyes and the tongues sticking out. If he'd been some puny English homesteader in the nineteenth century, he'd have been terrified to meet a bunch of those guys, even if they did carry wooden clubs instead of rifles.

So his guys did a variation of a Maori war dance. Nobody laughed. Nobody thought it was comic or over the top. It was dead serious and for a serious purpose.

Today they were working on shooting drills. That meant even the defensemen were using short sticks.

After fifteen minutes nonstop practice—the length of a quarter in a game—David called them in.

"Assume the position," he snapped.

To fraternities, that might mean bend over and get your butt beat by paddles. To David and his Rams, it meant lie flat on the ground, feet facing toward the center, in a circle around him.

He began to speak, quietly at first. He'd first heard the speech from his own coach. Now he could string it out to forty-five minutes before tournament play, but usually he only spoke a couple of sentences.

He'd embellished it to suit himself and rewrote it depending on what he wanted to convey. This wasn't an actual game, or even an official practice. This was a bonding session. Bonding them to one another and to him. Setting them up for the other rituals he planned. The final ritual at Halloween that would bond them to him totally.

"We are the Spartans," he said. "Three hundred men held off the entire Persian army at Thermopylae. They were heroes whose deeds define heroism. We are the brave. We are the powerful. We are the dynasty of triumph. This year we must continue that dynasty against bigger men, faster men, but never smarter men. Never more skilled men. A Spartan mother would tell her son as he went off to war, 'My son, return with your shield or on it. Victorious or dead.'"

His voice resonated over their supine bodies.

"And guys," he added in his ordinary voice, "if you don't learn to shoot better than that, I promise you'll *be* on your damn shields. If your opponents don't murder you, I *will*."

When they opened their eyes, he stood in the center with his hands on his hips grinning at them.

They rolled to their feet. Daryl, six feet four and two hundred and sixty pounds at seventeen, grabbed David around his knees, lifted him high and ran around the field with him. The others ran after him, punching their sticks in the air and chanting.

When at last Daryl put him down by the water cooler, David gave each of them a high-five. He smiled. *A little touch of Harry in the night, as Shakespeare would say. One small token of love from the lord to the serf.*

God, they loved him.

After three more fifteen-minute sessions, they straggled to the sidelines, dropped their sticks, yanked off their jerseys and poured sports drinks down their parched throats.

"Hey, Coach," Daryl said. "We going riding in the bottoms on Sunday?"

"Sure. Rain or shine. Meet at the cabin with your ATVs at 10:00 a.m."

"Aw, coach, 10:00 a.m.?" said Scott, a sophomore middle. "It's Sunday."

"Yeah, which is why I didn't say 5:00 a.m." David walked into the stands and left them to shower. Always good to leave by going up out of view, away from them rather than with them. A little distance, a little awe. He'd learned that from his coach. He'd been a damned fine strategist who knew how to make them willing to die for him on the field if that's what it took to win.

Winning the tournament championship this year was simply a test of David's power. The first of many he'd set for himself. They could do it.

They'd have to do it. He didn't ever plan to fail.

As they were leaving the locker room, Daryl fell into step beside Jason. "You coming Sunday?"

"I don't have an ATV. Even if I had a flatbed to trailer it, I don't have my driver's license yet, remember?"

"Hey, you can ride with me. What say I pick you up about nine?"

"Where are we going? What are we doing?"

Daryl guffawed. "Sheee-ut. I keep forgetting you're a newbie. Hey, Scott, Jason here wants to know about Sunday."

Scott ran his hand through his damp hair. "David's dad owns a couple thousand acres up along the Tennessee River he uses for a hunting preserve. Deer and stuff. We're going up there to ride ATVs in the bottoms. It's a giggle, you know, man?"

"Oh. How far away?"

"About an hour, I guess. An hour to David's, Ken?"

Ken swaggered by with his lacrosse bag slung over his shoulder. "I guess."

"Is everybody invited? The whole team?"

"The ones with ATVs. Duh," said Ken.

"Oh."

"Hey, you got that land. Get your dad to buy you one. Tell him you need it to check out the farm." Ken snorted and rolled his eyes. "E-I-E-I-O."

"How often do you go?"

"Whenever David invites us. Duh."

"Shut up, man, stop being a butthead." Daryl meandered along with the others toward the shiny SUVs and convertibles in the parking lot. "Maybe once a month. It's better in the fall."

"We ride all over, you know?" Ken said. "How about we come visit *you* next weekend?"

"Yeah. Hey, man, great idea," Daryl said. "Toss the kayaks on top of the Land Rover. We can swim and kayak and check out your farm."

"I don't know. I'd have to ask my dad."

Ken rolled his eyes. "He'd have to ask dear old Daddy the

teacher," he said in a high-pitched whine. "Please, Daddy, can my friends come over and drive everybody nuts with their ATVs?"

"Knock it off," Daryl said and shoved Ken, who whirled around with his fists up.

"You do that, David'll kick your sorry butts off the team," Scott growled. "Come on, Ken. Go home and whip up on your little brother."

Ken grumbled, but went.

Daryl gave him the finger, but only after his back was turned.

Jason followed Daryl to his Tahoe, and tossed his stuff in the back with the boxes of CDs, books, athletic gear and the leftovers of half a dozen fast food meals.

"Sorry," he said as he fastened his seat belt.

"You did right. Remember what David says. Always fly beneath the radar. Ask your old man. If he says no, we ride someplace else. No biggie."

He reached over and ran his big hand over the inch long dark stubble that covered Jason's head. "Man, your hair still sucks, you know?" His own hair was slightly longer than his collar, expensively cut and fell at a carefully casual angle across his forehead. The whole team wore their hair that way, even Calder, whose hair was so thick and curly it stuck straight up if he waited an extra week to have it cut.

Jason had been willing his hair to grow out faster. What had possessed him to shave his head in Chicago? Or to wear those goofy big clothes? God, the idea of letting his underwear show now made him physically sick.

Daryl reached over and turned up the collar of Jason's polo shirt. "I keep telling you, man, we all wear our collars up. Don't be a dork."

Jason was flattered that Daryl, a junior, had taken him under his wing. Daryl was a good guy and a talented player. He was also a stud, and swore he could drink the entire Ole Miss football team under the table after enough Wild Turkey.

Jason wished he enjoyed the taste of Wild Turkey or any other alcohol. He didn't mind a couple of those fortified fruit things, but he'd never admit that to Daryl. Those were girlie drinks. Men drank bourbon.

He could hardly wait for his birthday in November so he could get his learner's permit. Six months later, he'd be able to call himself the designated driver. Then he'd have an excuse not to drink.

Jason would tell them he was patterning himself after David.

Then they really would think he was a dork. And a kiss-up.

Maybe he was. He'd never known anyone like David. He made you feel like it was a privilege to run get him a bottle of water. He made you feel like a man, not some kid who couldn't be trusted to be out on his own after dark.

Jason brought his short lacrosse stick home. It was the one he already felt pretty comfortable with. He could get in at least an hour's practice before his dad made him come in for dinner.

David had made him promise to force Eddy and Angie to help him clean up the kitchen so that his dad didn't have to.

He'd even started hanging up his clothes and making his bed in the morning. David said neatness of one's surroundings reflected neatness and efficiency of one's mind.

David said eating saturated fat slowed you down on the field. Jason was eating a bunch more salads.

David said the only way to get into a good eastern college and keep playing after graduation was to make straight A's and ace the ACTs and SATs.

So far grades were a snap. David required all his players to get good grades, never get in trouble. Be respectful. Not smoke. No drugs. Definitely no steroids.

David called that flying under the radar.

"Follow their rules, my man. Pretty soon they'll start to trust you. Then you can do whatever you want when they're not watching."

David was right. But then he always was.

CHAPTER THIRTY

"YOU LOOK WONDERFUL," Tim said the following evening when he met Nancy at her front door.

"I decided I could really use a couple of new pairs of nonrunny panty hose," Nancy said. "I seldom wear an actual dress. Be surprised. Be very surprised." She turned with her arms out so he could admire the black dress.

He pulled her into his arms and kissed her. "You smell good, too."

"No essence of operating theater?"

"Nope. More like Woman Number One."

He slid his hands down her bare arms. "You're taller."

"Heels. I'll probably fall off them and break my ankle. Then you'll have to carry me home."

"My pleasure."

"Want to bet?"

As they drove away, she asked, "Jason babysitting?"

"He and some of the guys from the team. I'm surprised you can't hear them from across the street. They brought over a lacrosse goal, and they're outside practicing. We've got lights out there now."

"And they study when?"

"In study halls, according to Jason. These guys are smart. Straight A's from me and every other teacher, including Mrs. Martini, the Latin teacher. She's no pushover. Ninety-nine and nine-tenths of Maybree graduates go to college. Seventy-five per cent of them go to *top* colleges—mostly Ivy League. They have a leg up. Not only are they smart, but their parents can pay full tuition."

"Spoiled rich kids?"

He pulled onto the highway and headed south. "I don't know enough to say for certain yet, but most of them seem to be pretty good. A little lazy, a little blasé. I've already identified a few I'm sure are stoners and burgeoning alcoholics. We'll see how the rest of the year goes."

"Animals behave true to type. They're easier to deal with than human beings."

He pulled onto the interstate and headed south toward the Mississippi line. "Is that why you avoid people?"

"I do not."

"Yeah, you do."

"I'm not avoiding you." She glanced up. "Where on earth are we going?"

"You'll know when we get there, and yes, you are avoiding me. The banter is fine, but you use it to keep everybody at arm's length. Anybody gets too close, you make a joke."

"I'm a funny girl. Everybody says so."

"Everybody's right. Doesn't alter the fact that you use humor as a shield."

Nancy was beginning to wish she'd never come on this date. They seemed to be headed for New Orleans, and she was getting both hungry and annoyed. Did she do that? "So, I'm supposed to take everything seriously?"

He didn't say anything. They pulled off the interstate onto a country road. Soon they were running alongside white board fences that looked newly painted. Then he turned into a long driveway between a pair of stone pillars. The drive wound through old trees and across a hump-backed bridge over a stream. They followed the stream to a lake.

"Look, swans!" Nancy said. "Where are we?"

"Where we're going." He pulled under a columned portico

and turned off the engine. A white jacketed attendant opened Nancy's door and helped her out.

"Good evening, sir, madam. Welcome to L'Auberge Rouge."

"You're taking me to the Auberge Rouge? It's a four-star restaurant."

"I promised you white tablecloths and good wine."

The place was relatively new, but looked as though it might have survived Grant's retreat from Shiloh. High ceilings, broad center hall leading to a broad double staircase. Antique furnishings, Chinoiserie wallpaper, candles in tall silver candelabra.

The dining room held fifteen tables, which overlooked a wall of windows facing the lake. There were only three other couples having dinner.

"You do know how to impress a lady," she said as the maître d' seated her.

"It's a weeknight. I'd never have been able to get a reservation for dinner or a room on the weekend."

She froze. "Room?"

"L'Auberge Rouge is a B and B. If we split a bottle of wine and have a couple of brandies, neither one of us will be fit to drive back to Marquette County until we're sober."

"But your children…"

"I told Jason we'd be late."

"You ambushed me."

He reached across the table and took her hand. "I didn't have a choice."

She gulped. "But…"

"Do you want to make love tonight? Here? Right out. Say the words."

She opened her mouth to protest again, then shut it. A moment later she said, "Yes. See? I can be serious."

THEY TOOK THEIR TIME over dinner, but skipped dessert. Then they walked up the grand staircase arm in arm. Nancy felt as though her skin was on fire. Her heart had given up the samba and was now doing a fast jitterbug.

"A canopied bed," Nancy said when Tim opened the door. "I've never actually slept in one before." She walked into the bathroom. "Wow. Are all the rooms like this?"

"Apparently. I couldn't afford the bridal suite."

"You couldn't afford this, either, probably."

"I couldn't *not* afford this." He held out his arms. "Come here."

This time they undressed each other slowly. Tim inched Nancy's zipper down until her dress was open and slid off her shoulders.

She undid his belt with the same care.

At last they stood naked, not quite touching, almost afraid to break the spell.

When his hands slid down her shoulders, she shivered. "You make every molecule in my body stand up. You make my bones melt. Like somebody hit me with a stun gun."

"You say the nicest things." He slipped his arm under her knees, picked her up and swung her onto the bed.

They savored the touch and smell and taste of each other's bodies. Finally Nancy ran her tongue down his chest, across the soft dark curls around his nipples, then lower until she took him in her mouth. He caught his breath and wrapped his fingers in her hair.

She teased and tormented him with her tongue and her fingers, pulsing her tongue against the most sensitive point of his penis. He tried to move her up his body, but she shook her head without breaking contact.

He began to make the sounds he'd made when he saw the snake. She loved the feel of him against her lips, the way the ridge of muscle ran along the tops of his hips and guided her down. Her own body ached for him, but she exulted in her power to pleasure him.

She moved faster. He bucked against her. She knew he was close. She wasn't about to stop now.

When he came he dug his fingers into her shoulders hard and cried her name.

As he relaxed she felt his belly heave as he tried to breathe. After a few seconds he drew her up his body so that she curled once more against his chest. He kissed her hair and held her so hard she could barely breathe.

"No wonder the French call it the little death," he whispered.

"Don't die on me," she whispered back. "I couldn't pay the bill."

He chuckled. "It's already paid. No more jokes."

"It's a habit."

"You don't need to be funny with me. Promise. Talk to me straight. At least for tonight."

"You know, there's a great big whirlpool bath in yonder."

"At the moment, I would probably drown."

"So would I." She turned so that she was spooned against him. She felt certain he had fallen asleep.

She was wide awake. She had all but ravished him and loved every moment of it.

He kissed the nape of her neck, then moved to her ear.

She giggled. "That tickles." She turned in his arms.

"What's a four-star meal without dessert?" he whispered.

"What, indeed?"

"I thoroughly enjoyed mine. Now, madam it's your turn." His lips moved to her breast.

She caught her breath.

He whispered against her belly, "Next time, remind me to bring the whipped cream." His lips moved lower.

She abandoned rational thought in favor of pure sensation, peaking time after time until the final explosion left her spent. He held her until she no longer shuddered, then he pulled the duvet over them.

Tim needed to get home. They couldn't hide forever in this sanctuary where cell phones didn't ring, children and animals didn't make demands.

Where the real world stayed outside with the swans.

CHAPTER THIRTY-ONE

"YOU REALIZE this was a one-shot deal," she said as they walked up her front steps. She'd slept all the way home and was wide-awake now. Reality was biting bigtime. "If nothing else, you can't afford it."

"You're right. I can't."

"I can't, either." She opened her door and went in. "Where's Lancelot?"

"Helen and Bill bedded him down in the barn for the night so you wouldn't have to deal with him when we got home."

"Thank God." She didn't bother to turn the light on in the living room. "What's the alternative? We sneak off to a sleazy motel for a thirty-minute nooner?"

"No, we don't." He took her in his arms.

"Then how do we manage?" She broke away from him. "We're not teenagers. Neither of us is married. We're consenting adults. We shouldn't have to hide in the back of my Durango or pitch a blanket in the woods."

He ran his hands around her waist and pulled her back against him. "Not that either of those venues wouldn't be kind of fun."

She twisted away to face him. "You wanted serious. So here goes. Tonight was so wonderful, but it's no good. Maybe if I didn't live across the street from your family, we could figure out some way to manage without proclaiming what we were doing, but I do."

"You think Jason doesn't know what we we're doing until two in the morning?"

"He'll probably be too embarrassed to tell his friends," Nancy said. "Children are always horrified to think about their parents and sex. And it didn't happen under his nose. What do you think the odds are you could sneak across the street in the middle of the night more than once, make hasty love, pick up your pants and sneak back without one of them spotting you?"

"Thereby blowing your reputation straight to hell."

"*My* reputation? My friends would probably give you a trophy. You're the high school teacher, pillar of the community, first in line for the vice principalship of Maybree."

"And an unmarried, consenting adult."

"From what you've told me about Dr. Aycock, he'd probably be horrified just the same."

"Then marry me."

"What?"

He sat on the sofa and pulled her into his lap. "Marry me. It's the perfect solution."

She held herself stiffly away from him. "You are out of your mind."

He stroked her back. "Married people sleep together, same bed, same bedroom. They make love when and how they choose. If they want to check into a motel, sleazy or not, for a night of wild abandon, they find a babysitter and go."

"You're serious, aren't you? You'd actually propose marriage to a relative stranger just to get into my bed? Correction. To get me into yours."

"You're not a relative stranger."

"Then no." This time she made it to her feet and out of his reach.

He followed her, took her by the shoulders. "I mean it, Nancy. I've known since that first moment I held you in my arms that you were the woman for me. For us."

She closed her eyes and leaned back against him. "And I've known since that first moment that you make my knees turn to water and my gut turn to lava, but that has nothing to do with marriage. You don't marry for lust."

"That's all you feel? Lust?"

She shoved away from him with both hands and went to the far side of the room by the fireplace. "No, don't come over here. I can't think when you're close. Maybe what I feel is more than lust. I don't have much frame of reference. I warned you I'll never be a stepmother again. Didn't you listen? Didn't you believe me?"

"The kids adore you."

"They do not. They like me well enough as a neighbor. Angie likes me all right as a coach so long as I'm not too hard on her. Don't you see that the instant I become a fiancée or a wife, I become an authority figure with no authority? A woman trying to take their mother's place?"

"What do you think a coach is if not an authority figure?"

"When Angie is on a horse, she respects me fairly well, although she still fights. I have some leverage. I can tell her if she doesn't shut up and do what I tell her, she can get off her horse and not get back on again. What happens the first time I tell her she can't ride because she hasn't finished her homework? Or tell Jason he can't go joyriding with his buddies because he hasn't taken out the garbage? I can hear it now, 'You're not the boss of me.'" She dropped into the chair. "If I had a nickel for every time I heard those words from my ex-stepdaughter." She raised her face, and he saw silver trails of tears in the moonlight. "They're right. I can't be their boss. Even Eddy wouldn't accept me. He wants his grandmother."

"Helen gives them orders."

"She's an employee. Her commands are your commands and enforced by you."

"It would be the same for you if you marry me."

"No!" She sat on the club chair and drummed her fists on her knees. "Things that drive me crazy wouldn't bother you. Stupid stuff I wouldn't mind would be important to you. I already don't agree with you."

"About what, exactly?" He heard the anger and frustration in his voice. He sank onto the sofa. This wasn't the way he'd envisioned this night. He'd offered a gift. He didn't expect her to throw it back in his face.

"Angie's jumping, for instance."

"We're back to that. It's *my* choice, dammit. She's my daughter. *I* make the rules." He groaned and rubbed his face. "Oh, God."

"See?" It was a whisper. "And what about Eddy?"

"What about him?"

"Do you even know *why* he hides in his closet with JustPup and cries every time his grandmother calls him from Chicago?"

"He misses his mother."

She pointed at him. "Helen finally got him to talk. It's not that he's grieving for his mother, Tim."

"Of course—he's grieving for both his grandmother and his mother. I know that."

She shook her head. "He's miserable because he can't *remember* his mother at all. He sits on the floor of his closet with her picture and tries to remember her and cries because he can't. He thinks that makes him an awful person. He doesn't want you and the others to know."

Tim leaned back against the couch and ran his hands over his hair. "He was only four when she died. It's not surprising that he doesn't remember much. Poor little guy. I'll talk to him."

"Don't you dare! He'd never trust Helen again."

"All right. That's two down. What other decisions do you disagree with?" *Bring it on, lady.*

"You're entirely too lax with Jason. Half the time you don't know where he is, or what he's doing with those boys."

"Of course I know. He's at lacrosse practice or with the team. David Grantham's always there to look out for them all."

She shrugged. "Oh, David Grantham. Jason's idol."

"How'd we get started on him anyway? We were talking about marriage, remember?"

"We were talking about *stepparenting*. So far we have disagreed about everything. If I were to marry you, who'd override who?"

"We'd sit down and work it out. Present a united front."

"You mean I'd agree with your judgment and back you up, no matter how stupid I thought you were."

"Now I'm stupid?"

"I'm not saying I'm right and you're wrong…"

"Sure sounds that way to me."

"I'm not. You adore your children, and they know it. But I don't."

"Don't what?"

"Adore your children. I like Eddy, and I think Angie has real talent and Jason is a good-looking kid who's shaping up better than I thought at first, but they are not *mine*. You'd worry about where Jason was when he didn't come home on time, or when Eddy was bullied at school or Angie ignored you and jumped a five bar gate. When they screw up and do something truly dumb, you remember what they were like when they were cooing at you from their cribs. You can dial up your memories to get you over the times when you'd like to hang them up by their thumbs."

"I suppose that's true. Parents do tend to have total recall."

"I never heard a single coo from one of them. I can only see the people they are now. When I discovered Peter, my husband, had a stepdaughter just a few years younger than I was, I figured we could be buds." She walked to the kitchen counter and pulled out a stool. "Wrong. Peter felt guilty about walking out on Poppy's mother, so he gave her anything she wanted. When she came to visit us when we were living in the horse trailer, Peter would send me over to sleep in the other trailer with the grooms."

"And you went? I can't believe that."

"I went. He said it was too crowded with Poppy, but he never considered sending *her* away." Nancy shrugged. "As for being buds, she hated me from the get-go and did everything she could to cause trouble. If she gave in the slightest bit, she figured she was being disloyal to her mother." She picked Otto up off the

counter and cuddled him under her chin. "In case you're wondering, Peter had been divorced for years when he married me.
I did not break up Poppy's happy home."

"You have one bad experience with a spoiled brat and an
abusive husband," Tim said.

"Mac says that if at first you don't succeed, quit and try something you're good at. I'm good at what I do now. The problems
with Poppy weren't all her fault. I was the star rider, remember.
With everybody but Peter I expected to be treated like a star. I
was the one who got to have the tantrums when my horse's mane
wasn't braided on time. When she was around, I resented the attention he paid to her and all the gifts and affection he lavished
on her. We had some rip-snorting rows about her."

She shrugged. "Let's face it. Poppy and I were too close to
the same age to be anything but competitors for Daddy's love.
She always won."

"You shouldn't have had to compete with her."

"Should, schmould. I'm telling you we both behaved badly,
but I learned my lesson. I've got enough in my life. I come home
to get away from worry and pain, not to walk into more."

"Sooner or later you're going to marry me."

"So we can live happily ever after?"

"Nobody lives happily ever after. But whatever we face, we'll
face it together with love and respect. Whatever happens, that
love won't change."

"You can't guarantee that."

"People don't change. They intensify. The things I love about
you will get stronger."

"The things that drive you crazy will intensify, too."

"So you'll make more jokes?"

"Now who's not being serious?"

CHAPTER THIRTY-TWO

FOR THE NEXT two weeks, Tim spent his evenings grading papers and doing lesson plans while Nancy trained Angie and the other riders at the common until dark.

Haley and Meghan had become Angie's best friends. Seeing them jump made Angie even more anxious to begin jumping small fences herself, but Haley and Meghan both backed Nancy up when she said Angie wasn't ready to take Cloud over even small fences.

"I didn't jump for ages and ages," Haley said. "Mom and Dad didn't let me hunt in the first field with the adults who jump until last season, and *I've* been riding since I got my first pony when I was seven." At thirteen, Haley was already as tall as Nancy, with long straight pale hair, blue eyes and a willowy body that seemed part of her horse when she rode.

"And I'm *still* riding in second field where nobody jumps," Meghan said. "But then I didn't start riding until I was nearly nine." Meghan was a little chunky. The same age as Haley, she had unruly dark hair and brown eyes, and her short legs barely reached below her saddle skirt. She didn't have nearly Haley's grace, but she had a dogged determination to stay on her horse at all costs that made her a formidable rider.

If Nancy was right, Angie would combine the good points of both girls, but whereas Haley was Nordic pale, Angie's beauty would be smoky and Gallic like her mother's.

Tim had finally agreed after much cajolery and pleading to let the three girls go trail riding together on Sunday afternoons.

"There's a great path around the lake," Haley said. "And Henry and Herb have cut some fresh trails back into Nancy's woods. We can't get lost. We've all got our cell phones."

"I won't fall off Cloud," Angie pleaded. "We won't even trot, we'll just walk."

The first time they went, Tim watched the three ride out of sight up the hill and down the gravel road that backed Nancy's property.

He sat on his front porch and graded papers until they came back two hours later from the path around the lake he hadn't even known existed.

For Tim and Nancy, getting together even for a meal was difficult. Getting together for anything else was impossible.

Angie conscientiously took care of feeding, mucking and turning Cloud out every morning. Nancy never had to remind her. But she also never knew precisely when Angie would show up in her backyard and in the stable.

Phil and Phineas were now able to work Herb and Henry longer each day since temperatures had dropped from the high nineties to the high eighties.

"Making good progress, Nancy," Phil said as they turned the big horses out in the pasture for the evening. "Got us a bunch of big hardwoods cut way on back in the woods, nearly to the hind end of your property."

"I haven't seen your log truck," Nancy said. "You planning to leave them back there until they rot?"

Phil laughed. Even Phineas cracked a smile. "Seasoning, sugar. We call it seasoning. No, ma'am, we are not. We done took two loads to the mill already."

"When I wasn't here? How'd you get them through my yard without leaving tracks?"

"We didn't take 'em through your yard. Phineas and me, we cleared out a path in from that old gravel road used to go back to the Hawkins place. Since old Miz Hawkins went to the nursing home, don't nobody live down there no more. Road's pretty rough, but once it's dry, we can get the truck and trailer down there, turn around in her yard, point her on back this a'way, and old Henry and Herb drag them logs straight to the road and load 'em."

Nancy wiggled her eyebrows. "So, Phil, how much money have we made?"

"Not enough." He grinned. "You need a little bit on the front end?"

"Nope. We'll settle up at the end the way we said. Won't you even give me a hint?"

He leaned over and whispered in her ear, "We done paid for those fancy kitchen cabinets of yours, I bet."

"Already?"

"Uh-huh. Few more logs big as the ones we done cut already and left lying on the ground back yonder, and you'll have a nice little nest egg."

"How long will it take?"

"Shoot. Long as it takes, I reckon."

"I'll miss Henry and Herb when you move to another job. I love seeing them out my bedroom window when I get up in the morning. Cloud's going to miss them, too."

"Don't plan on missing 'em yet a while. Come on, boys, let's go get you some oats."

"IT'S THE PERFECT place for the Halloween party," Angie said to her brother. She was sitting on the back steps watching him practice goals with his short lacrosse stick. "Nobody'd even know you were back there."

"Like they wouldn't hear the music or see the lights."

Angie rolled her eyes. "At night in their houses with the TV blaring and the curtains closed? As if."

"I keep telling you, it's not a party. That's later," Jason said. He wiped the sweat off his face with the bottom of his T-shirt. "The guys are coming over with the ATVs Saturday afternoon. We'll check it out."

"Haley and Meghan and I want to come to the party. We, like, found the place, you know?"

Jason glared at her. "It is a *ritual*."

"There's a party afterward at Daryl's." She nodded and sniffed. "Think the whole school doesn't know?"

"Like I'll bring my thirteen-year-old ugly *sister* to a Halloween party with the team? Dad wouldn't let you anyway. By the time we get to the party, it'll be way past your bedtime."

"I am *so* not ugly. David says I'm already a beauty."

Jason snorted. "David? Try calling him David to his face, why don't you? All you brats hanging on his every word." He whined, "Yes, Mr. Grantham, no, Mr. Grantham, can we get our noses a little browner please, Mr. Grantham?"

Angie stood up with her hands on her hips. A second later she dived at Jason from the steps, hit him squarely in the chest, knocked him flat and began to pummel him.

"Hey!" He grabbed her arms and shoved her off. "Cut it out."

"I hate you!"

"The feeling's mutual."

"Jason, Angie, stop it!" Tim's voice came from the back door.

Angie rolled away and wiped her eyes.

Jason sat up and rubbed his chest. "If she's broken a rib, I'll kill her."

"He called me an ugly little brat," Angie growled and hit her brother on his shoulder with her fist.

"Ow!" Jason grabbed her and tossed her away.

"Jason, apologize to your sister. Angie, apologize to your brother. Behave yourselves or I'll lock you in your rooms until you're forty-two. Get cleaned up. Dinner's on the table."

"IT's PERFECT, Mr. Grantham," Daryl said the following Monday. He and Scott and Jason and several others were gathered around David in the locker room in their street clothes. "The path into the woods is plenty wide for the ATVs. We carry the booze down there ahead of time, circle the headlamps after it gets dark and do whatever we want. We can build a bonfire right in the middle. The trees are too far away to catch even if it's dry."

"Angie found it?"

"Yeah, riding with Haley and Meghan. Only thing, they want to come to the party afterward." Daryl held up his hands. "I know, you said no girls under sixteen, but they know where we'll be holding the ritual back in the woods. They could tell. And there'll be freshmen guys at the party. More guys than girls. Not like everybody's bringing a date."

"I'll talk to the girls," David said. "They'll keep their mouths shut."

The entire high school and most of the middle school knew at least something about the team ritual and the party after. They wouldn't talk. Not if they expected to be invited to future Halloween parties. Another reason to make the lacrosse team. David Grantham's famous Halloween party.

The past four years he'd held it at his parents' house in Germantown, but this year his father had refused. "What do you think my liability is if one of these thugs winds up dead or paralyzed?" his father had fumed. "They're drinking on my property. I could be arrested. So could you."

"Surely the famous Dr. Grantham can cure a minor ailment like complete paralysis," David said. "Why, all these years, I've thought you could bring the dead back to life."

Lately he hadn't bothered to be perfect around his parents. He didn't know when or how he'd slipped, but they had begun to look at him warily, almost fearfully.

Who cared? When he didn't need them any longer, he'd dispense with them. At the moment, they were still useful.

This year Daryl's father agreed to let Daryl have the party in *his* pool house. After all, David would there to chaperone. What could happen?

David had originally wanted to hold the team ritual at his

father's hunting preserve, but it was an hour's drive away and he didn't want anybody busted for DUI or getting themselves run over by a train on the way home. Too much publicity. Besides, drive time cut into party time at Daryl's. The girls would have curfew even if the boys didn't. After the ritual, the boys would deserve to cut loose at Daryl's.

Assuming any of them still felt like partying.

At his parents' place last year, the team had been forced to hide the beer behind the pool house. Daryl and the others brought their own hard stuff. This year, they could be more open about the booze.

Last year David began to create his Halloween ritual to bond the team to him. He'd added some demonic mumbo-jumbo and bizarre music to the usual hanging skeletons and cobwebs. This year the team members were expecting something far out. Something to scare the pants off them. Actually they were more interested in scaring the pants off their dates, but that wasn't till later.

Until it was too late to take any of it back.

This year's ritual would be under the stars and the moon. The moon would be full on Halloween, and the weather report said it would be about sixty-five and dry. Perfect.

Even more perfect, his chosen sacrifice would be delivered to him just like a pizza.

CHAPTER THIRTY-THREE

"MISS HELEN fixed us a great big roast," Eddy said. "Jason and Angie invited Mr. Grantham. And Miss Helen's staying for dinner cause Mr. Bill's going to a meeting. Daddy said to tell you it's safe to come over. What did he mean? Is our house dangerous?"

Nancy had finally agreed to have dinner with Tim and his children. He had sent Eddy and JustPup across the street to escort her. Make sure she didn't chicken out, more likely.

It was an early October Indian Summer, so she didn't even grab her jacket. Temperatures at night went down into the fifties, but so far there'd only been a week with daytime temps under seventy. Most days the mercury hovered around eighty-five.

As they crossed the street, a black Hummer pulled to the curb in front of Tim's house. So Grantham owned the car that had brought Jason home after curfew and half smashed. This was Tim's good role model for his son?

The instant he saw them, he flashed a smile.

And JustPup exploded.

Nancy gaped at the little dog. She'd never heard him utter more than a whimper when his burns were first treated. Suddenly he was barking so hard his front feet came off the ground. These weren't puppy yips. They were real barks. He started toward Grantham with his teeth bared for all the world like an attack dog instead of a half-grown puppy.

Nancy bent and scooped him into her arms. He wriggled and

snarled and snapped. Not at her, but in Grantham's direction. Eddy stared up at him in amazement.

"JustPup?" he whispered. "Nancy, what's the matter with him?"

"Eddy, go in the house and get his leash," Nancy said. She was afraid he'd bite her in sheer fury without knowing where his teeth were landing.

"Whoa," said Grantham. "Mean little guy, wouldn't you say?"

"No, I wouldn't."

Eddy came running back and handed Nancy the leash, which she immediately clipped onto JustPup's collar. "Hush," she said and gently set the little dog down.

He strained at the leash. His barking had turned to open-mouthed snarling.

"Sure doesn't like *me*." Grantham hunkered down and offered his hand a safe distance from those snapping teeth. "Hi, little guy. How come you don't like David, huh?"

"What's going on?" Tim asked. He'd come out onto the front porch and now trotted down the steps. "Hi, David. Eddy, what's the matter with your dog?"

"I don't know, Daddy," Eddy said. "He never barks, does he, Nancy?"

"Tell you what, Eddy. How about we take JustPup to my house. He can keep Lancelot and the cats company while we eat dinner."

"But…"

"Come on." She didn't wait, but trotted back across the street and into her house pulling the barking JustPup with her. The minute her front door shut behind the dog, the boy and her, JustPup became his old self. He flopped on his little fat rump, and licked at Eddy's face when Eddy dropped to his knees and cradled the little dog in his arms.

"He's shaking," Eddy said. "He's scared."

"He's mad as a hornet," Nancy corrected him. "Maybe it's Grantham's aftershave."

"Maybe."

Lancelot and the two cats had already joined them. Eddy petted each in turn, but kept one hand on the dog's head.

"JustPup, you stay here and keep Lancelot company, okay? Eddy, I think we'd better put both of them on the back porch so they don't destroy the house. Grab the water bowl and Lancelot's bed."

When they left five minutes later, JustPup tried desperately to beat Nancy out the door from the back porch to the kitchen, but she got past him and shut the pet gate firmly behind her.

He began to whine piteously.

"I can't leave him," Eddy said.

"Just for an hour or so. Your father's waiting dinner. He'll be all right."

As they walked across the street, they could still hear JustPup's faint wails.

DAVID EXERTED his charm over dinner. Helen what's-her-face, that cook housekeeper person, fell all over herself adoring him. So did Angie.

He was sitting between Angie and Nancy, the woman who'd saved him from the dog.

Angie wore an open-necked lacy shirt, one of those flimsy things that tied over a T-shirt. All the girls wore them after school with those rock star jeans that stopped just north of their pubic hair. Angie Wainwright had possibilities.

The kid was crazy about him. Probably would have stabbed her father with her steak knife if David had suggested it. She was besotted. So was Jason.

But not quite a hundred percent yet. Several times he caught Jason watching him watch Angie. He'd have to back off a little with the charm. He had never had a sibling, but he supposed a certain amount of vigilance from an older brother for a younger sister was standard.

He'd hit her with the charm when Jason wasn't there to watch.

He managed to kid Eddy out of his worry about his dog's attitude. Who'd ever imagine the scrawny thing would have survived, much less that it would remember who had tried to kill it? It had grown a lot, but he supposed puppies did grow fast. He knew elephants were supposed to have long memories, but mongrel dogs?

The only one he couldn't seem to charm was the neighbor, Nancy the kennel cleaner, or whatever the heck she was. Good-looking. Great bod.

The age difference didn't matter. He liked older women occasionally. They were so grateful, they'd do things he wouldn't dare suggest to his cheerleaders. He'd shown her the full force of his charm, starting with aw-shucks diffidence about the blasted dog.

She was pleasant enough to him. She had to talk to him. She was sitting beside him at the table, but she didn't fall for him the way women invariably did.

Wainwright was obviously having it on with her. You could tell the way he looked at her he was dying to get in her pants. She gave Tim one glance that said she was dying to get his *off*. Interesting. David didn't know how he could use that knowledge, but it might come in handy sometime. He consoled himself by assuming she was too absorbed in Tim to pay attention to him.

She owned the land they were going to invade for the ritual. He might just set her woods on fire after the others left. Terrible tragedy, particularly if a couple of houses caught fire at the same time.

Bad idea. Too much scrutiny. The whole thing could start to unravel.

After dinner, Angie said, "Can we go over to Nancy's, so you can see my new horse?"

"Wouldn't miss it," David said.

She turned to Nancy. "Can I go show David, Nancy?"

Nancy shrugged. "Sure. I'll come over with you. She's out in the pasture with the Percherons."

Angie ran ahead around Nancy's cottage and back to the pasture. David and Nancy followed more slowly. He wondered if she thought she was being a chaperone. One of those Spanish Duennas. Keep the little virgin safe.

"So when'd she get the horse?" he asked. "What kind?"

"A hunter."

No extra conversation there. He tried again. "She planning to show over fences? Ride with the hunt?"

"Not for a while."

"Here she is, David," Angie said. "Isn't she beautiful?" Angie buried her face in Cloud's neck.

David came up and ran his hand down the front of the mare's face. "She sure is. You know, I believe I know this horse." He turned to Nancy. "Isn't this Mrs. Crandall's Cloud? I didn't think she'd ever sell her."

"Angie's leasing her."

"I've seen her go. She never touches a rail in the field. Good horse for you to learn to jump on, Angie. Very safe."

"Angie's just started to ride. She won't be jumping for a long time."

"Forever!" Angie sounded exasperated. "I swear I could do it. Even Nancy says I've got a great natural seat."

That you have, little girl. "Take your time, Ange." *Always support the instructor, at least in public.* Another of his rules for flying under the radar. "Well, I'd better get home." He gave Cloud one more pat and turned back. "What'd you do with that yappy dog?"

"He's in my house."

They waited until Angie turned Cloud back into the pasture and slid to a stop beside them. "David knows a lot about horses."

"Really?" Nancy said.

"He used to play polo, didn't you, David?"

"For a while." He flashed Nancy another killer smile. She wasn't even wounded. "Gave it up for lacrosse."

He said his goodbyes and climbed into his Hummer. Angie looked as though she was dying to climb in beside him.

Not yet, little girl. Not quite yet.

NANCY WATCHED JustPup trot back across the street to Tim's house with Angie. She didn't know whether Tim would come over later or not. This was probably not a good night to talk to him, but sooner or later she'd have to.

He wouldn't believe her. The only evidence she had was Just-Pup's extraordinary reaction to the man. She felt sure Grantham had burned the little dog, tried to kill him, probably *had* killed his littermates. The dog remembered him and hated him. Had Grantham run down the basset hound as well?

Mr. Crandall was due at the clinic first thing in the morning to pick up Amanda, one of his polo ponies. So David had played polo for a while. If he was the David that Crandall said mistreated his polo ponies, Crandall would tell her. She had to know.

"HOW'S MY MARE?" Crandall walked into the back door of the clinic still wearing his polo boots and knee pads. His black shirt stuck to his back, and his white breeches were stained with grass and dirt. It might be October, but it was still plenty hot.

"Doing fine," Nancy said.

"Good. She's a handy little mare. I'd hate to lose her." He sat on the edge of the platform around the cow pen. "You've never come back to our matches after that first Sunday. How come?"

"The others are rotating. Until it cools off, I don't intend to unless I'm ordered. How'd the match go last Sunday?"

"We won." He walked into his mare's stall and ran a hand down her left foreleg. "No heat in her leg."

"She needs to be poulticed for a week or so, but you can take her home." She hesitated. "May I ask you something? You don't have to answer."

"Shoot."

"The afternoon I was there, I overheard you say something about someone not being allowed to ride your horses because he mistreated them. Do you remember that?"

Crandall nodded. "Not likely to forget."

"Do you feel comfortable telling me who you were talking about?"

He blew out his breath. "Why do you want to know?"

"Just checking a theory. It could be important."

He clapped his hands on his thighs. "I don't usually make mistakes about people. I've known the family for years. The father took out my aunt Griselda's gall bladder. The son's a fine young man, or so I thought. Loves sports, so I decided I'd give him a chance to learn polo."

"It didn't work out?"

"He could hit the ball from any angle the first time he picked up a mallet. He was a natural." Crandall leaned against the front of the stall and crossed his arms as though he was trying to protect himself.

"He hadn't ridden horses since he went to camp, but it's easier to teach somebody to ride than it is to teach them to use a mallet. I could see him becoming a real power player once he got some games under his belt."

"What happened?"

"The first few games, he was everything I thought he'd be. Couldn't afford a string of ponies, of course, although his daddy bought him the equipment. I've got talented ponies coming out my ears, so I could easily loan him half a dozen for an afternoon's matches." He shrugged. "He could be a bit rough on his ponies—ride them a little too long in the heat, that sort of thing. When I talked to him, he'd be more careful for a while, then he'd forget. I figured he didn't know any better and was getting too wound up in the competition. One afternoon late last season, we were playing a club from Florida. They had a couple of six-goal pros on their team."

He laughed ruefully. "Talk about way out of our league. They were eating our lunch. Every time this kid got within shooting distance of the goal, one of their men would ride him off hard. He stayed on his horse, I'll give him that, but he couldn't score.

"During the third chukka, the opposing backer tried to ride him off the same way he'd been doing all afternoon. David used his mallet to trip the pony."

Nancy caught her breath. The absolutely worst thing anybody could do in a polo match. The men knew they were at risk, but the horses were supposed to be protected at all costs. Hooking across a horse's chest was grounds for instant dismissal from a game. "You're sure?"

"I was looking right at him when he did it, saw his face. Twisted with rage. The pony and rider fell. The rider broke his collarbone. It was no accident. David's own pony was hurt, too. The opposing pony stepped on her and cut a big gash just above the coronet band on her near forefoot. He didn't even wait for the referee to kick him out of the game. Just rode off the field, tossed the reins to one of my grooms, jumped down, climbed into his car and drove off."

"Just like that? No apology? No making certain both ponies were all right? That the man wasn't badly injured?"

"Told you. Didn't even look back at the field. Climbed into that damned big Hummer and drove out like all the devils in hell were after him."

"Did he ever explain himself?"

"Oh, yeah. He called me that night in tears." Crandall shrugged. "Sounded like tears, anyway. Crocodile tears. He wanted the address of the man who was injured so he could write him an apology, send him flowers or something. Wanted to know how the horses were. Said he'd been so mad at himself, he couldn't talk to anyone until he calmed down."

"Maybe that was true."

"He was mad, all right. Nobody else saw what I did, Nancy.

He knew damned well what he was doing. I think he was mad because he didn't kill the guy."

"You haven't told me his name."

"Grantham. David Grantham. He's some kind of coach now."

CHAPTER THIRTY-FOUR

TIM HAD SLIPPED OUT of the house after the children were in bed, and now lay sated in Nancy's arms in her king-size bed. He'd finally convinced her to ignore the logistical difficulties, and concentrate on the pleasure they took in each other. So long as they were discreet, and he went home at a reasonable hour.

No doubt Jason knew what they were doing. Angie probably suspected. Tim would have been perfectly willing to discuss his relationship with them, but Nancy didn't want him to.

"I'm Angie's coach," she told Tim. "Besides, most kids don't like the idea of their parents having sex even when they're married."

So Tim had agreed not to say anything until his children brought up the subject. So far they hadn't. Now he looked down at Nancy and said, "So, what's up?"

"Why do you think something's up?" Nancy raised herself onto her elbow.

"I may not have known you long, but I have paid attention. Something is definitely bothering you. Just because I keep proposing to you..."

"Not that." She waved away his proposal entirely too casually for Tim's taste.

"Then what?"

She told him Crandall's story.

He heard her through, then lay back with his right arm under his head. "If I were a prosecuting attorney, I'd say you didn't have much of a case."

"I knew you'd say that." She sat up and swung her legs over the side of the bed.

He pulled her back. "But I am not a prosecuting attorney."

"I can't help it. He gives me the creeps. I'm not sure why." She held up her hands. "I know Jason and Angie are crazy about him."

"He's made a tremendous difference. Jason's grades are up, and Angie not only looks normal, she acts normal. She's even made a couple of friends at Maybree."

"What's that got to do with Grantham?"

"Her big brother's on the lacrosse team, so Angie gets to hang around. That makes Angie cool."

She pulled her legs up on the bed and sat cross-legged. "I have very strong instincts about animals. I sense things about them. In my business, I'd be minus a couple of fingers if I didn't."

"So?"

She looked away from him. "I think he's a rogue."

Tim laughed.

She frowned over her shoulder at him.

He pulled a couple of pillows behind his head. "All right. I'll admit you aren't either a dumb bunny or a nut case and that you must have good instincts." He reached down and picked up her hand. "All five fingers. I assume it's a matched set. But a rogue? David Grantham?"

"Peter tried to get me on a horse once that had a reputation as a rogue. He's the only horse I've ever refused to ride. Peter was furious. The horse later killed a rider and had to be put down."

"So how did you know he was a rogue?"

"I sensed it. Horses are big and powerful enough so that if they weren't even-tempered, we'd never have domesticated them."

"Was the horse mistreated when it was young? Brutalized?"

"He had been bred at a top farm and trained from the start with care and affection. He looked okay. Most of the time he acted okay. Then for no reason, he'd try to kill his rider or his groom or another horse. There was something wrong with him, that's all. A bad gene, maybe. The only thing I can say is that when I looked in that horse's eyes, I saw he wasn't quite a horse. He was something *other*. That's the feeling I got from Grantham. You're probably right to ignore me."

"I'm not ignoring you. I hope you're wrong, because nobody is going to believe you."

Poddy landed in the middle of Tim's chest. He grunted and began to scratch the big cat's ears as it butted against his chin. "Get down, your whiskers tickle." He shoved the cat off to the side, where it curled up and began to purr. "A couple of weeks ago, Jason came home long after curfew. He'd been drinking. He wasn't drunk, but he's fifteen. David brought him home."

"So you did see," Nancy said. "I thought you were asleep."

"You didn't bother to mention it to me?"

"I didn't want you to think I spent every moment staring at your house."

"David said Jason had one beer at Daryl's. He didn't want to rat Jason out for a single beer, so he brought him home because Daryl had drunk too much to be driving."

"Makes sense."

"How did he know Jason only had one beer? Or that Daryl was too drunk to drive?"

"He had to have been there for a while. To rescue Jason?" Nancy asked.

"And the other members of the team."

"So he's a hero," Nancy said.

"Depends on your point of view. In any case, if Aycock knew about it, he'd have a fit. David is an adjunct faculty member. The school might well have some liability in the matter, and Dr. Aycock freaks at the notion of liability or bad publicity."

"But it wasn't on school property."

"Right. I have no proof David was at the party except Jason's word that he came early and stayed late. Which do you think Aycock would believe? His idol or my nearly bald ex-thug newbie?"

"What can you do?"

"David denies everything except the rescue part and swears he lowered the boom on the team."

"You believe him?"

"I did before tonight. I assumed it was one instance of bad judgment on David's part."

"So did Charlie Crandall. At first."

"Yeah. You know about microexpressions?"

She shook her head.

"The latest thing—better than polygraphs. Any psychopath can beat a polygraph. I went to a course in Chicago last year to train teachers how to spot and use microexpressions. When you say something, anything, just for a nanosecond your face registers what you're really thinking. Then the smile or the frown or the blank comes down. When I asked David why he hadn't stopped the party, just for an instant, he looked ugly."

Nancy slid around so that she lay once more in Tim's arms. "That's what Crandall said."

"So, let's assume you're right that Grantham's what you call a rogue. He seems to have his tendencies under control at the moment. There's certainly no proof that he's doing anything wrong at Maybree on a continuing basis. The kids adore him and he seems to give them good advice. I don't see what I can do except watch him. Jason and Angie are my kids, but in a sense I'm responsible for all the students."

"That's all you can do."

They lay quiet in each other's arms while Tim nuzzled her neck.

"How about I change the subject?" he asked.

"Sure. To what?"

"Did you know you have a lovely pair of dimples on each side of your spine?" He ran his hand over her hip. "Right here." He bent and kissed her. "And here." He kissed her again. "And the way your hip curves to fit my hand cannot possibly be happenstance."

"Happenstance? Ooh, I don't think that's your hand."

"I am cutting, as they say, to the chase."

She caught her breath and slid back against him. "Be my—oh, my—guest."

Later, he pulled his clothes on. She ran a hand down his arm, but made no move to get out of bed.

He bent to kiss her, then sat on the end of the bed. "Confession time."

Her eyes opened wide. A moment later she sat and pulled the sheet up to cover her naked breasts. "You have three wives and a dozen other children? You're wanted by the police?"

"I took you seriously tonight because I spent too many years not taking Solange seriously. In a sense I killed her."

"Whoa." Nancy sat up. "Just because I unloaded about that Grantham person doesn't mean..."

"I've put it off too long as it is. I've asked you to marry me. You have a right to know how badly I screwed up my marriage to Solange."

"No, I don't. Not unless I agree to marry you, which I haven't and probably won't."

"Hah!" He pointed at her. "You said *probably* won't. That means possibly *will.*"

Nancy swung her legs out of bed and kicked him solidly in the thigh on her way by. "Don't play word games. I'm no good at them." She padded to her closet, pulled out a blue silk robe and tied it around her waist. "If you are determined to do this, then let's do it over hot chocolate. I never thought I'd say this, but I definitely need the sugar boost."

As she assembled the milk, cocoa, vanilla and sugar, she asked, "So, the police are after you for murder?"

"Serious, remember? No jokes."

She turned with the milk jug in her hand. "What am I supposed to say? Serious is scary."

He pulled up a stool and pushed Lancelot, who had gotten out of his bed when the refrigerator door opened. "No pigs."

Nancy turned her back to him and went about assembling the chocolate.

"You may have noticed that there's almost seven years between Angie and Eddy."

"Uh-huh."

"He was definitely not planned. When Solange found she was pregnant for the third time, she begged me to get us out of Chicago. Take a job in a small town where we could afford a house with separate bedrooms for the kids, room for a garden, bicycle paths. Maybe even a dog."

"You didn't hear her?" She dumped heaping tablespoonfuls of cocoa into the saucepan, added milk, vanilla and sugar, then turned the burner on low.

"I heard her, but I didn't heed her. When my grandfather died, Solange and I drove down for the funeral. Solange fell in love with the farm. Said it reminded her of the countryside outside of St. Nazaire where her mother came from."

"She wanted you to move down here? I thought she was the reason you stayed in Chicago."

He shook his head. "We couldn't afford to walk out on our lives in Chicago and move to the middle of nowhere. She said she didn't mean move down here, but someplace close to her mother that was *like* down here. But Solange wouldn't let me sell Granddad's place. She said it would keep going up in value."

"She was right about that."

"That's French practicality. If and when we did move, we could sell Granddad's place and our condo in Chicago to put down money on a really nice house in Illinois or Wisconsin. Maybe if I'd just blown her off, I wouldn't feel so damned guilty. I promised. In a year or so, when I had a couple of more publications to my credit, I'd start looking for a headmaster's job in the 'burbs. When I had chalked up another year as an assistant principal in an inner city school. More money, more perks. Give the kids the education, the advantages they deserved."

"That makes sense. Everything takes time." Nancy pulled a couple of mugs from the cabinet to the left of the sink and set them on the counter beside the stove.

Tim laughed at her comment, but there was no mirth in the sound. "Seven years of 'Take another class, Solange. Finish your master's so you can teach French in high school or at a community college. We need both salaries.' In the meantime, I told her, think of all the advantages we have living in Chicago—one of the greatest cities in the world. Museums, symphony, ballet, theater." He came and stirred the steaming chocolate. "Not that we had money or time to take advantage of them. We also had her mother to watch the children when we weren't there, so we weren't spending a fortune on childcare.

"I didn't even look for another job. I worked eighty hours a week. When I told her I could expect to make principal in another year when our principal retired, I think she realized I'd never move. The next week she signed up for classes at the university to get her master's in French. A month later she started an affair with her French professor."

Nancy caught her breath. "Uh-oh."

"Yeah. Uh-oh. She gave up on me. On *us*. I was too blind and stupid and self-centered to see what was happening. She was getting her ducks in a row to take the children and walk out. She told me that night—the night she died when she finally admitted the affair—she didn't think I'd notice they were gone."

He leaned on the counter, his eyes down. "I was furious. I told her to take the children and go to hell if that's what she wanted. Then I put her out of the car and drove off."

"I'm so sorry."

"Two joy-riding thugs shot her and another student on the steps of the building where their classes were held. You know where I was when the police finally found me? In my office at school working on teacher reports."

"You still aren't responsible for her death." Nancy moved

him gently out of the way, turned off the heat under the saucepan, stirred the contents and filled the two mugs. "Don't drink that right away. It'll burn the roof of your mouth."

"She wouldn't have been there if I'd picked her up after the class the way I was supposed to. She was waiting for a cab." He sank onto one of the bar stools and dropped his head into his cupped hands.

"I was prepared to pick up and leave the minute her funeral was over with no job and no prospects. My principal talked me out of it. Said I couldn't leave in the middle of the school year. I had a contract. Nobody would hire me."

"He was right."

He took a deep breath and raised his head. He still couldn't look at Nancy. He didn't want her to see the tears that threatened to overflow. "Then the perfect job opened up. A school outside of Philadelphia. Co-ed. Kindergarten through grade twelve. Prestigious, but not too prestigious. A faculty row where we could have a decent house on the central green. Surrounded by parks, big campus, but still close enough to Philadelphia to take advantage of the culture."

"You didn't get it?"

"I was the second choice." He took a tentative sip of his hot chocolate. "You're right. That's hot."

"Told you. Trust me, why don't you?"

"They hired a guy with a Harvard degree, but without either my experience or publications." He shrugged. "Harvard trumps even the University of Chicago, at least on the East Coast. Thing is, I had my hopes up. When I found out I wasn't selected, it was too late to search for anything remotely like that."

"So Maybree was your fallback position? Nice for them."

"Maybree's a good school, even if I had to drop back to teaching from administration. And I get free tuition for all three children. I could have taken a position with the Memphis City school system, but I didn't want the commute, and I didn't want my children in three separate public schools with three schedules. Aycock says I'm in line to become assistant principal next year. Finally, we're out of Chicago and in the country, the way I promised Solange, in a place she liked."

Nancy took a single ice cube from the ice maker in the door or her refrigerator. "Want one?"

Tim nodded.

She handed him the ice cube and took another for herself. They dropped the cubes into the chocolate. Nancy watched hers melt, then said quietly, "What's the difference between working eighty hours a week in Chicago and eighty hours a week in Marquette County? Is that what you promised Solange?"

"I'm spending as much time as I can…"

"Helen is looking after your house and mothering Eddy. I'm teaching Angie, and Jason spends all his time with David Grantham and his crowd. What's *your* role?"

"Trying to keep our heads above water financially," he snapped. "My salary dropped like a stone."

"Living expenses are lower. You own the house."

"Clothes, school supplies, gas and car expenses are not lower. Groceries are actually higher."

"So you get paid time and a half when you work overtime?"

"That's not the way it works. Doesn't work that way with you, either, does it?"

"Not usually. You'd rather stay in your office working on other people's kids and leave your own to other people? The same thing you did in Chicago."

"Those other kids are my responsibility, too. I love my family. I'm doing the best I can for them."

"I'm sure you love them, but you sure don't like them very much, and they don't like you, either."

"How the hell can you say a thing like that?"

"It's true. They're not very likable, besides, they don't trust you. You dragged them off to Marquette County away from their friends and the only family they have to fulfill some crazy promise to your dead wife because you feel guilty."

"What are you, some kind of psychiatrist? Listen, after Solange died, we all went to family counseling, grief counseling for the kids. With actual professionals."

"Ouch." She poured her hot chocolate into the sink. "Suddenly I'm not very thirsty."

He set his cup down and came over to put his arms around her.

She shook him off. "We have great sex. We enjoy each other's company. Then either my phone rings or your phone rings, and the world out there busts in. There's no room for *us*." She walked to her bedroom door. "Go home to your family and leave me my animals."

CHAPTER THIRTY-FIVE

"THE HALLOWEEN PARTY'S gonna be back in the woods the other side of the lake, isn't it?" Angie whispered.

"How'd you hear that?" Jason glared at his sister. "Besides, it's not a party. It's a ritual."

"I knew I was right."

"Who cares? You're not going."

"David invited me himself."

"He was kidding. You're not going. No girls. Just the team."

"But you're all going over to Daryl's after to meet the girls, aren't you?"

"What if we are? You're too young."

"I'm only two and a half years younger than you and I look older."

"Big flaming deal."

"I'll tell Dad about the party."

Jason bounded up from his bed and slammed his door. Angie cowered away from him. He was so angry with her, he was afraid he might hit her. He'd failed her once in Chicago, when he'd given in to her blackmail and almost got her killed. Not this time.

"You tell anybody, and I mean anybody, about the party and you'll be invisible for the entire rest of your high school career. I guarantee it. Nobody at Maybree will even notice you exist."

"But David..."

"Never mind David. Get over yourself. He's ten years older than you are. He screws women, not little girls."

"He does not!"

Jason grabbed her and tossed her onto his bed. "Listen, little girl, David's screwed every cheerleader in Maybree. He takes a different girl to bed every night."

She was crying now. Big, fat tears rolled down her cheeks carrying black streaks of eyeliner with them. "Why are you saying those things about David? I love him. I thought you did, too."

"He's a great coach. Lately, I'm not so sure he's such a great person."

She flew at him with her red nails out in front of her like a hawk's talons.

"Hey!" He grabbed her wrists. "Listen. I'm on the team so I'm going. I have to be there. It's part of the ritual so we can win. But you are not going, you hear me? I don't care if Dr. Aycock himself invited you. You take Eddy trick-or-treating like a good little girl and let the grown ups party down."

The hatred in her look would have thawed the polar ice cap. She flounced out of his room. He expected her to slam the door. Instead she closed it very quietly.

He flopped onto his bed. What had he gotten himself into?

"THE WHOLE SCHOOL thinks it's gonna be down by your lake," Daryl whispered, then snickered. "Gimme some more of those cobwebs." Daryl flung the plastic cobwebs at the crepe myrtle tree at the side of his pool.

"Daryl!" called a feminine voice from inside the French windows on the other side of the pool.

"Yeah?"

"You and your friends are going to have to clean all this up after Halloween."

"Yeah, yeah, yeah." He turned back to Jason and raised his eyebrows. "That's my stepmom." He grinned. "She and my dad are going to a big all-nighter on Halloween." He pulled some of the cobwebs down so they floated across the space beside the tree. "Karen walks into this, she'll scream and throw herself into my waiting arms."

"You wish," Jason said. "So there won't be any adults here?"

"Man, David'll be here. My dad's cool with that." Daryl climbed down from the ladder, moved it to the next tree and snapped his fingers for more cobwebs. Jason handed them over to him.

Daryl climbed the ladder and began placing more cobwebs. "Anybody looking for us is gonna be back there with the water moccasins while we're two miles away down in that clearing. Man, me'n Scott and David brought our ATVs over last weekend and stashed 'em in this old, abandoned barn down the far end of that gravel road. We've been bringing stuff over there and loading up all week. Saturday night, good buddy, we grab the jugs, the ice and the kegs, and we will be ready to rock-and-roll."

"I'm still not sure this is a good idea."

"You crazy? David says it's the way to win. He's got the whole thing planned. Once we go through the ritual, nobody'll beat us."

"So we keep the girls waiting at your house until we decide to get there? They'll all have to be home an hour after we show up. I don't understand this ritual anyway."

Daryl sighed cavernously and backed down the ladder. "It's like this, newbie. You want to play on this team, you do the ritual. Period, end of story." He laughed and punched Jason none too lightly in the stomach. "Besides, by the time we get back to my house the girls will all be smashed. Karen and Michelle and the others can probably drink *me* under the table. It's not like we're forcing it down anybody's throat." He gave Jason a light slap on the cheek. "Not even you. Somebody's got to stay sober to put me to bed, am I right?"

"Who's going to put the girls to bed?"

Daryl raised his eyebrows. "You mean *afterward?* Man, you know David never drinks. We'll stack 'em in the Hummer like cord wood, and drop 'em off at home one at a time. Hell, man, David says we'll be through with the ritual by ten anyway. That's when the signs are strongest. That'll give us at least until one with the girls. You need that much time to get your rocks off, newbie?"

"What signs?"

"David's got this new ritual all lined up. He says he's gonna scare the pants off us. I mean, man, it's Halloween. Nobody'll be able to beat us after Halloween."

Jason laughed. "You hope."

"Shee-ut, man, with David handling this, I know."

CHAPTER THIRTY-SIX

"I DON'T LIKE IT," Mrs. Martini said. She sat on the wooden chair in front of Tim's tiny desk in his tiny office. "Something is definitely coming down on Halloween."

"Vandalism?"

She took a deep breath. "I wish I knew. You can cut the atmosphere with a knife. The students are whispering and snickering and going quiet every time an adult passes within ten feet of them." She sighed. "One year they moved Dr. Aycock's wife's new Mini Cooper up the steps and into the assembly hall. Took three days to figure out how to get it out."

"Clever. Not particularly destructive."

She grinned. "Unless you count Dr. Aycock's near apoplexy. It's always the jocks that plan it and carry it out. They have the brawn, and a number of them have the brains, as well."

"The lacrosse team?"

"Ringleaders. I keep thinking David will tumble to what they're planning and head them off, but he swears he doesn't know anything."

"It may simply be a big party at somebody's house," Tim said.

"A few of our parents do not have a brain in their heads. They figure the kids are going to drink anyway, so why not provide the liquor and the beer and take their car keys away so they don't kill themselves."

"You don't agree?" Tim asked.

"Certainly not. You don't, either. I've heard you in the common room."

"No, I don't. It's not just the possibility of alcohol poisoning or falling into the swimming pool and drowning—or committing assault."

"Or rape."

Tim nodded. "Dammit, it's illegal, immoral and stupid. We ought to plan a party at the school where they can dance and stay sober."

"Dr. Aycock frowns on any official observance of Halloween."

"Then we'll just have to find out what's going down and where, and if possible, head it off."

That evening, he cornered Jason out by his backyard lacrosse goal and grilled him.

Jason stared at him with blank, innocent eyes. But Tim could tell his son was worried and perhaps a bit frightened.

"You know what would happen to me if I rat out my friends?"

"You know what will happen to you if you don't?"

"You can't do anything to me as bad as they can." Jason pushed past his father and walked up the back stairs.

"What if somebody dies?" Tim called.

Jason stopped with his hand on the doorknob. "Get real. It's no big deal. It's a team party. Period."

Tim sighed. So there *was* a party.

"I assume it's on Halloween night. Where?"

Jason's shoulders slumped. "No way."

"Jason, I don't issue many orders to you. This is an order. Tell me where the party is taking place."

"Daryl's gonna kill me. Okay. Down on the other side of the lake by the picnic tables."

"*Our* lake? What picnic tables?"

"You don't even know what's on the other side of your own lake," Jason snarled. He yanked open the door, stalked in and slammed it behind him.

Tim walked down to the dock. It was already too dark to see the path around the lake that Meghan, Haley and Angie used for trail riding. He didn't even know how to get to the other side of the lake except by canoe. He took out his cell phone and dialed Sheriff Mike O'Hara.

"Mike, I may have a problem I need help with."

SINCE NANCY HAD told him her feelings about David, Tim found himself watching the young man surreptitiously. The problem was that he and Tim only met occasionally in the lounge. David always said good things about Jason.

"He's really coming along fast," David said. "A natural with a stick."

That afternoon, Tim was supposed to take Jason and Angie home. But Angie said she had a paper to research in the school library, and Jason had lacrosse practice.

Tim walked between the bleachers to the field and stopped in the shadows to watch the end of practice where Jason couldn't see him and get distracted.

He was watching Jason take the ball away from Scott when he saw David talking to Angie beside the entrance to the locker room. She stood propped against the side of the building with her book bag in her arms.

Tim knew Angie had a major crush on David. All the girls did. She was staring up at him with stars in her eyes. Tim wasn't worried. David was expert at fending off adoring little girls.

Then David did something that startled Tim. He put his hand against the brick over Angie's head and leaned forward. Just slightly. There was still plenty of distance between them.

But not quite as much as Tim would have preferred. His gut lurched.

He'd seen that posture a million times. He'd stood that way himself probably half that many. It was the "so, baby, what's your sign" attitude. Between a twenty-three-year-old coach and the thirteen-year-old sister of one of his players.

Tim retreated into the shadows, coughed, scuffed his feet and walked out into the light.

David was now standing a dozen feet away from Angie facing the field with his hands in his pockets. Angie was still leaning against the wall looking at David as though she could devour him.

Not like a little girl.

This time Tim's gut lurched and kept lurching.

Not *his* little girl. If he ever saw David hit on his daughter for real, he'd kill the son of a bitch.

In the meantime, he'd start documenting David's behavior.

And start to worry about Jason all over again.

OKAY, so he'd improved the ritual in the past few days. Added a little something extra.

David gunned his Hummer down the straight highway toward Somerton. He'd called his bootlegger. The grain alcohol was ready to be dumped into the Purple Passion tomorrow night before the big event.

He already had the GHP and the pot. He'd toss the pot in the bonfire. Make the team mellow, so he could handle them easier. The GHP was for Angie. She wouldn't remember a thing when she woke up. One ritual gulp from the fancy silver goblet he'd borrowed from his mother would be all it would take.

She was nearly perfect. It would have been better if she'd had long hair, but you couldn't have everything in a ritual virgin, now could you? Just finding the virgin was tough enough. He didn't think a wig would stay on her head once they got started.

The team would remember what they'd done.

They would never be able to tell. They'd be united in guilt. They would belong to him forever. The first step. The first converts.

The ritual sacrifice of the white mare was new. Icing on the cake. He owed Crandall that after the bastard kicked him off the

polo team. Mrs. Crandall loved that mare. She'd have hysterics
when they found the bloody carcass. David snickered. He would
really get off when he slit that mare's throat.

All part of the new team ritual, of course. Every Spartan knew
you had to offer sacrifices to the gods before battle. Every
Spartan knew you had to ravish every available virgin.

He'd spent enough time researching the Spartan customs to
be able to fake a fairly coherent ritual. Didn't matter. Those
bozos wouldn't know a Spartan ritual from a trapeze act.

By the time he got them to Daryl's house for the rest of the
orgy, they'd have come to terms with what they'd done. People
could justify ax murder of little old ladies to themselves.

He didn't bother, of course. He didn't require justification
for his acts.

ANGIE WOULD GET to that clearing as David had instructed, if she
had to walk barefoot over broken glass. She was going to be the
star. Well, she and Cloud.

Nancy refused to teach her to jump. All right for her. David
promised that if she'd take part in this ritual tonight, he'd set up
some practice jumps down in the clearing for her. He'd teach her
to jump. Screw Nancy.

She had been warned not to mention what David planned to
anybody, not even Jason.

Especially not Jason. He'd already acted like a snot about the
ritual. At least he'd told Daddy it was down by the lake. That's
what they'd all agreed. If they were forced to tell an adult, they'd
say the party was across the lake.

If Daddy planned to wait for them, he'd spend the whole
night in the wrong place. Chiggers and snakes and all.

What were they doing that was so bad? As David said,
what a hoot.

She and Cloud would be the center of the team ritual. Their
moon goddess riding her white mare. David had given her a blue

robe to wear, and a crown thingie for her hair with an upside down moon on top.

"It's a big surprise for the team," he'd said.

"What about Haley and Meghan? Can they come, too?"

"Of course not," David snapped, then he'd touched her cheek. Those stuck-up cheerleaders would know Angie Wainwright after Halloween, all right. For that night, at least, she was David's Moon. Let them beat that.

EDDY HAD TAKEN JustPup's word for Mr. Grantham's character from the start, and he knew something was up with Angie and Jason. They weren't speaking to each other. He hated that.

He hated Halloween anyway. Going out in the dark to knock on strange people's doors to beg for candy really scared him. He and JustPup would spend the evening at home watching TV side by side on the sofa.

Jason said he had to go to the ritual. He'd also begged to go to the party. He swore nobody would be drinking. After all, the coach would be in charge. David was picking a bunch of them up to take them to the party.

Eddy didn't know what party, but he knew his father wasn't happy about it, and had cautioned Jason not to have so much as a beer, and to call his father to come get him at the first sign of trouble.

Tim told Eddy he was going out for a walk down by the lake.

Okay, so that left Angie to babysit, plus he could look out the windows and see Nancy in her living room reading a book.

She said they didn't have treat-or-treaters since the neighborhood kids moved away. Nobody had banged on their door, and now Tim had turned the porch light off. Eddy turned off the living room light, too, just in case somebody saw him through the front window and came up anyway. More candy for him.

He picked up a handful of miniature candy bars out of the bowl beside the door and turned to go upstairs.

He froze for a moment, then stepped deeper into the shadows.

Angie was sneaking down the stairs. He started to speak to her, but something about the way she moved warned him to keep his mouth shut.

She was leaving him alone! Going out to that party, he'd bet. She even had on some kind of big floppy blue costume and a crown on her head.

He remembered when she'd been in the hospital. He'd been scared then, too. He didn't want anything to happen to her. He knew she wasn't supposed to go out.

Maybe he should follow her.

Into the dark? Eddy shivered at the thought. He'd better stay where he was.

He worried for a long time, at least it seemed long to Eddy. If he put JustPup on a leash, maybe he could track her like a bloodhound.

But he might bark again. No, JustPup needed to stay inside where he was safe.

Eddy picked up his navy windbreaker and a flashlight, then slipped out and followed Angie through Nancy's yard.

He watched from the corner of Nancy's house while Angie disappeared into the dark barn. Five minutes later, she led Cloud out into the pasture. She hadn't even turned on a light.

Since the middle of October Henry and Herb had spent the chill nights in their stalls and worked outside during the day. The pasture gates were closed anyway. Angie opened the front gate softly, slipped through and used the mounting block to climb up on Cloud's back.

She didn't even have her saddle on. And that costume dress thing wasn't made to ride in.

He watched Cloud walk across the pasture like a white shadow under the full moon. Angie unhooked the pasture gate without getting off, opened it and rode into the woods.

Eddy shivered. He didn't know where she was going, but he

knew she was doing something she wasn't supposed to. She was going to get in bad trouble unless he stopped her.

His daddy might take Cloud away from her. Angie'd die without Cloud just like he'd die without JustPup.

The harvest moon was so full it was almost like daylight until he hid under the trees. He was so scared. A branch touched his cheek and he squeaked with terror.

An old branch couldn't hurt him.

He couldn't see Cloud any longer, even though she was white and ought to show up. But he could still see the path going straight ahead. Henry and Herb didn't much like detours.

Then he heard sounds. That crazy thumpy music Mr. Grantham played in the locker room. And he started to see lights and shadows moving in the trees. He froze. Fairies?

Wasn't such a thing.

He got down on his tummy and crawled forward.

He'd found the lacrosse team's Halloween party. The one Angie wasn't supposed to go to. Why had Jason driven off with Daryl? He could have walked down here.

They were in a big clearing. A bunch of ATVs sat around the edge of the clearing with their headlights aimed toward the center.

They had started a bonfire, too. Maybe for marshmallows and hot dogs and stuff. Nancy wouldn't like that.

These were Nancy's woods. She'd be real mad when she found out they were down here.

They were all doing some kind of dance around this big stump in the middle. It had a black cloth on it and some other stuff. He couldn't see much because of the smoke.

Angie rode into the clearing on Cloud. That funny dress thing she was wearing was kind of blowing in the breeze.

The dancers stopped. Somebody turned off the music.

Eddy didn't know any of their names except for Daryl and Scott.

"Hey, Ange, what're you doing here?" Daryl said.

"Hey, kid, what's with the horse?"

"Yeah, Angie. Jason, tell your baby sister. No girls allowed."
That was Scott.

"Not till after the ritual, right? Coach?"

"Angie!" Jason stepped forward. "Didn't I tell you not to
come down here? Go home *now.*"

David stepped out from behind the fire. He was dressed really
funny. Maybe he was wearing a choir robe. He put a hand on
Jason's arm. "Chill, Jason. It's okay. I invited her." He smiled up
at Angie. "Right on time."

"My dad thinks I'm still watching Eddy," Angie said.
"Daddy's down by the lake."

Everybody laughed. "Right," Daryl said.

"David, I don't want her here," Jason insisted.

"Man," Daryl said. "David invited her. She stays." He sounded
kind of mean, not like he usually did.

"We need her for the ritual. Don't worry so much, Jason. Everything will be fine."

"Angie, go home. Now." Jason grabbed Cloud's bridle.

Angie pulled back. Cloud threw her head up.

Daryl grabbed Jason and pulled him away. "Jason, man. David
said chill."

"Yeah. You want to win? We do the ritual, right, David?"
Scott again.

"Right." David clapped Jason on the shoulder. "I promise,
nothing will happen to Angie or Cloud." He turned to Angie.
"Okay. Climb off Cloud onto the altar. I've still got to set up, then
we'll get started."

"David," Angie said. She was looking around the circle of
light. "Am I really the only girl?" Her voice trembled a teeny bit.

She's scared, Eddy thought. I don't trust that David. He looked
into his brother's eyes across the clearing. He didn't think Jason
saw him, but he didn't think Jason looked happy, either.

"You're the only girl we need," David said with a laugh.
"You're our Goddess of the Moon."

"Yeah. The other girls are over at Daryl's. You can come over with us after," said Scott. "Right, guys?"

"Hey, man, she's just a kid."

"We'll see about that after the ritual," David said. "Angie, climb up on that stump and drink the wine from that silver goblet. I'll be back to start in a few minutes." He put his hand around Angie's waist and helped her to the stump. "Hang onto Cloud, okay? The goddess needs her steed to ride across the sky."

"All right, David," Angie said in a very small voice.

As he started toward the woods, she cried, "David, don't leave!"

"I'll be right back. Got to get ready." He waved. "Guys, turn up the music."

Eddy couldn't see Jason any longer. The music boomed, and the boys started bouncing up and down again.

Eddy backed away into the darkness before he stood up.

Suddenly a hand came across his mouth so that he couldn't squeak, an arm snaked around his body and lifted him up.

"Go get Dad," Jason whispered. "They won't let us leave. Bring him down here. Now."

He swung Eddy around and let him go. Eddy took off as fast as he dared without turning on the flashlight. He glanced back once to see Jason step back into the circle of dancers.

He ran out into the moonlight, through the gate, across the pasture and up Nancy's back steps. He banged on her door and shouted, "Nancy! Nancy, it's Eddy. Nancy!"

"Eddy?" She opened the back door, and he fell into her arms. "What on earth?"

"Jason says get my dad. He says to come. The party's in the woods down there." He pointed. "And Angie's got Cloud down there."

"What?"

"She's wearing some kind of funny crown thing and a big floppy dress. She looks crazy."

CHAPTER THIRTY-SEVEN

"YOUR FATHER'S down by the lake with the sheriff. Tell him Jason lied to him," Nancy said. "Tell him the party's down in the clearing in my woods. Tell him to bring the sheriff and bust it up now. If I call 911, it'll take the dispatcher half an hour to get anybody out here from Somerton."

"The lake. I can't…"

"You *must*. Do what I tell you right now."

Without waiting to see if he obeyed, Nancy ran toward the woods. She didn't even have her cell phone or a flashlight. She didn't know why David wanted Angie and Cloud, but she didn't like her suspicions.

Tim had told her about the rituals and the speeches David gave. All that malarkey about the Spartans he obviously made up from scratch.

She'd seen a couple of TV shows about ancient Greece and the Spartans. Their ceremonies always seemed to involve the sacrifice of some living creature. Might be a single dove. On the other hand, the ritual might involve a full-grown bull.

Or a white mare.

Nancy should have stopped to get her gun. If that bastard made a move toward either Angie or Cloud, Nancy would shoot him without a moment's hesitation. If she had a gun.

But surely it wouldn't come to that. It was just a stupid, teenage keg party for a bunch of impressionable high school jocks.

Wasn't it?

She ran through the back gate and down the path the Percherons had worn into the woods with their big hooves.

At first, she could follow the path fairly safely because the earth was lighter than the fall of leaves on the ground on either side. The minute she stepped deeper into the woods, however, the leaves remaining on the trees diffused the light. It had been a warm autumn. Although many of the leaves had already fallen, many had barely begun to turn.

Her eyes didn't adjust as well to darkness as they once had. She ran headlong into a tree trunk, banged her forehead and cursed under her breath. She touched it and her hand came away wet. Darn, she was bleeding. She'd have to be more careful. She put her hands out in front of her and walked fast. She didn't dare run. She guessed she'd penetrated at least a half mile when she saw the faint glow of firelight and heard the snap and crackle of green wood burning.

The idiots had built a bonfire in the middle of a forest. What were they thinking? Obviously they weren't thinking at all.

Loud, pulsating music, both hypnotic and somehow erotic, thumped from the clearing, but the woods were thick enough to dampen the sound.

Besides, everyone in Williamston was so accustomed to hearing the boom from radios as cars drove down the back roads at night with their windows open, they probably wouldn't notice. Televisions were on, houses were well insulated and nobody would be outside.

Any trick-or-treaters would be home in bed by now.

The lights wouldn't show, either—not all the way to the road or the nearest houses.

David and his crowd must have ridden their ATVs in from the back gravel road. No one lived down that way any longer, so no one would have seen them come. Once deep in the woods, they might as well have been in a cave.

She stopped and listened. Her breath soughed in her chest so loud she was certain they'd hear her even over the music.

With luck they wouldn't expect intruders and hadn't set out guards to warn them. Hadn't they conned the adults into watching the wrong location? Back here in her woods, where nobody except the loggers ever penetrated, they would feel completely safe from prying eyes.

The circle of light from the fire and the ATVs cast gigantic shadows of the dancers against the trees. Silhouettes rose and fell and undulated to the drumbeat. Not ordinary dance music. This was eerie—voices chanting hypnotically in a language she couldn't understand.

She stepped behind the last trees at the edge of the clearing.

Phil and Phineas had cut several large hardwood trees, trimmed them and left the logs lying on the ground, ready to be dragged to the road as soon as the paths were dry enough for Henry and Herb. The giant logs formed a rough semicircle at the far side of the clearing. Piles of discarded clothes and folded blankets lay on top of them, and half a dozen ice chests sat on the ground beside them. Nancy hoped they were full of innocuous picnic fodder like hot dogs, marshmallows and sodas.

The music was even louder here. The back beat from whatever disk was playing hurt her ears. Her whole body vibrated with every thud from the big drums.

She crept closer. Once she knew for certain what was going on, she could figure out what to do about it. At best, they were only trespassing on her property.

At worst… She didn't want to think about the worst.

The music was like nothing these kids would normally dance to.

Not that they were dancing normally.

The sound of the drums and stamping feet made the hairs at the back of her neck lift. There were fifteen or twenty of them. The whole lacrosse team. All male.

Tough to keep the numbers straight when they kept wheeling and dipping in and out of the shadows. The night was chill, so they were dancing close to the fire, but judging from the sweat gleaming on their bodies, they weren't feeling the cold.

They weren't quite naked. They wore jockey shorts or Speedo bathing suits with their heavy athletics shoes. Wouldn't do to get their feet dirty or stub a toe.

Except for the unearthly rhythm of their movements, they looked pretty silly dancing in their underwear with their clunky shoes on.

Then she spotted the beer kegs and milk jugs on the far edge of the clearing. The milk jugs were probably filled with the current version of what she knew as Purple Passion. She remembered it as a seemingly harmless but lethal concoction of grape and lemon juice, sugar, seltzer and as much grain alcohol as would fill the jug. No wonder everyone was already a little unsteady.

She prayed nobody had added Ecstasy or Ruffies to the mix.

Even if there were no drugs, there was probably enough raw alcohol to cause serious poisoning. David could kill somebody tonight.

Where was Tim? The sheriff?

Why hadn't Jason just taken Angie and come home?

Had he tried? Had they stopped him?

A giant stump, all that remained from one of the big oaks the brothers had cut down, stood almost in the center of the clearing. It was about three feet across, three feet high. There was a shiny black cloth like a tablecloth tossed over it, and two tall silver candlesticks with black candles. The candles were lit, but their puny light barely showed against the brighter light from the fire.

Angie stood on the stump with a silver goblet in her hand. She wore a flimsy blue robe, which fluttered perilously close to those candles when the breeze blew, and a rhinestone coronet with a crescent moon on the top.

She kept turning in a circle, trying to keep the dancers in view. She was shivering, obviously scared.

Nancy felt her head spin, turned away and took some deep

breaths. The smoke was starting to make her dizzy, burn her eyes and her lungs.

Had David tossed drugs into the fire? Something that would excite them and make them pliable at the same time, willing to go along with what they probably thought of as a big Halloween joke?

Where was he? Waiting to make a big entrance in a puff of smoke? Firecrackers, maybe?

Cloud kept turning her head and jigging in place, nervous and uncertain. Horses often sensed threat long before people did. She wore only her bridle, and Jason held her reins. He kept petting her, but his eyes searched the edges of the clearing. He had no way of knowing whether Eddy had found his father or not. He must be afraid he was on his own. How could Jason have gotten Angie—gotten them both—into this?

He was basically a good kid, even if he had lied to Tim to protect his status with his friends. Nancy didn't believe he'd go along with anything that involved hurting his sister. Big said he wouldn't hurt an animal, either…. Nancy prayed Big was right.

Jason was in way over his head.

But then so were they all, though the others hadn't realized it yet.

Where was Tim? She'd sent Eddy off to find him a million years ago.

She glanced at the luminous dial of her watch.

She'd left the barn only ten minutes ago! Eddy might not find Tim, and Tim might not be able to get the sheriff for an hour or more.

She didn't have that kind of time. The dancing and the music were reaching a fever pitch. Soon David would commence whatever ritual he planned.

She didn't dare simply step out of the trees and tell them to stop the nonsense and go home because they were trespassing and were too young to drink. Under normal circumstances adult intervention might have worked, but these kids were already half drunk and probably more than a little high. She could be in big trouble the instant they spotted her.

Jason's teammates might be teenagers, but they had the big, muscled bodies of men. She couldn't fight them.

The music stopped suddenly. "Hey," one of them said plaintively. One boy started toward the boom box, as David stepped out from the trees across the clearing.

His blazing eyes seemed to look directly at her. She shrank back into the darkness and prayed he hadn't seen her.

He was wearing some kind of long black robe—it looked like something he'd borrowed from a church choir. She couldn't tell what he had on under it. Maybe nothing. She was pretty sure he intended for everybody to be naked before the party was over.

Everybody froze when he stepped out of the shadows. A couple of the boys tittered, then were silent. If they'd been in a normal state, they probably would have kept laughing, but tonight they knew instinctively that nothing this man did could be considered funny.

For a moment Nancy couldn't figure out what David had on his head. Some sort of mask with something...

The missing ram's horns. Jason must have given them to him.

David Grantham had turned himself into some kind of goat-headed god, or priest, or *something* bizarre. Wasn't the goat head a symbol of Satan?

She knew what the black candles were about. The guy really was nuts. He was planning a Black Mass.

This was evil. Foul. So was he. Why couldn't the others see it?

"Hey, what happened to the music?" one of the boys said. Several shushed him.

"Come on, man, let's party." The young voice was plaintive.

"Shut up, Scott." It was Jason's friend, Daryl. "We're here for the ritual. Party after."

"Shee-ut, man, I'm hungry. Break out the hot dogs."

"Hey, David, man! What's with the horse?"

Jason stepped in front of Angie protectively. Nancy could see the set of his jaw and his tight muscles from across the clearing.

"Yeah, and why's she wearing that weird costume? What's she duded up for, David?"

More snickers. A couple of full-throated guffaws.

"Hey, anybody want to play Lady Godiva? We got the horse right here."

Nancy couldn't see which one of the boys had asked, but nobody answered.

Then David stepped forward. He seemed to have grown a foot. Nancy wondered whether it was the smoke she was breathing or whether he was wearing some kind of elevator shoes. In any case he looked huge. The horned shadow behind him seemed taller than a two-story building. The way it moved in the firelight, it seemed alive.

He smiled at them and raised his hands as though in benediction.

Too creepy. But none of them seemed to realize that.

When at last he spoke, his voice came from some deep recess of power that Nancy had never suspected. He spoke gently, but nobody moved. "We need a virgin, Scott. I didn't think you'd qualify."

"Hey, David, I'll bet Jason's a virgin. Right? Jason?"

Daryl turned to the speaker and snapped, "Watch it, Ken. Don't be ragging on my man, here."

"Enough!" David's voice cut through the group like ice. "This night we will truly become Spartan warriors, princes, unbeatable. This night we will join the power of All Hallows Eve with the power of the old gods. On All Hallows Eve demons have power and dominion over the puny human species. Tonight we will do them homage. We will call on the power of the old gods, of Satan..."

"Satan?" Came a tenor voice from right behind David. "Man, I'm not messing with Satan even for fun. My daddy'll kill me."

David quelled him with a look.

This wasn't a Black Mass. It wasn't anything Nancy had ever heard of. David had made it up. He was probably making it up right now as he went along.

The others had grown restive.

"Hey man, let's do it, whatever it is. I'm freezing my balls off." That was Jason's friend Scott.

David was on the verge of losing them, and from the look on his face, he knew it. For an instant, Nancy saw such a glare of rage and fury that she shrank even farther back into shadow. This guy was nuts. Capable of anything.

But they were really just kids. Decent, normal kids out for a naughty, slightly scary night they could brag about for weeks.

"Cease!" he snarled and raised his hands above his head.

They stared at him with their mouths open and their bodies swaying.

"Hey, guys," he said with his old charm. He raised his hands, palms up, smiling, easygoing. Just the right note. "Lighten up. It's a team ritual. After this, nobody will be able to beat us. It's Halloween. If everybody doesn't get into it, how can we prove we're not scared of all the Ghoulies and goblins and demons?"

"Yeah! Lighten up. *De*-mon, *de*-mon, *de*-mon," Daryl chanted.

The others took it up, raising their young voices as though they were leading cheers at a game. "*De*-mon, *De*-mon!"

The boy called Scott pumped his arm. "Come on, demon. We're gonna whup your sorry demon butt."

Only Jason kept his eyes on David. He wasn't drunk and he wasn't fooled. He obviously wanted to get away, but not without Angie, and so far he couldn't figure out how to do that safely.

Nancy saw him look toward the closest ATV, but it was too far to run. They'd stop him. All for the team. Don't screw up the ritual.

But they were drunk and half-drugged and growing truculent.

At any moment the party could erupt into ugliness. Acts they would never commit by themselves would seem right and proper with their friends to back them up. Any spark could ignite viciousness. They could become a mob between one second and the next.

Still no Tim. Maybe Eddy had run home and hidden in his closet with JustPup, the way he always did when he was scared. Maybe he couldn't face the lake alone at night.

Jason wanted the same thing Nancy did. She simply had to help him make the decision to try to escape. She had to get Angie out of there fast. If she could cause enough ruckus, Jason could run into the trees in the panic.

David was speaking again. He was back in his goat role, his voice deep and demanding. "Come, let us begin. Tonight, we offer up a blood sacrifice to the old gods. Tonight we are conquerors. Tonight we dance sky clad and offer up the blood of the white, the pure, the virgin."

"What's sky clad?" asked Scott.

"Naked, dumbo."

The one named Scott snickered. "I'm up for that." He pointed at Angie. "Long as she gets skyclad, too."

"Yeah, man."

Jason started for Ken, but Daryl held him back.

"Hey, man, he didn't mean it," Daryl said.

Jason shook him off. "Angie's leaving."

"I think not. Neither are you." David's soft voice raised the hair on the back of Nancy's neck. Jason froze and stared at him openmouthed. David smiled his lovely smile at Jason, then at Angie.

"It's all right, Angie. Nothing to worry about," David said.

David was playing them masterfully. Simplifying for his kids, drawing them along with them, making it seem like a big Halloween joke.

But it wasn't a joke.

From somewhere inside that black choir robe he pulled a long narrow knife.

This was David's own weird brand of evil. It was all to do with power to David.

Was he truly planning to sacrifice Cloud? Slit her throat and let the blood pour down? Maybe he just planned to nick her so she'd bleed a little.

Unacceptable. He mustn't be allowed to shed even one drop of blood. He might even be crazy enough to try to sacrifice Angie, although Nancy didn't think even he would go that far. He might be nuts, but he wasn't stupid.

Sacrifice Angie? Probably not. But once they were drunk enough and stoned enough and ecstatic enough, they might consider a gang rape part of the ritual.

This was a first step for him with these kids. Tomorrow they'd be hungover and horrified and unable to tell anybody what they'd done.

He'd count on Angie not to remember and not to tell if she did.

But David would know. And he'd own them all.

He must not succeed.

She closed her eyes, took a deep breath and waited until David was looking toward the sky with his hands raised while all the others swayed and laughed and nuzzled one another. She poked her head out and waggled her fingers. Jason, no longer staring at David, seemed to be searching for a way out. At last he saw her, jumped and took a step toward her.

She stopped him with a hand. Angie hadn't seen her yet.

She pantomimed putting Angie on Cloud, then pointed to herself and Cloud. At first he didn't understand. She pantomimed riding, hands on reins, bouncing up and down as though she were cantering a horse.

He stared at her.

She raised her hands, pointed once more at Angie and Cloud, then at herself, then pointed toward the woods and gave him a two-thumbs-up sign.

Suddenly his face cleared and he nodded.

He grabbed Angie around the waist. She kicked at him. He whispered to her.

"What the hell are you doing? Not yet!" David said. "It's not time!"

Nancy ran from the trees, shoved a couple of the boys out of her way and reached the altar just as Jason swung Angie aboard Cloud.

"Hey!" one of the boys said as he hit the dirt. "What the hell?"

The instant she reached Jason, he swung Nancy onto the altar and held Cloud while she straddled the horse behind Angie.

"Hang on," she whispered to the girl. "For God's sake, don't fall off."

"No!" Jason shouted and dove at David.

She caught movement out of the corner of her eye and saw David's enraged face as he swung the knife.

She felt fire across her ribs.

He'd *cut* her, the bastard.

She dug her heels into Cloud's sides. The mare, already frightened, wanted nothing better than to get away. She leaped forward.

As her front hooves struck the ground, Nancy was jarred all the way to her toenails.

She dug in again. "Yah!"

Cloud broke hard toward the edge of the clearing. The players on that side jumped out of her way, shouting and cursing as she flew past them. She felt a couple of hands claw at her, but they didn't unseat her.

"Bitch! I'll kill you," David screamed.

Behind her, she heard everyone shouting and laughing. They thought it was part of the ritual. If she and Angie could make it into the trees, nobody would catch them.

Behind her an engine roared to life.

An ATV! He was coming after them.

Cloud could never outrun an ATV.

And then she saw disaster ahead. One of the logs Phil and

Phineas had left on the ground stretched across the only opening between the trees she could spot on this side. The trunk was at least twenty feet long and a good three feet in diameter. She didn't have time to go around it. David was too close.

She galloped straight for it.

"Angie, lock your fingers in Cloud's mane and hold on! Whatever you do, don't fall off."

The sense memory of all those years she'd ridden over fences bareback flooded her cells. She held Angie with one hand, the mare's reins with the other, and pressed her thighs into the mare's sides.

For one horrible moment she thought Cloud would stop and send them both flying over her head into the trees. The mare wasn't used to jumping logs with two people aboard.

"Go!" Nancy shouted.

The mare cleared the log and landed with a terrible jolt that nearly blinded Nancy

Behind her she heard the crash of metal.

Then somebody started to scream.

She didn't stop or look back, although once safely under the trees, she pulled the mare down to a fast walk so they wouldn't run headlong into a branch.

Then they were out of the woods and trotting through the pasture gate. She'd left it open on her way out.

Tim was running across the pasture toward them.

"Nancy, Angie! What the hell's happening?" Eddy and JustPup ran behind him. JustPup was barking.

She pulled Cloud up beside Tim. Angie slid off. She hadn't made a sound since Jason slung her aboard.

From the far side of the pasture she heard Jason call, "Dad! Dad!" He was running toward them. There didn't seem to be anyone chasing him, thank God.

And through the trees she saw the lights and heard the sirens of half a dozen squad cars converging on the clearing from the other direction.

She threw her leg across Cloud's withers, slid into Tim's arms and down and down into a pit of blackness that had no bottom.

CHAPTER THIRTY-EIGHT

NANCY WAS SURE she'd been scalped. Her face hurt, her teeth hurt. Her side *really* hurt. As if someone had branded her rib cage.

When she could no longer avoid the pain, she opened her eyes. They hurt, too.

She was lying flat on her back. She knew that smell. Hospital. No matter what town she'd been hurt in or whether the hospital was large or small, they all smelled the same.

And looked the same. Hospital-green. The color of fungus and mold.

She could feel the IV drip in the back of her hand. She hated that feeling. They said it didn't hurt, but it did.

She managed to move her left hand—the one not attached to a tube—up to her throat.

Cervical collar. No wonder she couldn't turn her head. Well, she'd known the chance she was taking, but she didn't see that she had a choice.

When she opened her eyes again, a tall blond man in a lab coat was leaning over her.

"My toenails hurt," she croaked.

"Good thing, too," he said with a grin. "According to the tests, that little stunt you pulled didn't do any further damage."

"Tell that to my neck."

"I'm telling it to your entire body. You shouldn't ever get on a horse."

"No kidding. I didn't do it on purpose."

"I see. Somebody forced you."

"Something like that. Am I going to be all right?"

"In spite of yourself. You'll be wearing that collar for at least a month, maybe longer, and I want you in my office in a week. My people will call you to set up an appointment."

"Who *are* you? Where am I? What day is it? What the hell happened?"

"I'm not certain what happened myself. I've had conflicting reports."

"Can I sit up?"

"Sure." He hit the button to raise the head of the bed to a nearly ninety-degree angle. She groaned but signaled him to keep cranking.

"How long have I been here? I could eat an entire cow."

"Not on our menu, I'm afraid, but I've ordered you a liquid breakfast."

"Liquid? Come on!"

"You have a gash along your ribs that took twenty stitches. It's not deep, but I'd prefer that you not cough. You would prefer it, too, trust me."

"Oh."

"I'm Dr. Wickham. Orthopedic surgeon. You're in a room at Baptist Collierville. You came in last night around 1:00 a.m."

"When can I go home?" She stopped. "Oh, shoot. My car's still back at my house."

He laughed. "As if I'd let you drive. Forget that at least until I see you again."

"I have a job. Responsibilities."

"You're on sick leave as of this moment—for a week. And you're going to be on major league painkillers for at least that long."

"No way! Mac'll kill me."

"If that's the Mac who's been yelling at the nurses, he'll have to make do without you for a while."

"You don't know Mac."

"He and a guy named Wainwright who says he's your fiancé have been fighting over who gets to see you first. There are also three kids and half a dozen other people who came and went all night and all morning. Got any druthers as to which one you see first?"

"Tim, I guess."

"You don't sound too happy about it. Not a happy engagement?"

"Not an engagement at all."

"By the way, the sheriff of Marquette County is out there waiting, too. What did you do, kill somebody?"

The door opened, but Sheriff Mike came in instead of Tim. He was carrying a big basket of flowers.

"These are from Hayley and Meghan and the Greens," he said, and set them on the windowsill.

"Am I in trouble?"

"Not in my book. You are one crazy woman. Why didn't you wait for backup? Any good cop knows that."

"I'm not a cop and I didn't think I could afford to. What took you so long anyway?"

"Eddy couldn't find Tim right away. How'd you know they were in your pasture?"

"Eddy told me. Poor baby, he's so scared of that lake. I should never have sent him down there alone."

"He did what you told him to. He keeps telling everybody about it. Pretty proud. We moved fast, but not fast enough. We did get there in time to round up all the kids."

"I'm surprised they didn't scatter when they saw the lights and heard the sirens."

"They were pretty blasted. Hell of a mess."

"I don't know what happened. I thought I heard a crash behind me…"

"Yeah. Well." He dragged his heavy hand down his face. "Jason apparently tried to pull Grantham off the ATV, but Grantham knocked him out of the way. Tried to cut him with that knife he had. Hell of a blade on that thing."

"I think it was some kind of sacrificial knife. It would have to be special for David."

"He apparently planned to use it on Cloud. Maybe on Angie, too, for all I know. How come a guy that crazy could slide under the radar for so long?"

"Ask Tim."

"He says you didn't trust the guy from the get-go."

"He mistreated animals. I think he may have been the one that burned JustPup and hurt the basset hound."

"The stress gets to them," Sheriff said. "Have to break out or go nuts. That's why eventually they kill *people*. I've been through all the serial killer psych courses at Quantico. They escalate when hurting and killing animals doesn't do it for them. Then they do it oftener and oftener. Only thing that stops 'em is getting caught or killed."

"But all he did was trespass in my woods and cut me," Nancy said. "He could say that was an accident when Jason shoved him. Holding a party on Halloween isn't illegal, as far as I know."

"Furnishing alcohol to underage kids is."

"Big deal. With the money his father has, he'll never be convicted of anything. He'll come after us. We won't be safe."

"No, he won't."

"He will! And don't tell me any kind of a peace bond will keep him from doing anything he wants to do."

"Nancy, he's dead."

That stopped her. "Dead? He can't be. What? How?"

"ATVs can't jump logs. When you cleared it, he didn't have time to stop or change direction, so he hit it. He was thrown over the front and into a tree trunk. Killed him instantly."

"Oh, Lord. His poor parents. Oh, God, Mike. It's my fault."

"No. It's his fault. Listen, Nancy, this guy was bad news. He knew how to seem normal. I hate to say this about another human being, but we're better off this way."

Tim stuck his head in the door. "Dammit, Mike, I'm not staying outside."

Nancy's heart turned over when she saw him. He looked like hell. He hadn't shaved and, from the rumpled look of him, hadn't showered or changed clothes or slept since she'd been brought in.

Actually, she was probably no pin-up, either.

"Come on in. I'm leaving." Mike squeezed Nancy's hand. "Don't worry. Get well." He let the door shut behind him.

Tim stood across the room as though he was afraid to approach the bed.

"You told them I was your fiancée," Nancy said.

"They asked if I was the next of kin. What else was I going to say?" He came closer, but slowly, as though he was waiting for her to stop him. "You could have been killed."

"So could Angie."

"Yeah." He came closer. "We both know you're the one who took the chance." He moved to sit on the edge of the bed and picked up her hand. "If anything happened to you, I wouldn't make it."

"Sure you would."

"The kids wouldn't make it, either. They've been outside the whole time. They won't leave until they can see you're alive and well."

"Alive, yes. Well?" She waggled her other hand. "Let them in. Oh, and what about Mac? Is he out there, too?"

"He's gone to the clinic, but he said he'd be back." Tim grinned. "He was ready to take out the entire emergency room staff before he knew you were being looked after, and he's been bullying anybody in a white coat ever since." He opened the door, motioned and stood back to let the children in.

They looked, if anything, worse than Tim. They still wore the clothes they'd been wearing, even Angie in her torn blue robe and coronet, but they were filthy and torn from the woods. Jason's cheeks showed dark stubble, and he sported one of the most richly colored and swollen shiners Nancy had ever seen. Angie sniffled and looked at the floor.

"You okay?" Jason asked, his eyes on the cervical collar.

"Sure. How'd you get the shiner?"

"Daryl didn't know what was coming down, so when everything went crazy, he thought I was messing up the party. When David knocked me out of the way, he decked me." Jason shrugged and grinned sheepishly. "It is kind of awesome."

"Just wait until it turns green and yellow."

"Hey, thanks." He took a deep breath. "At first I couldn't figure out what you were asking me to do."

"You did fine."

He ran his hands through his hair. His father's gesture. "Man, I didn't know Angie was going. I told her it was down at the lake. I sure didn't know she was bringing Cloud."

Nancy looked at Angie who stood with her head down, still silent. She hoped the experience hadn't left her like Eddy.

Eddy stepped forward. "I went down to the lake like you told me and found Daddy."

"I know. You're a hero."

Eddy hunched his shoulders and shook his head, but Nancy could see he was pleased. "Can you go home now?" he asked.

"Sure. I'm out of here today if I can find somebody to drive me."

"I got my learner's permit," Jason said with a grin. "I can drive us home."

"I don't *think* so."

"I looked after Poddy and Otto and Lancelot," said Eddy. "Miss Helen says to tell you they're fine. She'll bring dinner over tonight."

Angie raised her eyes. "He promised he'd teach me to jump Cloud if I did what he asked," she said in a very small voice. "I stayed on, didn't I?"

"Yeah. I never doubted you would."

She lunged at Nancy and wrapped her arms around her shoulders. Nancy let out a groan sound and Tim reached for Angie.

Nancy shook her head and patted Angie's back awkwardly.

"I was so scared," Angie whispered. "He was going to hurt Cloud."

Tim and Jason exchanged looks. Hurt her, too, possibly.

"I loved him," she wailed.

"You loved what you thought he was," Tim said. "He fooled us all."

"Jason wouldn't have let him hurt you," Nancy said. "He's the one who got you up on Cloud and gave us time to get away."

"That stuff he gave me to drink? Jason told me not to drink it. I poured it on the ground beside Cloud."

"Good thinking."

"Yeah," Jason said. He punched his sister in the shoulder. "Dumb kid."

"Go back to the waiting room," Tim said. "I need to speak to Nancy."

As soon as the door closed behind them, he touched her cheek. "I don't know whether I can kiss you or not."

"Me, neither. Give it a try. But gently. My teeth hurt."

He kissed her softly, and sat on the edge of the bed.

"What happened to the others?" she asked. "The rest of the team."

"They are a very sober bunch of youngsters," Tim said. "The sheriff is talking to them and their parents. I'm meeting Dr. Aycock tomorrow to discuss what we should do about the entire affair."

"Dr. Aycock? He must be devastated. He adored David."

"According to Mrs. Aycock, he's gone to bed. She's very worried about him. Not only because he cared about David, but because of the damage this could do to the school. Actually, *they* were only guilty of underage drinking, disorderly conduct and trespassing. That's bad enough, but Daryl says they didn't know about any of the rest of it, and swears there weren't any drugs in the Purple Passion."

"I'll lay you odds there was something in that goblet he gave Angie and in the fire. I kept getting flashes of color."

"The thing is, they didn't know the kind of ritual David planned. They thought it was going to be like some of the exercises they do to psych the team before a game. I don't think they had any idea what he was setting them up for." He sighed. "Neither did I."

"You caught on to him, Tim. You tried to stop him."

"I was almost too late. Jason conned me. He's pretty broken up. I'm not sure I can ever trust him completely after this... Angie, either."

"Kids lie. I did. I'm sure you did, too. Is there such a thing as being scared truthful?"

He grinned. "There certainly should be. I'm supposed to be a professional. I only caught onto David after you alerted me."

"He was an amazing actor. I think he would have killed me last night, if he could have gotten closer. God knows what he planned for Angie."

"I have a damned good idea. If he'd succeeded..." Tim dragged his hand along his jaw. His beard stubble rasped under his fingers. "If he'd succeeded in hurting you or Angie or Jason, I'd be in jail on a charge of murder." He stood, turned his back on her and jammed his hand in his pockets as he stared out the window. "I might well have been up on murder charges even if he hadn't succeeded. That's not easy to admit." He looked over his shoulder. "I would have killed him with my bare hands if anything had happened to you. Any of you. How do you admit you're glad someone is dead?"

"How's Angie?"

"She doesn't seem to understand what happened. Jason keeps throwing up." He shrugged. "So do I."

"Come back and sit."

He took her hand in both of his. "I never imagined…"

"Nobody sane *could* have imagined."

"I think he knew he wasn't sane. Sometimes I'd catch him looking at me with what I can only call yearning, as though he realized he was damaged and longed to know what it was like to be healthy. The funeral's tomorrow. I've already been over to talk to his parents."

"They must be brokenhearted. To them he was the perfect son."

"In a funny way, I think they're relieved." He leaned over and kissed her. When he sat up, he started to laugh.

"Oh, thank you very much! Nothing like a good kiss to break you up."

"It's not that," he said and kissed her again. "It just hit me, you said you couldn't give my kids orders. You seem to have done all right last night."

She glared at him for a moment, then she, too, began to laugh. "Yeah, I did. And wonder of wonders, they obeyed me."

"Now you'll have to marry me."

SHE WAS STILL HOLDING out a month later when Tim asked her to come over to his house for a family conference.

"I'm not family."

"You are whether you want to be or not."

When he had them all assembled, he said, "I have an announcement." He looked as though he'd just won the powerball sweepstakes. "Remember that school outside of Philadelphia that didn't hire me last year?"

All heads nodded.

"The guy they hired turned out to be a dud. They asked him not to come back after the Christmas break." He took a deep breath. "Starting January 15 next year, they want to hire me as assistant headmaster. Five year contract with an option for five more. Big salary, big house on the faculty common. We're moving to Pennsylvania!"

He dropped to his knees before Nancy. "Will you please marry me and come to Philadelphia?"

Jason stood. "Doesn't matter what *she* says. *I'm* not going." He stalked toward the kitchen.

"And leave Cloud?" Angie whined. "And my riding lessons? I'm staying here. You can't make me leave."

"Me, neither." Eddy moved across to sit beside Nancy. JustPup jumped onto the sofa beside them. "You go on to Pennsylvania. We'll move in with Nancy."

"Yeah," Jason said. "You can visit." There was a sneer in his voice. "When you're not too busy."

Tim frowned. "This is *good* news. You're supposed to be happy. It's everything we always wanted. It's not like Marquette County is the cultural center of the universe. How many times have you complained about the lack of pizza parlors and movie theaters?"

"What *you've* always wanted, you mean," Jason snapped.

Tim took a deep breath and tried to keep his voice level. "Look at the trouble we've had here. It sure as heck ain't Paradise." He smiled at Nancy, who sat stunned. "I love you, Nancy. I'm sure with a recommendation from Mac you can work at the finest clinic on the Main Line."

"Why on earth would you think you can uproot these children again when they've just gotten settled? Why would you think I'd pick up and move just because I love you? I won't. I'll die inside if you leave, and I'll be here whenever you visit, but I won't go with you."

"Neither will we," Angie said. "Nancy can look after us. Jason's sixteen. He'll have his license in a few months so he can drive us. And we have Helen. You go. We're staying." She crossed her arms and glared at her father.

His voice took on an edge of pleading. "It's a beautiful campus, a superb school. We'd have a great house right on the common. Angie can take Cloud and Eddy can take JustPup.

Nancy can take Poddy and Otto. Helen and Bill can move back into this house with Lancelot. The campus up there is beautiful. Graduating from there is guaranteed to get you into good colleges. I want what's best for us all. Nancy, talk sense to them, will you?"

She stood and walked around the couch. "If you try to drag them off to Philadelphia, they can bring sleeping bags and sleep on my floor."

"You don't mean that."

"Tim, nowhere is safe. You can't keep them rolled up in cotton. When you got here, your whole family was a dysfunctional disaster and you were halfway to being a basket case with guilt. You've done it, can't you see that? Look at them. They're straight and smart and moral." She began to cry. "I wish to God I didn't, but I'm afraid I love them as much as I love you, you blithering idiot, and I won't let you screw them over again."

"I thought…I hoped…"

"You thought you could pressure me into marriage. You can't."

"Can *we*?" Eddy said softly. "You love us. You said that. You love my dad, too. You can marry my dad and still live in your house. We won't bother you."

"I don't care whether we live here or in Philadelphia or in Timbuktu," Tim said. "As long as we're together. That's all that matters. I'll stay an English teacher for the rest of my life if that's what it takes."

"But marriage…"

"If you're married you can't go away so easy," Eddy said.

"I'm not going away. Look, if I marry your dad all of a sudden I become the wicked stepmother."

"Hey, you already act like that," Jason said. "Can't get any worse."

Angie snorted. "Tell me about it. She can be really mean."

"You still want me?"

"Might as well," Jason said, then he turned sober. "Yeah. Yeah, I guess we do."

"Then I guess I'm stuck with you."

"Even me?" Tim asked.

She held out her arms. "Especially you."

EPILOGUE

One year later

DARYL SAT on the deck behind Jason's house and watched the fairy lights strung in the trees around the Wainwright backyard. Jason wandered outside and slumped into the chair beside him. They clinked soda cans. Behind them the party was in full swing. All generations were involved in old-fashioned Halloween games like bobbing for apples.

At first the lacrosse team and their girlfriends had stood aside. Too sophisticated for such kid stuff. As the evening progressed, however, they shed their inhibitions and joined in. Nobody mentioned last Halloween.

"Great party, man," Daryl said. "Just needed a little air. Too much essence of jockstrap, if you get my meaning."

"Yeah."

"How come your folks gave this party? I mean, how often do I go to parties with my parents?"

"Dad's idea. I didn't think anybody'd come, but a lot of people did. Most of the team anyway, and all the cheerleaders. How come you're stag?"

Daryl shrugged. "Karen dumped me last week. Said the closer we got to Halloween, the more she didn't want to look at my face. Girls. What can you say."

"Yeah. It's not like anybody remembers what happened."

They both knew everybody remembered not only the evening, but the terrible aftermath. David's funeral.

And none of the attendees forgot the two-week suspensions from school or the dressing down they got from the sheriff, their parents, Dr. Aycock and eventually the judge that had them picking up trash around the lake and in Nancy's woods every weekend for a month. Not to mention painting all the jumps on the village green.

"Man, your step-mom's tree house turned out great. From the road you can't even see it's up there."

"Dad and Bill picked the biggest oak in the backyard."

"Way it's built, you could get a mortgage on it." Daryl snickered.

"Yep. Stairs, air-conditioning, sky lights."

"Come on, show me." Daryl began to struggle out of the deck chair.

Jason stopped him. "Nobody goes up without an invitation."

"Not even your dad?"

Jason laughed. "He gets the most invitations. Lots of times when the weather's nice, they'll spend the night up there."

"Come on," Daryl wheedled. "She won't even know we went up there."

"Listen, if your mom hadn't dragged you off to Spain for the summer, you could have helped us build it. Then you'd know what it looks like inside. Too late, man."

"Aw, is Jason scared of his wicked step-mother?"

Jason lunged at Daryl, who fended him off easily. "Hey, back off. Just kidding. So you get along with her?"

"Mostly," Jason answered. "It's better now I have my driver's license."

"I'm an expert, man. I'm on my third step-mom. This one's the best so far, but sometimes I wish *she'd* go sit in a tree and leave me alone."

"Nancy gets to leave us alone is the point, dum-dum. She needed someplace private after she sold her house."

"Yeah. I met the guy that bought it a few minutes ago." Daryl raised his eyebrows. "Deeply weird."

"What can I say? According to Kenny Nichols, most exotic animal vets are strange. I thought we'd wind up with the Halliburtons across the street, but they bought a house closer to town."

"They take that pig?"

"Yeah. He comes to work with Helen most days."

"He's kind of cute," Daryl said. "For a pig."

They leaned back in their chairs for a couple of seconds, then Daryl sat up and said, "Hey, man, I just saw Emma Lockhart come in."

"She's only fourteen," Jason said with a snort.

"Listen, my man, when you are twenty, she'll be eighteen. Think about that."

"Yeah," Jason said. He and Daryl uncoiled from their seats and sloped off into the house like a pair of wolf cubs after their first rabbit.

"PERMISSION TO COME aboard, sir." Tim stuck his head through the trapdoor and lifted a bottle of champagne and a pair of champagne flutes above his head. "I bear gifts."

Nancy rolled over on her stomach and took both from him. "Permission granted. I'm not easy, but I can be bought."

Tim climbed up and dropped the trapdoor back into place. The inside of the tree house was cozy from the small electric heater in the corner. The queen-size air mattress sat halfway along the back wall, and a dozen pillows of different sizes were propped up against the wall behind it to create a headboard. The tree house was about twelve feet square, and was anchored securely not only in the heavy branches of the oak, but with sturdy posts into the ground as well. The only light came from a small lamp on the floor beside the bed.

"I stole Halloween cookies from the leftovers," Nancy said with a leer. "You interested?"

"Ah, Halloween cookies and champagne. Food of the gods."

He sank onto the pile of quilts that covered the bed, leaned over and kissed his wife.

"Champagne and cookies first, hanky-panky afterwards," she whispered. "I'm starved."

"There was enough food for an army."

"I know. I can't ever eat at those things, especially when I'm hostessing and running back and forth to the kitchen." She propped herself against the pillows. "Besides, we were feeding the lacrosse team. They eat like an army."

He worked the cork out of the champagne, then poured Nancy a glass and took one for himself.

She held her glass out to clink with his. "I never thought you'd pull it off," she said seriously. "I was certain no one would come to another party here on Halloween. Not after last year. You're a genius. A little cracked, maybe, but still a genius."

"Modest, too," he said and slid up beside her.

"Did you see Jason and Daryl hitting on Emma Lockhart? Mac's going to have to get used to boys going after his step-daughter." She chuckled. "He looked downright murderous. He's not going to like it."

"Neither am I," Tim said. "I keep hoping Angie will prefer horses to boys. I guess it can't last." He looked questioningly at her, then topped up her glass without waiting for her answer.

She stretched and yawned. "I'm glad Jack Renfro's back full-time. I don't think I could go into work tomorrow if I had to."

"Drink up."

"Are you trying to get me drunk, sir?"

"Woman, I am your husband. I have rights."

"In your dreams." She cuddled against him and kissed his chin. "Privileges, maybe. Rights—no way."

He wrapped his free arm around her. A moment later he set his glass on the floor beside the bed and pulled her into both arms. "I know it was a crazy idea. I just thought if we could get the kids who were there last year with their parents and some of the other kids from Maybree and *their* parents, we might be able to replace some of the bad memories with good ones. They're still kids. Whether they know it or not, they need the emotional support of their parents."

Nancy laughed. "I hope the photos of Dr. Aycock bobbing for apples come out. He's a really good sport."

"Amazingly enough, he is. And Coach Lepage seems to have managed to get the boys on his side already." He lifted her chin and kissed her. "I have an announcement."

"Uh-oh. That sounds ominous."

"Dr. Aycock offered me the job of assistant headmaster."

"That's wonderful." She started to throw her arms around him, then stopped. "Isn't it? Why are you shaking your head?"

"I turned him down."

"You what?"

He took her hand. "It's more money—not a lot more, but some. It's a year-round position."

"So why did you turn him down?"

"This past year I've discovered I really do like teaching English. And I'll be teaching summer school, so we won't be losing much money."

"Uh-huh."

"Oh, shoot. The real reason is I'd rather spend time with you and the kids than hunched over my computer working on budget forms." He looked up sheepishly. "I know I should have discussed it with you first."

This time she did throw her arms around him. The cookies went flying.

He grabbed her and rolled her over beneath him. They tussled for a moment, then she went still. A second later so did he.

"I complicated your life," he whispered.

"Peace is boring. Besides, you brought me *back* to life. I love you. All of you."

"And I love you. Thank you for marrying us."

HARLEQUIN®

Super Romance

FOUR LITTLE PROBLEMS

by Carrie Weaver

You, Me & the Kids

The more the...merrier?

Patrick Stevens is a great teacher.
All of his "kids" say so—except
Emily Patterson's oldest son, Jason.
Which is too bad because Patrick would
like to get to know Emily better...if only she
didn't come complete with four children.

On sale May 2006
Available at your favorite retailer!

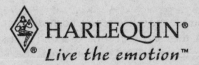

HARLEQUIN®
Live the emotion™

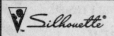

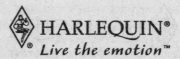

HARLEQUIN®

Super Romance

THE OTHER WOMAN

by Brenda Novak

A Dundee, Idaho Book

Elizabeth O'Conner has finally put her
ex-husband's betrayal behind her. She's
concentrating on her two kids and on opening
her own business. One thing she's learned
is that she doesn't want to depend on any
man ever again—which definitely includes the
enigmatic Carter Hudson. It's just as well that
he's as reluctant to get involved as she is....

By the award-winning author of
Stranger in Town and *Big Girls Don't Cry.*

On sale May 2006
Available at your favorite retailer!

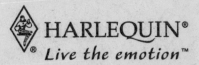

HARLEQUIN®
Live the emotion™